WHAT THE LUCK?

BRIAN CRAMER

WHAT THE LUCK?

Published by Brian Cramer Books
www.briancramerbooks.com

ISBN-13: 978-0-9961529-1-4
ISBN-10: 0996152911

Dedicated in memory of my mother and father, two people who not only gave me life, but also the freedom to live it.

And supplied the bail money when I lived it a little too freely.

Please go to
blog.briancramerbooks.com/what-the-luck-readers-supplement/
for bonus content, including pictures and video.

CHAPTER 1

Bill Brabham was at home, contemplating the universe. All the ingredients for contemplation were present: dim lights, sad music, and hard liquor.

Bill was not a religious man, but he was starting to believe that maybe there really was a God after all, and that this God person actually hated him for some reason. He always considered himself to be a decent man, so he wondered why, then, has he been the victim of so much misfortune recently?

He had once heard someone say that he was "down on his luck," whatever that meant. Well, here, alone in the dark and half drunk on whiskey, he was determined to figure it out.

It seemed to Bill that there ought to be such a thing as karma — the idea that what goes around, comes around. And deep in his gut, he thought that maybe there really was such a thing — probably not in a "mystical healing power of crystals" way, but maybe in a more explainable and rational way. After all, wasn't it natural for others to help you and treat you more kindly if they saw that you, in turn, were a kind person? And, of course, if you were a known bastard, well, you could just manage on your own, couldn't you?

Bill then reflected that somehow this karma thing didn't always seem to work in a nice, even manner. After all, he had been a steady worker and a faithful and loving husband. Nevertheless, here he was in the dark, drunk, alone, and unemployed.

Bill's whiskey-soaked brain reasoned that there must be a

randomness to the universe that is beyond the control of men. The more he thought about it, the more he realized that this randomness did exist, and its name was luck — and he was apparently down on it. He really hoped that he would be up on it soon.

After all, wasn't there something called "regression toward the mean?" If you flipped a coin only three times, it may land on tails each time, but if you flipped it one hundred times, then the number of heads and tails should move toward 50/50. Bill had certainly flipped tails a few times lately and was really hoping that his luck would even out soon.

In actuality, it was only a single, unlucky event that had caused all of Bill's recent misfortune. He thought about it again and shuddered. He had been working as a financial analyst for a large hedge fund in Houston. Life had been great, and he had been making money faster than even his wife could spend it.

He had met his wife, Julie, there as well. Julie was also an analyst, but she specialized in fundamental analysis while Bill was strongest at technical analysis. They made the perfect complement to each other both professionally and personally.

If there was one sticking point in their relationship, it was their boss, Miss Trezzor. The reason for this was simple: Miss Trezzor was beautiful. Julie was good looking too, in a mousy secretary sort of way, but Miss Trezzor was good looking in a super model sort of way, and it made Julie uneasy.

To Bill's credit, he was always the perfect gentleman and was always very careful to avoid anything that could be remotely construed as sexual harassment. Besides, as Bill was the first to explain at home to Julie, Miss Trezzor was a major bitch and trying to be romantic with her would be like trying to get cuddly with a porcupine. This view was reinforced by the fact that no one in the office even knew her first name.

And then one day *it* happened. Miss Trezzor had been in front of her desk tidying up some paperwork. Bill had walked into her office to ask for clarification on an assignment. As he had approached her, he had tripped on god-knows-what and had pushed into Miss Trezzor from behind, bending her over the desk with her skirt flipping up in an oh-so-indecent way. And then Julie had walked in.

It was as simple as that. Just one stupid mishap had ruined his life. And boy was it stupid, thought Bill, as if his life were some cheesy sitcom.

And like most cheesy sitcoms, no one had laughed at it. Miss Trezzor was particularly not amused. In fact, she was very embarrassed by the situation and also fearful of a potential lawsuit. In her mind, she felt that if she did not play hardball with Bill, then Julie would think that she was a willing participant, which would then expose her to legal risks. To prevent this, Miss Trezzor preemptively filed a lawsuit against Bill, which turned the severity of this stupid accident up to eleven, and made Julie take it even more seriously.

The end result of this one stupid event in Bill's life had been a large settlement paid, a job lost, a divorce granted, and a reputation in the financial world ruined. Oh, and just now, Bill was vomiting on his shoes.

CHAPTER 2

Bill woke up slouched over his computer desk with the classified section of the newspaper stuck to his face. It had been a full three months since he had lost his job, and he was starting to feel like he was somehow unemployable.

He still had a decent amount of savings even after the large settlement he had paid to Miss Trezzor, but it was not going to support him forever. He toyed with the idea of playing the financial markets, but without Julie's help with the fundamental analysis he was worried that he would pooch things up royally and leave himself broke. It was one thing to gamble with a stranger's money, but quite another to gamble with one's own.

After peeling away the newspaper, Bill checked a few online news sites to see what was going on in the world. An article about the Fukushima power plant caught his eye, and so he read it. The article summed up the continuing difficulty they were having with cleaning up the wreckage at the power plant, even after all these years had passed since the earthquake/tsunami combo had destroyed the plant and sent several cores into meltdown.

It was a sad story and Bill did not want to think about it, but something in the article spoke to him. That something was money. The article explained that the plant was willing to pay top dollar for workers to aid in the cleanup. It was difficult for the plant managers to find workers for the cleanup because of the inherent danger of the job. This was a shame because they were in constant need of fresh workers since the men had to be continually rotated to prevent exceeding "safe" levels of exposure to the radiation. The average tour of duty was a mere month, but a man could earn a year's wage in that small amount of time.

Bill sat back in his chair and stared at the ceiling while weighed the pros and cons of taking the job. He thought, OK, so what are the pros? Well, it was a boatload of money. That was a big plus. And he had traveled overseas many times and was good at picking up new languages, so that was probably not a problem. Also, he had worked in construction when he was younger, and, thanks to his former company's gym, he was still in decent shape for a 35-year-old financial consultant. And lastly, there was nothing keeping him in Houston — no job, no kids, no pets, and no wife.

OK, now what are the cons? Well, cancer was certainly one of them. And there was also that whole language barrier thing. Quick study or not, he would still have to learn how to read all those weird, scribbly characters. Also, he did not enjoy seafood all that much, and he was fairly certain that it was popular over there in Japan.

He shook his head while mumbling, "Am I nuts for even contemplating this?" He then sat up straight again and looked around his apartment with disgust. He had only been living there for a few months since the incident, and he was already sick of it. He had spent so much time in his apartment while looking for work that it was starting to feel like a prison to him.

"Fuck it," he said to the world in general, "I'm going." He turned his attention back to the computer and thought, OK now to learn the language and culture of a whole other race of people I know nothing about apart from vague notions of samurai and harakiri. Oh, and that they build pretty good cars. And there was anime too — those cartoons with the characters with really big eyeballs. Maybe I'll watch a few of those.

CHAPTER 3

Bill heard the doorbell ring and answered the door. It was the UPS man delivering a package for him. Bill rushed to the table with the package and opened it up excitedly. It was a limited edition figurine of a character from an anime that he had been following for the last two months. The figurine was quite evidently female, and the creators seemed to have forgotten to give her much in the way of clothing. However, she made up for this in some small way by the excessive number of weapons that she was carrying.

Bill's friend, Kevin, had been watching him silently in disapproval. After watching Bill carefully put the figurine on the shelf next to the others, Kevin finally said, "Dude, don't you think you are taking things a little too far?"

Bill paused for a moment of introspection. He thought back to how he had gotten to this point in his life. It was not very complicated really — it all started from his desire to learn Japanese. After learning the basics from books and software, he thought that it would serve him well to learn to listen and comprehend the spoken language. And so it seemed only logical to Bill to start off with a medium that was meant for children, which prompted him to start watching anime. The end result was that Bill did actually improve his listening comprehension, but it also meant that Bill's spoken Japanese mainly consisted of anime catchphrases, and his apartment was now filling with what he called collectibles, but everyone else just called dolls.

Bill sighed. "Yes, I guess you have a point. At any rate, I

reckon I'm ready to hit the road."

"Air," Kevin volunteered.

"Yeah, whatever. Just water the plant once a week, will you?"

"Sure bro. I'll take care of things here. You just watch out for yourself over there, and try not to come back a mutant."

CHAPTER 4

Bill stepped off the plane at Narita airport and was welcomed by a sign which read in Japanese *"Okaerinasai"* and underneath in English "Welcome to Japan." He smiled at the Japanese version, which translated more like "Welcome home." Well that's friendly enough, he thought.

Bill was able to navigate to the baggage claim area using the airport signs, which were mercifully in English as well as Japanese.

After retrieving his luggage, he was off to customs. The customs official looked rather serious but he asked Bill little more than, "What is the purpose of your visit?" and then let him pass.

Bill was there as a visitor for the time being until he could somehow secure a work visa. He was not at all sure how to go about getting one, however, and was starting to think that perhaps he should have spent a little less time watching anime and a little more time on the logistics of the trip. He shrugged to himself and walked out of the airport and into a whole new world.

Bill was thirsty from his travels and was glad to find a vending machine just outside the terminal building. He fed the machine some of the fresh Yen that he had just acquired at the currency exchange in the airport, and then picked a selection at random.

He flinched a little when he grabbed the can — it was hot! Well, that's interesting, he thought. Coffee perhaps?

He opened the can by peeling the lid back like something you would find on a soup can. He smelled it. It smelled like soup made from long-dead fish. He waited for a moment when no one was watching and then he poured the contents in the garbage and dropped the can in the recycling bin.

This time with less nonchalance and more concentration, Bill bought some chilled green tea and was finally at peace with the world. As he sipped his tea, he noticed a glass room about the size of a small bedroom. He could not see inside the room because the glass had a smokey tint to it.

Bill wandered over to the room in the spirit of exploration and opened the door. Before he could take more than two steps inside, a wall of year-old tobacco smoke hit him square in the nostrils and knocked him backwards. Bill slammed the door closed but not before catching a glimpse of several men in suits. They were standing around and smoking with very little conversation but plenty of heavy lung work.

Bill had heard rumors that the suicide rate was high in the densely populated areas of Japan, but he was shocked that they would attempt it so soon after arrival.

He dismissed this thought and then, using a combination of broken Japanese and some miming, he was able to find the bus that was to take him to his hotel in Tokyo, which was about an hour away from the airport and also nowhere near the power plant.

Bill intended to spend a week in the capital to give himself a chance to adapt to his new surroundings before rushing off to play Homer Simpson at the nuclear plant. Besides, ever since he saw *Lost in Translation*, he wanted with all his heart to explore Tokyo and perhaps fall in love with a Scarlett Johansson look-alike.

He walked over to the loading area and waited for the bus between little painted lines that told everyone where to stand and kept everyone nicely lined up. How very Japanese, he thought.

The trip to Tokyo was mostly uneventful except for a couple of things. The first shock had been when Bill had discovered that the Japanese drove on the opposite side of the road. He had watched in horror as the bus driver exited the airport on the left-hand side of the road and was sure that the bus driver must have been one of those suicidal smokers that was looking for another way to end it all. The other shock had come after the sun had set, which had made the crash-landed flying saucers really stand out since they had been so brightly lit. Bill later discovered that these were just really, really big Ferris wheels far off in the distance.

CHAPTER 5

Bill stood on the sidewalk and shielded his eyes from the lights. He looked at his watch as if to check his facts — it was eight o'clock at night and he had been up for something like 24 hours in his own personal timescale, but thanks to the magic of time zones it had been more like 38.

The spring air was crisp and it kept Bill awake while the thousands of bright lights that lit the buildings and signs worked to burn a hole in his retinas. He was in Shibuya, one of the many distinct areas of Tokyo. Most of Shibuya was so brightly lit at nighttime that Bill supposed that it actually got darker there during the day.

He stood in a trance-like state with the murmurings of thousands of Japanese conversations hitting his ears and bouncing off with little recognition. He watched in fascination as all the traffic stopped at a very large intersection, and what looked like millions of people poured into the street from every direction at once. They then intermingled with each other and somehow arrived at alternate sides of one street or another just in time for traffic to resume. Amazing.

After watching the miracle of Shibuya Crossing a few more times, Bill struck out in a random direction in search of food. After a few blocks, he stumbled on some sort of Italian restaurant. He knew it was an Italian restaurant because there were exquisitely crafted plastic replicas of various pasta dishes on display behind a window. Bill later learned that there are only a few companies in the world that make these food props, the biggest of which was inexplicably called Yummy Plastics. The models were all created by hand, and it was something of an art form to make them. But for now his hunger outweighed his curiosity of such matters so he followed the signs down a narrow set of stairs and into the smallest restaurant that he had ever seen.

The restaurant was about the size of the living room in his former house. The tables were clustered together in groups and he was seated quite intimately next to two attractive natives. Despite being a six-foot tall foreigner wearing blue jeans, Bill felt just like one of the crowd as everyone else tried really hard not to stare at him. Good thing I didn't wear my cowboy hat, thought Bill, or else their poor little heads would explode.

As Bill worked to master the art of eating spaghetti with a pair of chopsticks, he overheard snippets of conversation between two women a few tables from his. Bill was far from fluent, but he could make out some words like 'tall' and 'foreigner' and 'cool looking.' Part of him wanted to strike up a conversation, but most of him was too worried about his third-grade vocabulary. He was also concerned that this was somehow a breach of etiquette, and so he merely smiled to himself as he ate the rest of his meal in silence and soaked up the strangeness of his surroundings.

After paying for dinner with a handful of coins, Bill arrived blinking into the brightness of the streets once again. He was beginning to get a headache from the bright lights, and probably from his brain trying to make sense of the Japanese that was constantly bombarding it through his eyes and ears. He decided that what he really needed now was a drink, and after a few more blocks he found a place that would likely give him one. A sign read "Tombstone Bar" and had a sketch of a girl wearing a bikini and a cowboy hat while sitting on a tombstone and putting on high heel shoes. Bill raised his eyebrows. My kind of place, he thought.

And so Bill found himself going down yet another set of narrow stairs and into what he could only imagine was some biker's living room in which someone had inexplicably added a bar top. It was even tinier than the previous restaurant and it had a certain outlaw biker motif going for it, with lots of associated posters and replica guns scattered along the walls. Oddly enough, 90's grunge music was playing in the background.

The bartender spoke a bit of English and Bill chatted with

him sparingly between drinks. The place had a really fun atmosphere and everyone was happily joking around with one another. Bill looked around and felt, for the first time in quite a while, that the world was a good and happy place.

This thought was broken by a couple of tourists who poked their heads through the door. One of them exclaimed, "Is that all there is?" and then they left. Bill was slightly disappointed that they had left because he was itching to speak English to someone who could understand him.

After another drink, Bill said his goodbyes and emerged back into the crisp night air. His lack of sleep, the potency of the beer, and the oddity of his surroundings were conspiring to make him feel as if he were watching himself from outside his own body. Or perhaps his brain simply could not process all of this strangeness all at once. Whatever the reason, Bill felt that if he did not strike out for the hotel now, he was likely to wake up either in the gutter or in jail. So he made haste to the train station only to find that the blasted system had shut down at midnight.

Annoyed, Bill tried to get into one of the many waiting taxis outside the station, but the door would not open. The taxi driver quickly rolled down his window and said something like, "Fast taxi, fast taxi," as he pointed to the front of the line of taxis. It took Bill a second to realize that the driver was not bragging, but rather trying to direct him to use the *first* taxi.

As Bill reached for the door of the first taxi, it opened automatically and smacked his hand out of the way. Bill got inside and stayed clear of the door as it shut itself. He then reached into his pocket and retrieved a matchbook that he had taken from his hotel, which had the name of the hotel written on the front cover. Bill handed it to the driver and said, "Here please," in Japanese. This seemed to do the trick, and in short order Bill was sleeping soundly in his bed while dreaming of neon and tombstones and Japanese women throwing spaghetti at him.

CHAPTER 6

Sakamoto Kenta finished his *tonkatsu*, a Japanese meal consisting of a breaded, deep-fried pork cutlet, some rice, and some shredded cabbage. *Tonkatsu* is usually splashed with a thick, brown sauce, and some of this was now also splashed onto Sakamoto's mouth and face.

One of the two girls attending him quickly bustled away the dirty plate while the second girl licked Sakamoto's mouth and face clean with her tongue. She then dried his face delicately with a fresh napkin.

She did not want to do this, of course. Sakamoto was a disgusting beast of a man and no woman would willingly do this for him. He was severely overweight, and he had a face very much like a Shar-Pei, only with even more wrinkles and some scars. Looks are not everything of course, but Sakamoto was a total package — he was as disgusting on the inside as he was on the outside.

Sakamoto was the boss of an up-and-coming crime syndicate called Yasei-kai. They specialized in drug and sex trafficking — two rackets that the larger, more established groups had moved away from as they grew into more white-collar forms of crime involving things such as stock market manipulation and the infiltration of mega corporations.

Sakamoto's group was a small one, but they were growing rapidly because of their ruthlessness. Their motto was "Honor holds you back," which might make sense for a criminal organization, but this motto had nevertheless sent shock waves through the Japanese underground, a large part of which considered themselves to be the protectors of the everyday man.

Indeed, the other organized crime families and syndicates of Japan often consisted of the outcasts of society, and as a result, they often felt that it was their duty to protect the downcast and to punish the oppressive.

To this end, the older, more established groups worked hard to prevent everyday citizens from becoming entangled in their sometimes violent world. In fact, the home town of the largest criminal organization was, quite surprisingly, considered the safest city in the country. This was attributed to the fact that all the petty criminals had been driven out by this large organization.

Of course, criminals are criminals, and what is a criminal but someone who does not follow the rules. So even in a society where many of the criminals tried to be at least civil about their activities, you will always get your low-life trash. And that was Sakamoto.

Nothing was taboo to Sakamoto if he could gain money or power from it. Take for instance his two serving girls. They came from the Yasei-kai sex trade in which young girls from other Asian countries like Vietnam and the Philippines would be tempted to come to Japan for lucrative careers in modeling, only to be turned into porn stars and prostitutes.

Sakamoto would frequently rotate his attendants as younger or more beautiful girls became available. He thought of them as furniture, and they were always called "One" and "Two". His current two were both about 17 or 18, tall, slender, and beautiful. They both could have easily been genuine models if they had not been so unfortunate as to have met Sakamoto and his crew. Now they were forced to serve his every whim under the threat of death to their families back home.

While Sakamoto was surely evil, he was not a stupid man. He directed his crew to ignore the runaways and the strays of society and instead focus on the pampered and wealthy girls with strong family bonds. This gave the group an automatic leash to control the girls, as well as an opportunity to make even more money by collecting a ransom from the families once the girls were used up in a few years' time.

The girl called One returned with a cup of tea for Sakamoto. She served it to him, and then both girls kissed his cheeks, one from each side, and stood at attention by his side. They then stood still with their eyes forward just like members of the Queen's Guard, only much more attractive and without the funny hats.

A moment later, one of Sakamoto's lieutenants arrived to give his daily report. He approached Sakamoto and bowed.

Sakamoto asked, "How is the new venture in America going?"

"Everything is going well, boss. The COUGARS are gaining in number exponentially. The women are signing up by the hundreds now. It was a brilliant idea of yours, boss, to incentivize them with profit sharing and referral fees. Once the first few were organized, the whole thing just exploded. It is doing so well that I think we will have to enlist more lawyers soon."

"Excellent. I will give your recommendation to the administrative branch. How about our main project?"

"That is also going well, boss. We have covered approximately fifty percent of all the relevant restaurants in Tokyo. I think we will be fully ready in about two months. We are going as fast as we dare, but as you know, we must not get caught while switching the products. Any slip-up could endanger the plan."

"I understand. Two months is acceptable, but no more. Continue with caution."

"Yes, boss."

"That will be all."

"Yes, boss."

CHAPTER 7

Breakfast. Yes, that's what he needs right now. But where to find it?

Bill asked the hotel concierge for a map of the area, and also where to find some breakfast. The concierge handed Bill a crudely drawn map of the area that surrounded the hotel. There were no street names to be found, which made it rather useless as a map in Bill's opinion. The concierge also pointed to a nearby room in which he could find his meal.

Bill, not feeling like fish for breakfast, went for a "Western-style Breakfast," which turned out to be bacon and eggs. Well, sort of. The bacon was Canadian bacon, and the eggs were a little runny and tasted like they were cooked in fish oil. Bill hazarded a few bites before his stomach lurched in protest. He managed to eat about half of the meal before he threw in the towel, or rather, the napkin.

Bill left the hotel and was still hungry. He saw a familiar place, 7-11, and decided to give that a try. The inside was very different from those in Texas. Not only was the store smaller inside, but the merchandise was completely different as well.

He moseyed around for a few minutes while trying to decide what might be suitable to his palate. He saw some *onigiri*, which were basically triangular-shaped balls of sticky white rice that had been pressed together with some sort of fish stuffed inside. He passed on the *onigiri* and was about to give up on 7-11 when he saw a glass cabinet on the counter near the door.

There were several dough-ball looking things inside of the cabinet, and the inside of the cabinet's glass walls were runny with condensing steam. There were a few different varieties of these steamed buns, but Bill was unsure of the differences. He

17

asked for one from the top row. These were apparently called *nikuman*.

Bill stood outside the store and started to eat his bun, but then was quickly reprimanded by the store manager and told not to loiter. Or maybe it was not to eat there. Either way, the person was clearly not happy with him, so Bill apologized with a bow and then walked the short distance back to his hotel to finish his second breakfast in his room.

The steamed bun was excellent. It was filled with something like pulled-pork, and it really hit the spot. Now satisfied, Bill struck out once again to explore the area.

The city was clean and most of the buildings were tall and modern, but not quite what he would consider to be skyscrapers, although plenty of taller buildings could be seen in the distance.

Bill checked the map and was reasonably sure that he was walking down the main road toward the train station. Sure enough, in a few blocks, he found it. He made a mental note of its location and continued down the road while soaking up the foreign sights.

While he was walking, he noticed a woman who was sort of fast walking or slow jogging down the road, as if she were late for work. She stopped suddenly when the traffic signal along a side road turned red. Bill watched as the woman waited patiently. No cars were coming, and the side road was really nothing more than an alleyway. Finally, the light turned green and she was off sprinting down the road again.

This seemed to be a common theme as he walked. No one jaywalked in Tokyo, it seemed. No, wait, Bill saw a group of five kids that looked as if they had tried to dress like delinquents but only had a Sears catalog to work from. They carefully looked both ways and then ran across a large but not very busy street. They made it safely to the other side of the street and yelled, "Rebels!"[1] in unison while looking at Bill and acting all smug. Bill waited for the green light before crossing and did not celebrate on the other side nor declare himself to be a rebel.

After a few more blocks, the road dead-ended at a cross street. On the other side of the cross street, there was some sort of large temple. Bill was about to cross when he noticed a small park and some blessed vending machines, so he took a drinks break while he toured the park.

---

1   OK, it was more like "Reburu!", but you get the point.

The park was nothing more than a small picnic area, or perhaps just a place to take a break. Off in the back corner was a large pedestal with a bronze head of some aristocratic Westerner on top. Bill could not make out the writing on the plaque, but while he was trying, he noticed something even more amazing in the background: a small, wooden, old-style, Japanese building (the type with the roof that curves upward at the tips) that was sandwiched between a modern apartment complex and a modern office building. Very odd.

Now refreshed, Bill crossed the street to explore the Shrine grounds. There were buildings to the left and right as he entered the grounds, but the focus was obviously the one straight ahead. All the buildings had that distinct traditional Japanese look to them.

As Bill approached the shrine, he saw something astonishing that was towering over the right-hand side of the building — it was the Eiffel Tower! But it was orange? And in Tokyo? Bill added this to his list of things to explore and made his way up the many steps of the shrine. Or was it a temple? Bill was not at all sure if it was Buddhist or Shinto or what. Probably a Buddhist temple, he guessed. At any rate, he walked inside stealthily and was welcomed by the sound of the priest/monk guy chanting and occasionally banging on some very big drums. Bill stood at the very back of the temple with his back against the wall and realized that he was having a *Lost in Translation* moment. He suddenly felt very out of place and sidled back out of the door.

As Bill walked down the steps, he noticed a few hundred little statues along the right-hand side of the building. He walked over to investigate them. No one was on this side of the building, and he wondered if he was desecrating the sanctity of something or another by walking there. He decided to risk it and inspect the statues.

There were two rows of little statues, all about a foot tall. They were standing with their hands together in prayer. They had Buddha-like faces, kind of fat and chubby like that of a child's. They all wore red knitted hats that looked as if maybe they had been knitted by hand. In front of each one were three vessels: a tall, fat vase with flowers inside; a tall, skinny vase that had a red, pink, and white pinwheel inside; and a small, squat holder that was empty but was probably used for candles. It was somehow a little creepy so Bill left promptly. Later on that day, Bill did some research and discovered that these were

Jizō statues, which were intended for people to pray to in order to protect the souls of their stillborn children. Creepy indeed.

After taking a few pictures, Bill made his way to the tower. It had looked to be only a block away because of the size, but the walk to the tower ended up taking Bill a good twenty minutes. As he approached the tower, he noticed a building at the base of it with a sign on the top-left corner that read "TOKYO TOWER" in blocky English letters. Bill wondered how he had gone his whole life not knowing that such a thing existed, and promptly went inside.

Once inside the building, Bill learned from a pamphlet that the structure was 333 meters (1093 feet) tall and had a main observation deck about half-way up (150 meters / 490 feet) and a smaller special observatory deck near the top (250 meters / 820 feet). It was, of course, modeled after the Eiffel tower in Paris but it was made nine meters taller, probably just for spite.

Its main function had been as a support structure for television and radio antennas, but because of the limitations in digital television signals, it was deemed unsuitable for television broadcasting after the changeover in 2011, and so an even bigger tower called the Tokyo Skytree had been built to replace it. Since then, the Tokyo Tower had mainly been a tourist attraction but it also continued to service a few radio broadcasting companies.

Bill bought a ticket and waited in line for the elevator. A person was there to meter out how many people went inside the elevator for safety reasons. There were actually several elevators, and they were quite large, so it did not take long before Bill was heading up to the main deck.

The view from this level was stunning, and it cemented in Bill's head that Tokyo was a vastly huge place. It was not merely a large city, but a conglomerate of intertwining cities. The word megalopolis is the sort of concept we are looking for here.

Bill took hundreds of pictures and then went up to the special observation deck. Surprisingly, the view was not quite as spectacular up there. The vantage point was just too high up — so high up that the eye could no longer make out the details of the city. Just the same, Bill thought it was pretty damn cool. He wanted desperately to come back here again at night.

By now it was well past noon, and he was starving. He left the tower in search of food, but stopped suddenly at the sight of a giant pink condom with arms and legs and a Band-Aid on its head. Or maybe it was a cone-headed penis? Or was it supposed to be a flesh-colored crayon? At any rate, it was hugging a little boy, causing Bill to wonder if he should alert the authorities.

But it seemed that this was OK with the boy's parents, so who was he to judge? He shook his head and continued his search for food, which ended at a Wendy's hamburger joint.

Some people at this point in the story may feel compelled to scorn Bill for his lack of adventurousness, but in his defense, he was starving and needed something familiar with lots of calories and, above all, not tasting of fish.

The Wendy's was very interesting. Bill walked inside, and after only two steps he hit an obstacle: the counter. He looked around. There was a long counter that stretched from wall to wall with several short lines of customers waiting in front of it. And that was it. No seats anywhere to be seen. Not even a condiment stand.

Bill gave his order by pointing to one of the choices on the menu that had been conveniently laminated to the counter top. The girl behind the counter asked him in broken English if he wanted the meal or just the sandwich. He ordered the meal and was asked for the size: S, M, or L. She actually said the letters. So he ordered the "S" size and was handed a placard with a number on it.

He stood there holding it like a moron for a good thirty seconds until one of the girls behind the counter found the time to stop giggling at him and pointed to the stairs over in the corner. Bill realized his mistake and felt like a complete tit. He went over to the stairs, which led both up and down, and so he chose up.

He sat at a table that felt as if it were three-quarters the size of a proper table. In fact, as the days went by, Bill came to realize that most everything in Tokyo was three-quarters the size of its counterpart in America, and close to half the size of anything in Texas.

Bill's meal was delivered to him in short order. He soon discovered that his burger, while tasty, was three-quarters the size that he was expecting. And the small drink was basically a thimble. And they gave him exactly five fries. Bill sighed. OK, mental note, "L" is your friend from now on.

While Bill was eating his meal, two girls sat down a few seats away from him. They were dressed like geisha, complete with the white makeup, red lips, and rolled-back hairstyle. Bill was very confused — he was pretty sure that geisha were from a bygone era. Perhaps these girls just came from a play or something?

After eating his meal, Bill encountered even more Japanese strangeness. This time it was in the realm of garbage disposal. There were all sorts of various receptacles intended to receive his garbage. Fortunately for Bill, he had been almost absentmindedly watching people dump their garbage as he ate his lunch.

The routine was this: remove the plastic lid and straw from the soda and place them in a special container, presumably for recycled plastic. Then dump your ice and left-over soda into a stainless steel receptacle. Then dump the paper cup, paper napkin, paper fry container, and paper sandwich wrapper into the more traditional-looking garbage receptacle. On reflection, this made so much sense that Bill was unsure why the rest of the world had not adopted this system.

Even though he had just finished lunch, Bill noticed that the afternoon was wearing on. This was not because of any weird geological or astronomical trick but simply because Bill was still jet-lagged and had started his day rather late, and as a result had been out of kilter with the rest of the world all day.

He wondered very briefly if it would be safe to be out at night by himself and then quickly decided that amongst a population of people who thought that jay-walking was the height of civil disobedience, he was very likely the scariest thing around.

And so Bill struck out for the train station. Just inside the entrance was a giant map of the entire train system on the wall to the right. Below it were the ticket machines. Straight ahead were the turnstiles that people were feeding tickets into. To the left were some vending machines. Bill hung back and examined the map. It was in Japanese. All of it. Bill was still sketchy with his reading and writing. OK, don't worry, he told himself, you are prepared for this.

Bill pulled an English version of the map from his back pocket and unfolded it. He was thinking how brilliant he was for printing it out before he had left Texas. He found his next destination on the English map, Shinjuku, and noted at which station it was located. Then he found that station on the big wall map and noted the Yen amount that was written next to it. This was the price of the ticket. Then it was a simple matter to press the button on the ticket machine with the correct price on it, and feed some coins into the machine.

He was rewarded with a tiny little ticket that was sort of thick and rubbery, very much like a refrigerator magnet. In fact, flipping it over, Bill saw the same kind of flexible brown substance and guessed that this must be the machine-readable portion of the ticket. He fed it into the gate, which opened for him obediently. As he walked through the gate, his ticket was waiting for him at the top of the railing up ahead. He guessed, correctly, that this was needed to get back out of the system.

Riding the train was very much like riding the subway in New York, but without the smell of urine and vomit, and without the lady that keeps coughing up blood, and without the guy who keeps talking to himself while getting angrier and angrier.

The seats were arranged along the side walls, facing inward. The center was empty of seats but had lots of hand straps above head that one could hold onto while standing. No one was talking. No one. No one was even making eye contact with each other. Most people stared down at their cellphones, or read books and magazines. It was very nice and polite, if not a little creepy at first. However, Bill grew to appreciate the silence and the politeness, and he had to admit that it was certainly an improvement over urine, vomit, blood, and noise.

Bill exited the rail system at Shinjuku station. The sun was almost completely down and the eye-popping lights of Shinjuku were already lit. He did not think it was possible, but Bill supposed that Shinjuku was even brighter and busier than Shibuya.

Not far from the station was a department store called Keio. Bill went inside with the hopes of maybe finding a nice pair of chopsticks. Keio turned out to be very much like Macy's but with a few interesting exceptions. Firstly, they had a wide variety of chopsticks for Bill to choose from. And Secondly, they also had a department where a person could buy very big, very beautiful, and above all, very expensive swords. Bill saw this and had to almost physically restrain himself from spending all of his remaining money on a sword. The only thing that stopped him was the thought of trying to get it through airport security on his way back home.

Bill avoided temptation and left the department store in search of more adventure. He walked around and explored for thirty minutes or so, but stopped when he noticed a very odd phenomenon. He kept getting really turned around and was increasingly starting to cross over places where he knew he had already been, but was expecting to be somewhere totally else. This was actually because the part of town he was in was bounded by a triangle, not a square — which is something he never discovered and continues to be baffled about to this day.

Nevertheless, he managed to free himself from the Shinjuku Triangle and stumbled into the seedier part of town, Kabukichō. Bill was fairly certain of this when he saw a store with a sign that read "Love Merci" and had some rather suggestive imagery to accompany the letters.

Bill was by no means prudish, but he always felt uncomfortable about going into sex shops. In his mind, they were places for deviants to go after they had worn out all the normal pleasures of life and therefore needed to amp things up with leather and rubber just to feel anything at all. It reeked of sadness and desperation. But Bill was also very inquisitive and he was away from home and away from everyone that knew him, which somehow gave him a little more fizz, shall we say. And so Bill shrugged and went inside Love Merci.

The place was very red and pink. There were handcuffs hanging from the ceiling — fuzzy ones. There was an entire aisle devoted to long, rubbery things of all shapes and sizes. There was even a Hello Kitty "neck massager." It was long and slender and it vibrated.

Bill was looking at some sort of contraption that was encased in glass, as if it were some sort of museum piece. Bill fled when he realized what it was for, which was to, eh-hem, "massage" certain parts of a man.

Bill darted into another aisle, and what he saw there blew the last of his circuits. With his mind blown, he stumbled back outside for some air. Bill would never get the sight of Japanese businessmen shopping for love dolls out of his mind for as long as he lived.

As he walked down the road, he was continually asked, in English, if he wanted some female companionship, or if he wanted to have a good time at some bar or another. Interestingly enough, most of the people doing the asking were not Asian, but rather black or white Westerners. In fact, Bill noticed throughout his trip that this seemed to be the sole job of the scant few gaijin (outsiders / non-Japanese) men in Tokyo — the vast majority of which were black. Bill wondered if this was somehow a racist thought, but decided that it was not. After all, it was reality. You had to call a spade a spade. OK, that was probably a racist thought.

Bill politely declined the offers and continued down the road when an elderly Japanese man suddenly sprung out from behind a sign and said, "Six?" to him.

Bill blinked at him. "Six?" he asked.

The man repeated, "Six?"

Bill thought for a moment and then he finally got it.

"Oh, you mean sex," he said, probably a little too jovially.

The man bowed slightly and said, *"Hai.* Six."

Bill answered in broken Japanese and a worried voice, "What? With you?"

The man practically choked and said, roughly translated, "No, no. Not like that. With pretty young lady."

Bill politely declined and continued his walk. He was starting to feel that he needed a beer to help him cope with the culture shock. He saw a place called "Sexy Bar," but given his last few encounters, he was a little wary of it. Instead, he stumbled into another random bar, this one slightly below ground. They were playing hip hop, which Bill was not fond of. He walked over to the bar and ordered a beer, which was three-quarters the size that he had expected.

As he sipped his beer, Bill surveyed his surroundings. He was actually the only person seated at the bar. Most of the customers were sitting at small tables that were scattered around the room. Three-quarters of the people, all men, were black. The other quarter were Asian, and female. Something seemed a little off to Bill. The hairs on the back of his neck were standing up and his imagination was starting to come to some interesting conclusions. After a few more sips, a rather scary-looking black man who had a messed up eye that was completely milky white (which was a large part of the reason why he was so scary looking) caught Bill's attention. He walked up to Bill and winked at him with his messed up eye, and then walked over to the other side of the bar and gestured toward a pretty Asian girl with his head. She was playing darts with her friend (or perhaps co-worker), and seemed oblivious to the scary black man.

Bill shook his head no, gulped down his beer, slammed down some money on the bar, and quickly scurried outside, all the while trying very hard to not make eye contact with the scary black man.

Bill was a little creeped out now, and felt that he really could use another drink. And then before he knew it, some guy, this time white, had talked him into visiting a place called Club Essex, which was offering free drinks.

The club was fairly big for a place in Tokyo and was furnished like a cross between a restaurant and a night club. Bill was shown to a table and served a huge gin and tonic, which glowed rather intriguingly under the black lights of the club. The only other patron was a Japanese man seated across the room who was chatting with a cute Japanese girl.

After a minute or two, a girl with pale skin, blue eyes, and short blonde hair took a seat next to him and put her hand on his leg. She started to speak some crazy gibberish, which Bill thought might be Russian.

Bill said, "Hey, whoa, who the hell are you?" but the girl kept gabbing away in her own lingo. When it was clear that communication was near impossible as the girl knew very little Japanese and even less English, she left and a few minutes later was replaced with a somewhat less attractive but still very friendly Filipino lady. To Bill's relief, she seemed more reserved than the first girl.

Bill introduced himself and inquired what all this was about, referring to the club, and asked what the catch was to the free drinks.

The lady, who had introduced herself as Tina, answered, "This is what we call a host club, a place where a person can come to have something like a guaranteed date. Our hosts are trained to stroke your ego, and while very flirty, usually do not stroke anything else. It is a place to unwind and relax with a member of the opposite sex who will go out of their way to make you feel smart, funny, and interesting — and also very at ease. This is something that is not usually talked about, of course, as it spoils the fantasy, but I can tell that you would not feel comfortable with fantasy."

Bill was amazed and responded, "That's actually very perceptive of you. You must be very good at this job."

Tina answered, "Actually, I work as a waitress upstairs. Sometimes I fill in when they need someone who can speak English. Things are slow up there at this time of night, so I came down here to make some extra money. Incidentally, you asked about the catch, right? The catch is that your drinks are free but mine are not. And that is how they make their money, by having me talk you into ordering overpriced drinks for me, and overpriced appetizers for the table."

Bill nodded. "Ah, I see."

Tina continued, "And with that said, that is also how I earn my money — I get a percentage. So do you mind ordering something for me?"

How could he refuse? Bill ordered some appetizers for the table and told Tina to get whatever she wanted to drink. Bill's empty glass was replaced with another pint-sized glass of gin and tonic. It was really very good. Bill could feel himself getting a little loopy already, but he was enjoying the company and it was nice to be able to speak English for a change.

"So tell me," he asked, "do any of you ever take these pseudo dates outside the bar?"

"Tina giggled and answered, "Sometimes, yes. A popular spot is Disneyland..."

Bill interrupted, "Disneyland?"

"Oh yes, there is one right here in Tokyo. I've been there lots and lots of times but every time I go, it is my first time."

Bill squinted at her. "What do you mean, first time?"

Tina giggled again and answered, "I mean, every time I go with a customer it is like, 'Oh my, this is my first time here — how exciting. Thank you for taking me!'" She smirked.

Bill laughed. "OK, you've just earned yourself another drink. What do you get the biggest tip from?"

"A bottle of champagne for the table."

Bill nodded. He flagged down the attendant and ordered a bottle of champagne like the big shot he was. He turned back to Tina and said, "You really are good at this, you know. Are you sure you don't do this all the time for the club?"

Tina smirked. "No, this is my first time."

Bill laughed again and almost choked on his appetizer. Bill was getting seriously drunk at this point and was enjoying himself to no end.

Tina asked, "So, is this your first time to Tokyo?"

Bill nodded. "Yes, this is my first time anywhere in Japan."

"So what do you think of it?"

"I really like it," answered Bill. "I didn't think I would like Tokyo because I'm not a fan of cities, but Tokyo is kind of awesome. It's so... clean. And cute. Everything here is so cutesy — like everything has a little cartoon character or a heart or some kind of silly mascot added to it. I'm trying to figure out if this is some sort of innate cultural thing, or if it is somehow pushed by the government as a form of manipulation of the group psychology."

Tina creased her forehead in a very cutesy manner and said, "I'm afraid you lost me there. Maybe you should drink a little more to get yourself down to my level."

Bill offered a hollow laugh and said, "Sorry about that. It's just something that interests me, group psychology. I used to work in the investment industry and I found that if you can understand the way that groups think and what drives them, then you can rule the markets — at least that is what my ex-wife used to say. She was pretty sharp about that stuff."

"Ex-wife?" questioned Tina.

"Yeah," said Bill, "We got divorced over a stupid accident."

Tina snickered. "Oh, what, like you tripped and fell and stuck your dick in someone else?"

Bill chuckled and said, "You laugh, but you aren't far from the truth. I did trip and fall on someone, and there were sexual harassment charges filed, but I promise you that my penis never entered into the equation — or anything else for that matter."

"OK, now you've got my interest. You better explain yourself."

Bill explained about his mishap with Miss Trezzor and continued to chat with Tina for some time, when suddenly she asked him where he is staying.

Bill's pickled mind was having a slurred conversation with itself in response to the question.

One part said, "Hey, maybe we are getting lucky."

Another part answered, "No, you idiot, it will probably cost us money."

The first part answered back, "Why don't you just ask her? She'll probably give us an honest answer."

To which the reply was, "No, you ask her." At which point his brain locked into an infinite loop of, "No — you. No — you. No — you..."

Mercifully, Tina broke the loop by adding, "If you are staying nearby and took the train here, you should probably leave now. The trains are going to shut down in fifteen minutes."

"Shit! Thanks," answered Bill, smoothly. He really, really needed to go to the bathroom and he was almost too drunk to stand. He pulled himself together the best that he could and settled his bill with the attendant, which because of the yen-to-dollar exchange rate made Bill feel as if he must have just bought a car — there were a good many zeros on the bill.

He waved goodbye to Tina and rushed out of the door. He bobbed and weaved around the black men trying to make a love connection and arrived at the station with five minutes to spare. He boarded the train, which was empty except for him, and promptly fell asleep.

"You go. Mister. Please. You go now. Mister?"

"Huh? Where am I?"

"Train closed. You go."

Bill glanced at the sign. He was pretty sure that this was nowhere near his stop. "This is not my stop."

"Train closed. You go please."

Bill got to his feet and held back an urge to vomit. He really had to urinate, too. He left the train and quickly found a bathroom, which was locked. He cursed and headed toward the exit, pausing only to vomit almost a gallon of slightly used gin and tonic on the steps of the station. He felt very bad about this, but he had nothing to clean it up with and felt that even if he tried, he would likely just add to the pile. And so he left the pile and found the exit. He entered a cab outside the station and again did the matchbook trick with the driver.

After a blessedly short (and smooth) ride, Bill left the cab and stopped at the 7-11 for another steamed bun, this time from the middle rack, and some other random items that looked interesting. He flirted briefly with the idea of asking to use the bathroom, but reasoned that it would take longer to try to ask in drunken Japanese than it would to just walk next door to the hotel and use the one in his room. And so that was exactly what he did.

After using the toilet, Bill tried his steamed bun. Instead of the heavenly pulled-pork filling, this one contained something that was gooey, gritty, and somewhat sweet all at the same time. It was not what Bill was expecting, and not anything he could readily identify, so he immediately spit it out and ate something else from the 7-11, which was a long and tasty piece of beef skewered by a bamboo stick.

Now satisfied, Bill quickly fell asleep and dreamed of Japanese businessmen chasing young girls around Disneyland with Hello Kitty vibrators while black men with weird eyes sat on nearby benches and grinned as they counted their yen.

CHAPTER 8

In a secret laboratory below a small shrine located in an unassuming town, two monks dressed in white robes sat at a workbench and drank tea while discussing the day's events.

The senior monk said, "I am not sure about that fellow. He keeps coming back here but all he does is poke around as if he were looking for something. He never prays. He does not seem any more spiritual. Actually, he looks annoyed to me. What do you say?"

The junior monk answered, "I am unsure, Master. He does look distracted when he comes here, but otherwise he seems to have chosen to walk the path. He has given away a fortune to aid others and now lives in simplicity and almost total isolation. I think it is working. Perhaps we should try again with a second subject?"

The senior monk stroked his long, white beard while he considered this. Finally, he answered, "Yes, I agree. One cannot draw proper conclusions from just one data point. We will try again in a few days. Please begin the preparations."

The junior monk bowed and said, "Very well, Master. As you wish." He bowed once more and excused himself.

CHAPTER 9

Today's breakfast consisted of *stroopwafels* and a semi-gelatinous energy drink called Weider-N-Jelly, which tasted like a mixture of Gatorade and grape juice. The *stroopwafels*, which Bill had found in his room, had apparently been imported from Holland. A *stroopwafel* was a foodstuff made from two small waffles that had been glued together with a sort of cinnamon-spiced caramel. Bill thought they were heavenly.

The energy drink had been bought the night before, and it had miraculous hangover-curing properties. It seemed to settle Bill's stomach, alleviate his headache, and provide him with instant energy. It was monstrously great stuff, and he felt that he could make a fortune if he could import it into the United States.

Bill took a moment to plan out his day as he ate his unusual breakfast. Today would be a day for some lighthearted exploring. Today's destinations would be: Harajuku (a sort of avant-garde fashion district), Hibiya Park (where there was rumored to be a statue of Godzilla), and Akihabara (which was also known as "Electric Town" and was known to be the epicenter of all things high tech as well as all things anime and manga). Several of Bill's "collectables" had originated from shops in Akihabara.

Bill took the train to the first of his destinations — Harajuku. He had picked a good day to visit this district because all the bat-shit-crazy kids who frequented the area were off from school today. And they really were crazy, or at least crazy looking, with odd makeup and elaborate costumes. Some were dressed like anime characters, a practice known as *kosupure* (cosplay), short for costume play. Bill had to admit that, crazy or not, they were kind of cute.

Bill walked further and then stopped suddenly when he saw a group of seven men wearing nothing but red leotards that covered them from head to toe, including their faces. They were not doing anything remarkable other than walking and attracting attention.

It was difficult for Bill to get a better look because the streets were terribly narrow and terribly crowded. The area actually reminded him of some cities he had seen in Italy. The narrow streets were reserved only for foot traffic and were bordered by a string of shops and dwellings that were all joined together to form two winding walls of commerce.

The crowd density in the valley between these two opposing lengths of storefront was almost inhumane. It was absolutely not a place for a person with either claustrophobia or agoraphobia. Bill had neither but was still feeling a little uneasy. Pausing only to buy a cappuccino and a strange hand puppet that made the sound of a hundred screaming Japanese schoolgirls when he opened its mouth, Bill left Harajuku in search of Godzilla.

On his way back to the train station he passed a pedestrian bridge lined with more bat-shit-crazy girls and decided to check it out. Several of them were young Japanese girls dressed as French maids.

Now, Bill thought that many of the Japanese girls were quite sexy in Tokyo, especially when they wore short skirts and long stockings, leaving only two inches of leg exposed between the two, which somehow contrived to be just about the sexiest thing that he had ever seen. Bill also quite fancied French maid outfits and thought they were incredibly sexy as well. But somehow, seeing an otherwise pretty Japanese girl in a French maid outfit was very, very unsexy. Surprisingly so, in fact.

There was something about a little Asian face poking out from all those frills that just seemed wrong. He supposed that somehow it was engrained in his Western head that the face should be, well, French. He smiled at them politely and walked on by.

This brought him to the entrance to some sort of park. At the side of the pathway near the entrance was a huge rack of barrels stacked three high and around twenty across. On the front of each barrel was a person's name. Bill cringed when he thought about the implications, but was relieved when he read a sign next to them explaining that they were wine barrels. Apparently, they had been donated by some fancy wineries in France during the Meiji period.

Bill began to tour the park, which turned out to be a flower garden. But since it was largely unfinished, he decided to move on to his quest for Godzilla, which was rumored to lurk in Hibiya Park.

Hibiya Park was very beautiful and very large. It was also, as Bill was coming to realize, completely free of anything Godzilla-like in nature.

The park was harmoniously landscaped. Natural stone was used to border the central lake, to form walkways, and to function as natural steps to assist in climbing the steeper hills of the park. The bridges were wooden and modest. The trees had grass skirts for some reason, but the look was pleasing. Bill wondered if they were to prevent insect or rodent infestation, to ward off evil spirits, or perhaps just to look pretty.

There were also a couple of smaller trees along the lakeside that were strung up with ropes. The ropes were tied to various parts of each tree and then converged to a single point above them, which formed a sort of cone shape. It was unclear to Bill if this was merely for decoration or perhaps to pull the trees in a certain direction as they grew.

And yet, there was still no sign of Godzilla. The closest thing Bill found so far was a couple of turtles floating along the edge of the lake. He scouted around some more and eventually found a map of the park, which was completely bereft of Godzilla — although he did laugh out loud when he noticed that there were two turtles on the map in the exact same spot that he had seen them. Obviously this map was very up to date and scarily detailed.

Bill noticed a fountain on the map and decided to head there in the off chance that Godzilla was immortalized in bronze while having a drink or shooting water out of his mouth.

Bill had been very reluctantly asking people in Japanese "Where is Godzilla?" or simply stating "I am looking for Godzilla," and he felt somehow that he was being racist again as he did so.

No one seemed to know what he was talking about, however. Maybe because of this, Bill was starting to feel isolated by his linguistic handicap. It felt like something oppressive was surrounding him, slowly depriving him of life in much the same way a drowning man might feel about water. He desperately yearned for someone to throw him a life preserver in the form of an English conversation.

Walking on, he finally came to a fountain where he noticed a tall blonde-haired gentleman who was wearing a tan suit and wire-rimmed spectacles. The man was sitting on the wall that surrounded the fountain while he unpacked his lunch.

As Bill approached him, the stranger said, "What's up?" in a friendly and inviting sort of way.

Bill answered back absentmindedly, "Oh thank God."

The man tilted his head. Bill continued, "I'm sorry to bother you on your lunch break, but can you tell me if you have seen a Godzilla statue anywhere in this park?"

The guy shook his head. "I'm sorry, friend, I come here almost every day for lunch and I have never seen a Godzilla statue in Hibiya Park."

Bill looked downcast. The man, seeing this, gestured for Bill to have a seat beside him and gave Bill half of his baloney sandwich. Bill ate it graciously even though he had had an aversion to baloney ever since he had gone to jail for two weeks for driving on a suspended license back when he was in his early twenties. The prison had fed him baloney and mustard sandwiches every day for lunch for two weeks straight. Sometimes, if they had made too many sandwiches, he would get one for dinner too.

Bill thanked the man and dejectedly made his way toward one of the exits. Just before leaving, he saw a prehistoric stone wheel, or at least that is what it looked like to him. The plaque next to it read in Japanese, English, and Braille as follows:

This round stone was used as money in Yap Island (the present Federal States of Micronesia) in the South Pacific. Such stone money varies greatly in size from about 6 cm to 3 m in diameter.

In general, the value was decided based on four characteristics: 1) diameter, 2) surface texture (smooth or rough), 3) shape, and 4) difficulty of transportation. This stone money is approximately circular, measuring 1.35 m across its longest axis and 1.0 m across its shortest. It was

regarded to be worth about 1,000 yen in 1924. (Contributed by Mayor of Yap Island Branch Office in January 1925)

Bill did the currency conversion in his head. At the present exchange rate, that would be worth $10 in America, which seemed a little low if a man had to lug a 1500 pound stone with him just to buy lunch. He could only assume and hope that thanks to inflation, 1000 yen went a lot further back in 1924.

As he left the park, Bill noticed a small *koban*, which was a sort of police box or guard station — basically a police station for one man. Bill approached the guard with a little apprehension because he knew what he was about to do. He asked the guard if he knew English. The guard's answer was an apology in Japanese. Bill was happy that the guard looked somewhat elderly and very calm — it would make this a little easier.

Bill switched to Japanese and told the man that it was not a problem. Then he asked him, "Where in Hibiya Park is Godzilla?"

Bill braced for a blow from the guard's baton while really wishing that he knew the Japanese word for 'statue'.

The guard looked puzzled, or at least Bill hoped it was puzzlement and not anger. The guard answered back, "*Gojira?*"

Bill nodded.

The guard then answered, "Not in Hibiya Park."

Bill nodded again and then was about to apologize and thank the guard for his time when the guard added, "It is close by." The guard pointed down the street and added, "Go two blocks, make a left, go one block, make a left. *Gojira* is there."

Bill was ecstatic at this turn of good luck. He bowed deeply to the guard and thanked him for his patience and his help.

And sure enough, after a short walk, there was Godzilla in all his glory. But somehow after all of this work, Bill was left feeling a little cheated.

Yes, OK, the bronze statue was fantastically detailed and obviously the work of a true craftsman, but Bill could not help but notice that it was only four feet tall.

To help with its height issue, the statue was on a large pedestal that was in itself about four or five feet tall, but somehow conspired to make the statue look even smaller. The statue was both beautiful and silly at the same time. Bill took a few pictures of himself with Godzilla in the background. He found that if he kept the camera low and shot upward, it created the illusion that the statue was much larger and was towering over him.

With another item now erased from his bucket list, Bill took the subway to Akihabara.

The subway turned out to be almost identical to the train — the same magnetic tickets were used, the cars were very much the same inside, and there was even the same sense of forced quiet while riding.

But there were also some differences. For one, the subway stations were, of course, underground. Also, it often took a kilometer's worth of walking through the labyrinthine station to get to the correct subway line. Bill frequently felt that had he simply walked the same distance on the surface then he would have arrived at his destination without the need for transport.

Another difference was, of course, that there was a lot less to see out of the windows of the subway car. Bill examined the signs inside the car instead. One of them featured a drawing of a young man slouching on a bench seat while taking up valuable sitting space with his belongings. He had some sort of girly magazine sitting next to him, and he was casually reading it while soda cans littered the area around his feet. The caption read in both Japanese and English, "Please do it at home."

Another sign, this one only text, caught Bill's attention. It read, "If you notice any suspicious unattended packages or people, please report them immediately." Not only was this funny because it implied that there might be suspicious unattended people hanging around, but it also piqued Bill's interest because it was written only in English. He wondered why this might be so. Was it because the Japanese already knew to do this by custom and practice, or perhaps it was solely for the benefit of foreigners as a very gentle hint that they are being watched.

Later on, he encountered another sign in the subway tunnel that reinforced his suspicions. It was again only in English and it read, "This subway station is monitored by camera." He half expected to see another one in English reading, "Please do not tempt the locals with sex and alcohol."

Bill emerged from the subway grateful that no one had felt that he looked suspicious or unattended. He was now in Akihabara, the epicenter of Japanese *otaku* culture. *Otaku* essentially means enthusiast, but it has evolved to mean someone who spends way too much of his time watching anime, reading manga, and collecting little dolls of the characters in both of them.

It was also the epicenter of technology and electronics, which Bill quickly found out as he made his way through the never-ending alleyways of Akihabara. There were stalls set up where a person could buy switches, capacitors, resistors, and other assorted electronic components by the kilogram. There were stores selling high-end cameras, stores selling all sorts of robotics, and there was even a store selling used computer parts, stun guns, spy cameras, and porn under the same roof. It was like a stalker emporium.

Exploring further, he stumbled on a shop selling manga, or if you wanted to be crass about it, you could call it a comic book store. But it was unlike any comic book store that Bill had ever seen. For one thing, there were glass cases throughout the store featuring highly detailed dolls of the sort that Bill was so very fond. He was beginning to drool.

He looked at a few price tags, and even subtracting the required two digits from the end, the prices still did not make sense. These were no ordinary dolls, these really were one-of-a-kind collectables and some listed for thousands of dollars each. And for that price, they still wore very little clothing — some were even topless.

Bill managed to restrain himself from adding to his collection and made himself leave before he did. As he was leaving the building, he noticed a set of stairs leading down to below street level. Over the stairway was a picture of a young girl, too young, with ripped clothing and tears in her eyes. Bill did not go down the stairs.

He then visited Yadabashi-Akiba to lighten his mood. This was a giant retail electronics store in the center of town. He traveled through floor after floor of gadgets. Everything in the store was familiar yet odd — mostly the same things he could find in Texas except with different brands. A lot of things were somewhat smaller, while others were completely new to him — like microprocessor-controlled rice cookers and fancy toilet seats that washed and dried your butt automatically.

Eventually, Bill felt dizzy and disoriented from constantly trying to figure out the Japanese that was assailing him non-stop, and also from simply trying to identify all the strange things around him. His brain was overloaded and he needed a break.

By now it was getting late, and Bill was considering heading back to the hotel when he saw, well, another hotel. But this one was a special sort, a capsule hotel. He had read about them online and was dying to try one. These were super cheap hotels in which your "room" was a 1x1x2 meter box — essentially it was a kennel for people. They were affectionately known as coffin hotels. OK, it was obviously not everyone's cup of tea, but Bill was inquisitive to a fault.

He walked into the place, and within a few paces of the reception desk, he was immediately yelled at. The man motioned toward the doorway and told him to take off his shoes. Bill looked back and saw a few other pairs lined up by the door, presumably belonging to the other people who were checking in. Bill sighed and walked back to the entrance. Great, he thought, I've already desecrated the sanctity of the lobby. I wonder if they are going to cane me?

Now in socked feet, he made his way back to the desk to check in, where he was immediately sent back to the doorway to get his shoes and put them in one of the available lockers by the door. He did this and once again returned to the desk with the key to the locker in his hand.

The man now took the key from Bill, which worried him slightly. The man then attached the key along with a second unknown key to a cloth wristband and handed it to Bill, who hesitantly put it around his wrist, hoping this was the right thing to do. There was no shouting, so he supposed that it was.

After some paperwork was signed and some money was exchanged, Bill was pointed to the elevators and told not to go to the 7th floor under any circumstances, which seemed a little ominous.

He heeded the advice and instead went to the 2nd floor, which was a large open shower of the sort you might picture to be in a prison. He searched for a locker with the same number on it as his wristband, pausing only to let a bare-assed Asian man streak passed on the way to the showers.

The locker opened with the second key on his wristband. Inside of the wafer-thin locker was a robe that felt like an over-starched hospital gown. There was also a toothbrush and a towel.

Bill glanced back and decided that a group shower was not in his future. He changed into the gown and locked his clothes and all his other belongings in the tiny locker, although he kept his cellphone with him.

Now it was off to the 6th floor to find his "room". He noticed on a map in the elevator that the 7th floor was for women only, so that solved that mystery.

The sixth floor consisted of a single hallway, and on each side of the hallway, stacked two-high, were the "rooms." They were nothing more than fiberglass boxes approximately three feet high, three feet wide, and six feet deep. They had bamboo blinds for doors. This later proved fortunate because Bill was a little taller than the average customer, so his toes stuck out of his room.

Bill pulled up the "door" and crawled into his capsule, which was on the top row. He flipped over onto his back and hesitantly sat up. There was enough headroom for this, which was a relief.

He surveyed his surroundings. A small TV was built into the right-hand corner of the capsule. To the right of the TV, on the wall, was a panel containing a radio and alarm clock, as well as controls for the TV and the light.

Above and slightly behind his head were a light and a fresh air vent. To his left was a map of the 6th floor that indicated the location of the stairs in case of an emergency. Straight ahead of him were his feet. And finally, below him were a comfortable mattress and a pillow that was stuffed with hard plastic beads that ended up being quite comfortable.

Bill took a few pictures of his room and his feet and emailed them to Kevin, who later wrote back asking if he should send bail money.

Bill reflected that this was not far off the mark. After all, they had taken his shoes, his clothes, and his stuff. They had put him in a scratchy robe, given him a toothbrush and a towel, and confined him to a tiny cell. The dull yellow lights outside the cell never went out at night. The showers were communal. He had heard several people snoring (as well as making some other disturbing sounds). Really, all that was missing was a baloney sandwich and it would have been just like being back in jail again.

CHAPTER 10

The senior loan officer of Tamiya Bank sat in his office and played with his executive toys. Right now he was fiddling with the Newton's Cradle.

He was not only the senior loan officer for this branch, but also happened to be the branch manager's nephew. It was his first week on the job and he was a little confused about what he was supposed to do because recent changes in the bank's policy had eliminated the making of loans — at least to the "poor" people who needed the money. That would be silly.

No, most of their working capital was now loaned to serious men, men that had drive and were gaining serious political pull.

In fact, although he did not know it yet, this was now his de facto job — to loan money to these serious men, and then as they paid back the loans he was to channel a portion of the proceeds to some well-connected people in the political arena. This arrangement seemed to be a win-win for all involved. The serious men ensured that the political leaders had the backing of the common man, and the political leaders ensured that the serious men were left alone to do so. And the bank received a percentage of it all. Win-win-win. It was so easy.

CHAPTER 11

Bill woke up way too early for his liking and unceremoniously checked out of the coffin hotel, vowing to work hard from now on to earn enough money to never have to stay in one again.

He picked the absolute wrong time to take the train, and probably the worst line for this time of day as well. He was on the Yamanote line during the morning commute. The Yamanote line formed a loop around the core of the city and was a hub for several other lines. He was crammed inside the train tighter than a pig in a can of Spam, which made the short ride rather unpleasant.

While riding the train, Bill noticed several men who were holding their hands up, as if they were waiting to be called on by a teacher. He had watched enough anime to know what this was about. The object was to demonstrate that they were not perverts. Groping was sometimes a problem on crowded trains, and false accusations were on the rise, so these men were taking preventative measures against them. Bill followed their lead and folded his arms in front of him.

Back at his normal hotel, he packed up his things and decided that for the next day or two he was going to spoil himself by staying in what was arguably the nicest hotel in Tokyo, the Park Hyatt. This was to reward himself for the stay in the coffin hotel, and also to get himself back into a professional, high-roller frame of mind.

He had a shower, a shave, and put on a suit to aid in his self-improvement and then had the concierge call him a taxi, which next to a limousine was the only proper way to arrive at the Park Hyatt.

The ride was swift and pleasurable. When the taxi arrived at the Park Hyatt, a fleet of bellhops descended on it like a formula one pit crew. One person collected Bill's luggage while another escorted him to the front lobby. Two others were on standby simply to bow and open the doors for him. Oh yes, this is more like it, thought Bill.

His escort took him into the elevator and pressed the button for the 41st floor. The hotel occupied the top floors of a modern skyscraper. On the way to the hotel lobby, his escort stopped several times to show him some attractions like a library filled with literary classics that was open for use by the guests, as well as a stunningly elegant (and probably staggeringly expensive) dining hall. The escort then guided him over to a desk where a blonde girl with a British accent walked him through the check-in process.

After the paperwork was sorted out, she handed Bill a room key on a sterling silver keyring. There was a time when mag cards were something special and added an air of sophistication to a hotel, but now that they were ubiquitous, there was something exceedingly elegant about getting a standard key.

Bill was now escorted to his room on the 43rd floor by the one remaining bellhop who had his luggage. He did not speak much, but walked around the room pointing and turning things on and off. The last switch he flipped was near the bed, and it triggered an electric motor which opened the massive curtains.

This revealed a window the full length of the wall. Bill stared out of it and gibbered. The bellhop gave his leave and backed out of the door, bowing several times as he did so. Bill felt the need to tip him but stopped himself when he remembered that there was no tipping in Japan, which came across more like an insult to the receiver.

Bill thoroughly approved of this as he often felt that people already got paid for the work they were doing, and so why should he have to pay them extra just for doing their job? In fact, a tip used to be given ahead of time as a sort of bribe for preferential treatment. Now it has devolved into a custom where everyone expects the bribe just for doing their regular duties.

Now alone in his room, Bill set about exploring it. The décor was Western with an Eastern flare. The bathroom was huge, and Bill noted with amusement that the shower stall in the bathroom was bigger than the capsule he had stayed in the night before.

He walked back to the giant picture window and marveled at the scenery. He was in one of the tallest buildings around, and so the scenery looked very much like that from the Tokyo Tower. In the center of it all was a giant patch of green, some sort of very large park he guessed.

It was funny how different Tokyo looked from other cities in America, such as Houston or Manhattan. It looked cleaner for lack of a better word. The buildings looked more modern and somehow both whiter and more colorful as well. Bill's impression of Manhattan had always included words like 'gray' and 'deteriorating', and Houston was even less impressive.

Tokyo even managed to look smarter at night, with sleek black silhouettes punctuated by crisp white lights and red beacons on the top of each one. Manhattan at night just looked like a sea of sickly yellow lights and nothing more.

Bill decided to celebrate by going up to the lounge on the top floor of the building. He had another *Lost in Translation* moment when he realized that he was sitting in the very same seat as Bill Murray in the movie, which was filmed in the very same hotel. He ordered a Suntory whiskey just to be cute, and patiently waited for Scarlett Johansson to show up but she never did.

The low lights and the smooth jazz coming from the live band conspired to put Bill in a reflective mood. The whiskey helped as well. He wondered how an unemployed nobody from Texas had found himself here in the nicest bar on the highest floor of the best hotel in the biggest city on Earth.

He caught the eye of the beautiful jazz singer and flicked her a smile. He wondered briefly if he was going to have a fling with her, but this never came to be.

Now feeling somewhat lonely, Bill paid his tab and left both the lounge and the hotel in order to do some more sight-seeing. He paused to admire the fountain beside the hotel which was constructed like an infinity pool with the water level even with the surrounding walkway.

The water in the fountain's basin split at one end and traveled along trenches on either side of a cut-out in the ground. The trenches each made hairpin turns on the other side of this cutout, which turned out to be a stairway leading to an underground shopping mall. The water then splashed down its own set of stairs on either side of the normal stairs where it disappeared at the bottom of the stairs. From here, it presumably got pumped up and squirted back out of the fountain high above. It was marvelous to see something like this constructed just for the sheer beauty of it.

As he was admiring it, the wind kicked up and drove a speck of dirt deep into his eyeball. He rubbed his eye to get it out and accidentally knocked out one of his contact lenses, which dropped to the ground and was immediately stepped on by a passerby.

Bill sighed because he was wearing his last pair of contacts. He went back inside the hotel to ask the concierge for directions to the nearest eye doctor. The concierge quickly found the address on the Internet and then drew Bill the most extraordinary map.

The map was drawn in a 3D perspective from above the city and, while Bill was not familiar with the area, it seemed to contain many of the actual buildings, trees, mailboxes, vending machines, and even some little people going in and out of the shops. It was hastily sketched but still amazingly detailed considering it was drawn in under three minutes. Bill was speechless.

Bill took the map from the man with both hands, as if it were a precious thing. He then said to him, "This is extraordinary — you have an amazing talent. Do you mind signing it for me? I'd like to frame it." The concierge seemed very pleased with this and agreed to Bill's request. He looked almost as if he were coming alive again, or as if he had just rediscovered his purpose in life.

The concierge took the map back from Bill and signed it with a flourish. He then looked at Bill for a moment and studied him, as if trying to reach a decision about him. He then quickly scribbled something else on the map and handed it back to Bill and asked, "What is your name, friend?"

"I'm Bill Brabham."

"Nice to meet you, Brabham-san," said the concierge with a smile. He bowed and said, "I wish you good fortune in the future."

Bill, slightly flustered, said, "Thank you. I wish for your good fortune as well."

He thanked the concierge for the map one last time and left the hotel. He began to follow the arrows on the map, which themselves were drawn in 3D and were shown to be floating above the sidewalk, marking the correct path. He walked for a few blocks and stopped suddenly when a burst of music caught his attention. It was Bob Marley's "Three Little Birds," and it was being sung in a Japanese accent.

Bill followed the music and realized it was coming from an Apple store. Apparently they were having a grand opening or something. Bill listened until the end of the song and then continued to follow the arrows.

In short time, he made it to the optometrist's office. He was wondering how healthcare worked in Japan and hoped they would take a random foreigner as a patient.

He went inside and was greeted by a charming lady who spoke English most eloquently, although Bill noticed that when she got overly excited about something she would occasionally slip in a random 'like' into the sentence, which led him to believe that she had been educated in California.

She introduced herself as Kawaguchi Natsuko. In Japan, it is standard to give your family name first followed by your given name, the reverse of how it is done in America. Bill gave his name as well and both of them exchanged the usual set of pleasantries when meeting someone for the first time.

Bill took to calling her Natsuko-san, which for reasons of culture was somewhat forward of him. It is standard practice to use family names, even among co-workers or classmates. When people become friendly, they will then switch to using first names. To call someone by their first name is very much like admitting them into your inner circle.

In addition, the suffix 'san' is usually applied to the names. This is sort of like saying mister or misses. Other suffixes also exist, such as 'kun', 'chan', and 'sama'.

'Kun' is often used towards young men by their peers (if they are close) or by superiors. 'Chan' is a very cutesy sort of suffix and is typically used with either girls or very young boys. It is a diminutive, and is very much like affixing a 'y' to someone's name, as in going from 'Bob' to 'Bobby' or from 'Susan' to 'Susie'. It too would be used by close friends or superiors. 'Sama' is the ultimate ass-kissing suffix and would be used only toward superiors, such as the president of your company, the Emperor of Japan, someone of great accomplishment, or in some cases a customer whose ass you are trying to firmly smother with kisses.

After switching to first names, very close friends or lovers will then usually use only their names with no suffix whatsoever.

Even closer than this would be the use of nicknames.

With all this in mind, Bill felt like 'Natsuko-san' was a happy medium between politeness and his Western sense of friendliness. He also knew that as a *gaijin*, he could get away with it. Natsuko did not seem to mind, although since she found Bill attractive she felt herself blush a little every time he said it. If he had forgotten to affix the 'san', she quite possibly would have fainted.

After the introductions were over, Bill explained his problem. "I lost one of my contacts today and they were my last pair. I don't know how things work here, but can I just order a new pair? I know my prescription."

Natsuko shook her head slightly and answered, "I am afraid not, Mr. Brabham. You will have to have an exam first." She saw the disappointment creeping into Bill's face and added, "But not to worry, because the exam is free and it does not take much time. After that, we can sell you contacts."

Bill lightened up again, "Oh, excellent. Thank you Natsuko-san."

-Blush-

Natsuko led him into a back office and administered a few standard tests, most of them fully automated. Afterwords, she verified the prescription by having him look through a contraption with about a thousand interchangeable lenses on it. He did so and could see perfectly again.

During the testing, Bill occupied the time with idle chitchat about what he was doing in Japan, and a very abbreviated version of what happened in his life to push him into the decision to come there in the first place.

Natsuko listened intently and was surprisingly sympathetic to his plight. She even offered to help him with his relocation if he needed it, and she gave him her cellphone number to that end.

The exam ended and Bill was sold a few boxes of contacts at a very reasonable price — much cheaper than he would have been charged in Texas. He thanked Natsuko for the exam, and for her offer of help. Natsuko walked him downstairs and to the front door. It was clear that both of them wanted to spend more time together, but it was equally clear that there was also no real justification for it at the present time. Bill took solace in the fact that he had her digits and vowed to use them as soon as possible.

Bill said his goodbyes and went back into the hustle of the

street. On a lark, he looked again at the hand-drawn map. It really was excellent. He noticed that over one of the buildings the man had written "Here Be Dragons" and decided to see what that was all about.

It was a long walk to the building, a few kilometers. When he finally arrived, it turned out to be a bar called Gaspanic, which was devilishly named after the 1995 sarin gas incident in the Tokyo subway. He did what any self-respecting man would do when warned of danger, he entered it.

The first thing he saw when he entered was two girls, both very drunk, hugging each other — although it could be possible that they were using each other for mutual support. They stopped hugging and the one said something cheeky to the other, who retaliated by gently smacking the first girl on the forehead, which seemed to upset her world just enough to cause her to fold in two and throw up just in front of Bill (who took a hurried step back). The second girl then helped her up and they both made haste to the restroom.

Well, this looks promising, thought Bill. He walked up to the bar and ordered a beer. There was a young Japanese guy sitting on the bar top. He was wearing a completely white suit and a white hat, along with two thick gold chains around his neck and two gold studs in each ear. He had a bottle of champagne in his hand and was pouring it into several glasses on the bar. He saw Bill and exclaimed something slangy that Bill could not understand, and then slid a glass of champagne over to him.

Bill said thanks and picked up the glass. The guy on the bar immediately yelled out, "*Kanpai!*", clinked glasses with Bill, and then guzzled down the champagne. Bill screamed out, "*Kanpai!*" and guzzled his down too. Hey, this is fun.

Much later that night, Bill returned to the hotel, although he could not remember how. He really hoped that he had not made a spectacle of himself, although if he really concentrated he could vaguely remember throwing up behind one of the bookcases on the way to the lobby.

CHAPTER 12

The concierge waited outside of Bill's room until he heard snoring. He then quietly let himself inside with a spare room key.

Once inside, the concierge located Bill's keys, which were sitting on top of the dresser. He picked them up and quietly added another small key to the keyring.

The concierge then set the keys back down, took one last look at Bill, bowed to him silently, and then left the room.

CHAPTER 13

-RING- -RING-

"Tamiya Bank loan department, how may I help you?"

"Hello? This is Sakamoto. They tell me you are in charge of loans now, am I correct?"

"Yes, that is correct, Sakamoto-san."

"Great. Do you know that YP company? I think they might be a good company to invest in — say to the tune of three million yen. I hear they have a great new product that is about ready for launch, and they just need some last-minute funding to make it happen."

The senior loan officer looked puzzled. "YP? Oh you mean Yum..."

"Yes, that one," interrupted Sakamoto.

The banker answered in a business like tone, "Well, I sincerely appreciate the tip. I will request a full financial statement from..."

"Are you joking? Are you new to this? Just send the money," snapped Sakamoto, impatiently.

The banker stammered, "I am new to Tamiya Bank, Sakamoto-san, but I never joke about money — things need to be done properly. Now, do you by chance know the company's estimated gross revenue for next year?"

Sakamoto was getting livid at this point. "Listen you little paper monkey, I know you are new, but I have a close relationship with the bank. You do not need paperwork because you have my word. Now please send the money."

"I cannot just send money without the proper paperwork," he explained. "It is simply not done."

Sakamoto was so angry at this point that he blew through furious and emerged back on the other side, super calm. "Fine. No problem at all. Someone will be around to see you directly with the paperwork. Sorry for the confusion."

"That will be great, Sakamoto-san. I am sorry for the trouble. Unfortunately, bank rules are very strict. Talk to you soon." -CLICK-

On the other side of town, Sakamoto turned to his Second Lieutenant and said, "You know that new loan guy over at the bank?"

"Yes, boss."

"Apparently he doesn't understand that we are a valuable customer. Please send some men over there right now to educate him — and the bank manager who trained him. And after he is educated, tell him to send the fucking money like I asked or I'll cut his fucking balls off and feed them to his wife as I rape her while he watches."

"Yes, boss."

CHAPTER 14

Bill had managed to spend the last few days in one of the most wholesome cities on Earth sniffing out questionable people in questionable areas, drinking with those questionable people to excess, getting sick in public places, and otherwise behaving in a manner that would have earned him a good smack on the head by his mother had she still been alive to hear about it. It had been fun, Bill reflected, but it was probably time to stop acting like a feral teenager and rejoin the world of responsible adults.

To that end, Bill was once again wearing a business suit in order to keep himself in an adult frame of mind, although it clearly had not worked the night before. He sat at the hotel desk and scanned the map of Japan for a suitable city in which to relocate. He was looking for a town close to the electric plant, but for obvious reasons not too close.

With the power plant sitting right on the eastern coast of Japan, Bill began by looking for towns about 50 kilometers inland. He stumbled on the town of Funehiki and immediately fell in love with it because he thought it would be amusing to tell people that he lives in "Funny Hickey," even though that was not, strictly speaking, how it was pronounced.

Also, strictly speaking, it was no longer called Funehiki. If one can believe the Internet, it was merged with several neighboring towns in 2005 to form the city of Tamura. Knowing this, Bill made it a point to find a place in the old Funehiki part of the city.

-KNOCK- -KNOCK-

Bill heard the knock at the door and looked at his watch; it was three minutes until noon. He smiled to himself and said, "She's punctual, I'll give her that." He crossed the room and opened the door.

Bill smiled when he saw Natsuko and said, "Oh, hey there, right on time. Thanks for helping me out with this."

Natsuko smiled and then looked a little conflicted, as if she were trying to figure out exactly how to address him. Finally, she settled for, "No problem, Mr. Brabham. Thank you for the opportunity to continue to practice my English."

"Please, call me Bill. No need to be formal — I'm not your boss."

Natsuko tried not to blush. She knew it was common for Americans to use first names so soon after meeting, but the Japanese part of her brain still made it feel like he was asking her to call him by a pet name. After she composed herself, she turned back to Bill and said, "I'm still a little uncomfortable with that, Mr. Brabham. I am Sorry."

Bill raised his hands up defensively and said, "No, no, that's fine. I think I understand. Whatever makes you comfortable. I understand that we aren't that close yet." He smiled and added, "Even though you did just meet me in a hotel room."

Natsuko looked shocked at first, and then forced a smile and said, "You tease me, Mr. Brabham."

"Yes, sorry. Please, come on in. *Douzo, Douzo.*"

Natsuko walked into the room as if she were a gazelle that had been invited over to the lion's house for dinner and was now a little worried about what might actually be for dinner. She kicked off her shoes and said, "*Ojamashimasu,*" which was the polite thing to say when entering someone's house, and it more or less meant "I am going to be a bother."

Bill looked down and realized that he was still wearing his shoes and wondered if he had desecrated the sanctity of the room, or some such thing. He quickly kicked them off behind Natsuko as she entered the room.

"So, have you picked a place yet, Mr. Brabham?" asked Natsuko.

"Yes, I think so. What do you know about the town of Funehiki in Tamura City?"

Natsuko's forehead wrinkled for a moment and then she said, "Not much. I am sorry. I think Tamura was one of the areas that were evacuated during the disaster, but I think the people were allowed to return a year later. You will probably be able to find a place to rent there. I am sure some people preferred not to come back. What made you choose Funehiki?"

"Um, I don't know," lied Bill while shaking his head. "I guess I liked the name."

"Funehiki... Ship Pull?" questioned Natsuko.

Bill shrugged. "I like boats. They draw me in."

They took their seats at the computer desk and did a virtual tour of the city using Google Street View. Bill thought the neighborhood of Funehiki looked nice enough, and so with a lot of Internet searching and detective work, they were able to find an apartment for rent. It was small, maybe the size of his current hotel room, but it would serve for the time being.

Bill was amused and delighted that the Japanese word for apartment was "mansion". Now he could tell his friends back home that he was living in a mansion in the town of Funny Hickey.

Natsuko worked her linguistic magic on the telephone, wheeling and dealing for Bill's new apartment and even arranging for ground transportation as well.

Bill was amazed at her fluent Japanese, and then had to remind himself that she was a native and he should be more impressed with her fluent American English. It was just that this was the first time that he had heard her speak Japanese since they had met, and so it came as a bit of a shock.

Natsuko hung up the phone and bowed slightly to Bill. "I was able to get you a place for 48,000 yen a month. It was 59,000 but I talked them down."

"*Sugoi*, Natsuko-san, well done."

"It was nothing, Mr. Brabham," answered Natsuko while staring down at Bill's feet. "I also arranged for a car to take you to the town tomorrow after lunch. I hope that was not too presumptuous of me."

Bill looked shocked. "No, no — that's awesome Natsuko. Thanks again for your help. Can I take you to lunch as a thank-you?"

Natsuko felt her face get hot but kept her composure. She bowed slightly and answered, "I would be honored, Mr. Brabham."

Bill was starting to feel like he somehow didn't just gain a friend, but a secretary as well. This thought prompted him to say, "Something tells me you were not always an optometrist.

Were you some kind of secretary before that?"

Natsuko simply answered, "Yes, I was some kind of secretary before." She seemed to smirk slightly at the recollection and then added, "I was known in my organization as 'the woman who gets things done.'"

"It sounds like a perfect job for you. What happened?"

"One time, I did not get something done." Natsuko looked down. "It was important, and my failure cost the organization dearly."

Bill did not answer immediately, and before he spoke, Natsuko suddenly snapped back to attention and forced a polite smile. "But enough about that, Mr. Brabham. Shall we do lunch now?"

Bill, amused at her formality, answered back, "Yes, let's do lunch, Natsuko-san."

They walked to a restaurant called Kirin City, which was presumably named after the Japanese brewery. Bill thought he could half do with a beer to ease his social anxiety. Natsuko was easy enough to talk to, but something about her made him tense. He watched her as she led the way to the restaurant. The grace that she exhibited as she moved in public, the dignity that she projected as she walked, the formal way in which she spoke, all of it put Bill in mind of royalty. But at the same time, she was also subservient. It seemed like such a contradiction.

They arrived at Kirin City and were lucky enough to get the last free table. The restaurant was not particularly fancy, but it still had a trendy and expensive atmosphere, which tended to draw a crowd.

Right now Bill was starving because he had been too engrossed in his search for an apartment that morning to eat a proper breakfast. His blood sugar was dropping too, which was causing him to become more than a little irritable.

They both sat there patiently for twenty-five minutes while waiting for the waitress to take their order. Natsuko seemed content to wait and make small talk, but Bill spent most of his time staring at the waitress, which did him no good because she seemed to be purposefully ignoring him.

Bill was trying to decide between tackling the waitress and setting fire to the table when he finally spoke up and asked Natsuko, "Are we supposed to ring a bell or raise our hands or something?"

"For what?" asked Natsuko.

"To get the waitress to take our order. I'm starving."

Natsuko answered in a businesslike tone, "I will take care of it, Mr. Brabham." She turned to the waitress, who was facing them but was also on the other side of the restaurant, and called out loudly but somehow politely, *"Sumimasen!"*[2] The waitress promptly came and took their orders.

Bill looked at Natsuko with a mixture of admiration and interest and said to her, "You are an interesting woman. You carry yourself like nobility, but can still be very humble. You seem meek, but you can also be pushy and yet still not be offensive. You can appear helpless, yet you are clearly someone who gets things done. In short, Natsuko-san, you are an incredible person. I get the feeling that you could probably rule a country and still find time for mundane domestic duties such as cooking and cleaning for your family — and you would probably give equal importance to both. No, actually, you would most certainly put your family first, wouldn't you Natsuko-san?"

Natsuko looked into Bill's eyes, something she rarely did, and answered, "I am just Kawaguchi Natsuko, Mr. Brabham. No more, no less. I do not think I could run a country, but it pleases me that you have such confidence in me. I can say with certainty, however, that I would always put my family first."

Bill nodded and left it at that. It took another forty-five minutes for their blasted meals to arrive. Bill was already to the point of chewing on his fingernails for the protein. Natsuko, of course, was composed and seemed indifferent to the idea of food.

Natsuko's meal was some sort of garden salad with tentacles on top. Bill tried not to look at it too closely, although nothing at this point would have made him lose his appetite.

Bill's meal consisted of steak and fries, or more specifically it consisted of exactly six quarter-sized pieces of steak and six french fries. He counted them twice to be sure. He gobbled down three of each right away, which did nothing to extinguish his appetite. He noticed that Natsuko was eating slowly and daintily, and then sighed inwardly. He made a rough guess as to how long it would take her to eat the salad — thirty minutes — and divided that by his six remaining pieces of food. OK, in another five minutes I can take a bite, he decided.

Bill turned his attention back to Natsuko and resumed the

---

2 Excuse me!

conversation, "OK, so you had some sort of pseudo-secretarial job at an organization which you seem reluctant to name, which you then had to leave because you made a single yet important mistake, which you are also reluctant to talk about. After which, you inexplicably became an optometrist. May I ask why you choose optometry, or is that a national secret as well?"

Natsuko finished chewing her food, which gave her some time to collect her thoughts. She daintily dabbed at her mouth with a napkin and then answered, "My past is not so mysterious, Mr. Brabham. But it is true, some of it I cannot talk about, and some of it I do not wish to talk about. As for optometry, that is quite simple. My father was an optometrist and he owns the office where I work. I grew up helping him at work, so it was natural for me to carry on the business.

"I had worked there for a few years after returning from college in America. One day some businessmen, who were friends with my father, stopped by to talk with him, and while they were there they took an interest in me for some reason. They named a ridiculous amount of money for me to work for them, which neither my father nor I could refuse.

"And so it came to be that I worked for their organization for nearly ten years. After that ended abruptly, I returned to my father's business so that he could retire."

"Very intriguing, Natsuko-san," said Bill while looking at his watch.

"Are you late for something, Mr. Brabham?" asked Natsuko.

Bill looked up. "Hmm, what? Oh, no. No, sorry. It's just a nervous habit." He ate another tiny piece of steak and mindlessly ate a french fry too. Great, he thought, now I'll have to wait ten minutes for the next bite.

"Is something wrong? You seem annoyed," asked Natsuko in concern.

"No, no. I'm not annoyed. OK, well, maybe a little but not with you. Sorry. I'm just really, really hungry."

"But you have barely been eating your food. Is it not to your liking?"

"No, it's damn good, actually. I'm just pacing myself."

Natsuko considered this. Finally, she sought out the waitress with another loud "*Sumimasen.*"

The waitress hurried over to them. Natsuko then motioned to her to come close, and then she whispered something into her ear.

The waitress immediately bowed deeply to Natsuko while saying, *"Kashikomarimashita, Ojou-sama. Shitsurei itashimashita."* Translated into English, this would be something like, "Certainly, young lady. Please humbly excuse me for the inconvenience," but said in a way that was the verbal equivalent of groveling on the floor.

The waitress glanced briefly at Bill and then rushed to the kitchen, after which Natsuko turned back to Bill and said, "Please, Mr. Brabham, enjoy the rest of your meal now. There is plenty more on the way."

Bill, despite having already consumed two beers (albeit two small beers that were mostly foam), was thinking quite clearly. And what he was thinking quite clearly about was this: Natsuko, this lady of infinite grace and means with a mysterious past, had only to whisper a few words to that rather slack waitress to cause her to treat Natsuko as if she were a visiting princess. Should I ask her about it? No, I think not.

Bill simply said, with a hint of a smirk, *"Arigatou gozaimasu, Ojou-sama,"* and then he ate the remains of his food. This was a thank-you fit for a princess (because Bill's American blood forced him to always be at least a little cheeky).

"Very funny, Mr. Brabham. 'Natsuko-san' will be fine, thank you."

"I'm sorry — you know I'm just kidding. My mom had continuously told me when I was a child not to be such a dumb-ass, and so when I grew up, I became a smart-ass instead."

Natsuko laughed naturally for the first time that day. It did Bill's heart good to hear it. It probably did Natsuko some good as well. However, this moment of levity was broken by the arrival of the waitress. She had a much bigger plate this time, and it was filled with twelve of the little steak bites, and countless fries.

The waitress left the table, bowing and excusing herself in the process. After she had left, Bill said to Natsuko, "I really want to ask what you said to her."

Natsuko replied, "Oh, that was very good, Mr. Brabham. Well done. That was a nice indirect question. We will make a Japanese person out of you yet."

"So, you are not going to answer it, then, are you?"

"And now you have gone straight back to being a pushy American. Tsk, tsk, Mr. Brabham."

Bill smiled. What else could he do?

Natsuko continued, "I am sorry, I am also just kidding around. Please, come here and I will tell you."

Bill leaned across the table. Natsuko leaned across too and whispered into Bill's ear, "I told them that you are the Prince of England and you would like some more steak right away. I also said not to make a fuss over you, as you were here for vacation and did not wish to be disturbed."

Bill exploded with laughter. Natsuko urged him to act more royally, which only made him laugh harder. After he finally contained himself, he said, "You really are an amazing person, Natsuko-san."

Natsuko shook her head. "No, I am just Kawaguchi Natsuko. Nothing more, nothing less."

Bill scarfed down more of his steak and fries while Natsuko demurely finished her tentacle salad. Bill was pleased to see that they had also brought him a proper-sized beer to wash it all down with. Natsuko watched him drink it and said, "Do you like to drink, Mr. Brabham?"

Bill wiped the foam from his face with a napkin (being careful not to use his sleeve, which would have been un-princely). "Yes, I enjoy it. Why?"

Natsuko suppressed a smile, which somehow made her look uncharacteristically mischievous. "It just occurred to me that your name in Japanese would be *Biru*, which would sound very close to the word for beer. I find that amusing."

"Very funny indeed, Ojou-sama," answered Bill sarcastically.

Natsuko smiled, and then frowned suddenly. "What time is it, Mr. Brabham?"

Bill checked his watch. "Almost two o'clock. Why?"

"I am very sorry, but I must leave shortly for work."

"No problem at all," answered Bill as he reached for his wallet to settle the bill. He was about to take out his American Express card, and then thought, crap, I doubt any of the princes of England have an American Express card. And so he was about to use another card when he thought, crap, my real name is on the card. I hope I have enough cash.

He studied the bill. It somehow looked even more intimidating than the one from the host club from the other night. He deducted two zeros from the end of the number to get an approximate dollar value, and the figure made him sweat. It was probably the most expensive lunch he would ever have. Eating that much Kobe beef in a hipster place like this had clearly been a mistake. Bill cried a little inside as he counted out ¥10,000 notes.

Natsuko, clearly impressed, asked Bill if he really were the Prince of England. Bill answered, "I'm not even the Fresh Prince of Bel-Air," but Natsuko did not get the reference.

They left the restaurant and walked together to Natsuko's office. "Thank you very much for lunch, Mr. Brabham. I had a great time. I wish you good fortune in your new job and your new apartment. Please call me any time if you need help. It would make me happy to stay in touch with you."

Bill gently grabbed one of her hands and held it in between both of his. He had seen that on TV once and the beer in his system was telling him that it was a perfectly normal thing to do. He said, "Thank you for all of your help, and for keeping me company. You have my word that I will keep in touch." He was going to say more, but he was starting to feel a little foolish, and so he left it at that and released her hand.

Natsuko bowed to him and said, "*Ja, mata ne,*" then turned and walked away.

That was very Natsuko-like, thought Bill — a formal bow and an informal goodbye, effectively a 'Whelp, see you later'. He called back to her, "Later, Ojou-sama."

Now feeling a little sad, Bill started walking back to his hotel. On his way he noticed, for the first time in the several times he had passed it, the entrance to a small park. The entrance was easy enough to miss because it was sandwiched between two buildings and set back away from the road.

He paid the small admission fee and entered the park. It was much smaller than Hibiya Park, but it had the same elegant minimalist landscaping and in some ways was even prettier than Hibiya Park, probably owing to the hilly terrain.

Bill walked to the top of a hill and sat down. He sat there for some time and contemplated his life while a soft, warm breeze tousled his hair. He looked back on all the adventures and people he had already met in Japan and he wondered what was in store for him next.

He was also feeling a little anxious about his new job. He knew that it would be a somewhat high-pressure one, and he was just a little worried that his poor vocabulary was going to be a handicap. He also worried that they may not hire him at all.

Well, whatever. I'm just going to take it one day at a time. If they do not accept me, then maybe it was not meant to be. And at the end of it all, at least I would have had a nice va... what the hell is that?

In the last few minutes, unbeknownst to Bill, some sort of elementary school trip had arrived in the park. He had looked up just in time to see thirty little kids, dressed in little sailor suits and red caps, screaming at the top of their lungs while rolling down a hill in unison and making a big pile of little kids at the bottom.

Bill saw two adults nearby that were also watching the children. He noted that the adults looked unworried, and so he could only assume that this was perfectly normal behavior and nothing to worry about. Unfortunately, the screaming was messing with his chi, and so he decided to push on back to the hotel in order to pack and to do some more research on his new town.

Before leaving the park, Bill contemplated rolling down the hill and screaming to see what it was like, but decided against it at the last moment because it did not seem like princely behavior.

CHAPTER 15

Breakfast this morning was instant ramen from the hotel room. It tasted like fish, but Bill ate it anyway.

He was all packed, the hotel room was clean, and he had nothing to do for several hours before the car was to come and take him to his new apartment. He might as well take one last stroll around town.

He left the Park Hyatt by foot and decided to explore more of Shinjuku. He was currently in the rich business section of town.

There were very few, if any, foreigners in this section, which somehow made Bill feel safer. Perhaps this was because Bill now considered himself to be Japanese. After all, he was starting to think very much like a Japanese person and he was also trying very hard to blend into their society. This was, of course, hampered slightly by him being tall, white, and American.

No, he was sure that he was Japanese on the inside. He felt Japanese, and all he saw around him were mostly Japanese faces, so naturally he began to assume that he was also one of them now in much the same way that a cuckoo bird that has been planted in the nest of another bird probably grows up thinking that it is the same as the other bird.

Yes, he was Japanese now, and from his time spent in Tokyo thus far, he did not trust those shifty-looking foreigners one bit and he was glad not to see them around.

He walked for a few blocks and found what he called a vending oasis, which was a place with a small park, some benches, and about ten vending machines. He ordered another bowl of ramen from one of them, which the machine actually cooked for him.

After inserting his money in the machine, Bill was instructed to wait for three minutes while the machine did its thing. A timer counted down the seconds. When it finally reached zero, the machine made some noises but Bill's soup failed to appear in the hatchway.

He thumped it to avail. He thumped it again. Nothing. He grabbed the edges of the machine and gently started to rock it. No noodles came forth, only a piecing siren.

Bill looked around in shock. A few people were taking his picture with their cellphones. He tried his best to pretend that all was well, and then he calmly but quickly walked away in a random direction. He ducked inside a random door, which by happy coincidence was a restaurant - an Irish pub to be exact. It was even called "Irish Pub."

Bill was still hungry and did not want to look a gift horse in the mouth, so he sat down at a table. A waitress was there almost immediately to take his order. He ordered fish and chips, but had his doubts about what they would be like. Bill was not a big fan of fish to begin with, as has been already noted, but he did enjoy a good fish-n-chip dinner if the fish was not too fishy and the batter was done right. Well, at least the waitress had been prompt.

In fact, the chef was up to snuff as well. Bill's lunch was served in under ten minutes. Very impressive, thought Bill, they should give Kirin City a few lessons in customer service.

Bill squeezed a little lemon juice onto the fish and took a nibble. It was fantastic — the best he'd ever eaten. He wanted to miniaturize himself and dive into his meal, burrow into it like a mole, and eat it until he could no longer stand it.

In reality, he simply ordered seconds, after which he told the waitress to give his compliments to the chef.

As if noticing Bill for the first time, the waitress suddenly had a look of recollection on her face. She bowed and scurried off to the kitchen. A moment later she and the chef returned and made a big fuss over Bill. The chef told him, in Japanese, how honored he was to meet him, and how he was so very happy that he liked the meal, especially because it was an English dish.

Bill was lost and confused, and so he just nodded and smiled and bowed and shook hands and posed for pictures with the staff. This was certainly a friendly place.

With his stomach now full of fish and potatoes, and his mind full of questions and uncertainty, Bill took note of the time, paid his bill, and legged it back to the hotel. As he approached it, he saw a sleek, black Bentley parked in front and wondered what rich, snobby bastard had arrived in it.

As he walked past the car on the way to the entrance to the hotel, a man stopped him by asking, "Mr. Brabham?"

Bill said, "Yes?"

"Very good, sir, I thought that was you. I saw your picture on the Internet earlier today." He leaned closer to Bill and said, "And I wouldn't worry about the vending machine, sir. We've all done it at least once in our lives."

"What?"

"Nothing sir, never mind sir. Please, step this way," said the man while gesturing toward the Bentley."

Bill stammered, "Wait, this is for me?"

"Yes sir, of course sir. Now, this way please."

"But my bags..." protested Bill.

"Not to worry, sir — we've got them already."

"You...what?"

"Right here, sir, see," said the man while opening the trunk, "Here they are, safe and sound."

Bill's mind, which was still partially frolicking in a fish-n-chip paradise, finally started to assemble the facts. "Wait, Natsuko sent you?"

The man smiled and nudged Bill in the ribs, "Oh, it's Natsuko is it? Well, well. I never thought I'd see the day. Does Kawaguchi-sama really let you call her that?"

Bill realized his mistake and back-peddled. "No, I'm sorry, I meant Kawaguchi-san. We've only met twice, after all. Although I do admit to calling her Natsuko-san because it sounds way too impersonal to call someone by their family name in a social situation — at least to my American ears, it does."

"American ears, sir? Are you not a prince of England?" inquired the man with a mischievous grin.

Bill decided to play along. "Figure of speech, my dear chap, figure of speech. There's a good man."

The man shook his head slightly. "Very good, sir. Well done. And extra credit for not trying to squeeze in a 'pip pip' or a 'cheerio'. You know, we don't all talk like that, your grace."

Embarrassed, Bill snapped back, "Yes, yes. Of course. And

just call me Bill."

"Very well...Bill. Please, step this way. Time is money. Let's be off."

Bill nodded and got into the back of the car. He was happy to see a privacy window between the front and back seats. It was not that he disliked the old man, but he somehow felt that, like Natsuko, the driver was part of something...big, so he felt it was best not to get involved. Instead, he spent the three and a half hours of the trip playing video games in the back of the limo. He contemplated a drink, but decided against it both because he wanted to be alert when he arrived in his new town, and also because he thought it best not to take advantage of the hospitality being offered to him.

Something caught his eye as they drove through the city limits, a sort of giant African-voodoo-witch-doctor kind of something. It was well over four meters tall, made of wood and straw, had a painted face that looked very angry, and it held a sword. Its other arm was jutting out straight ahead with the hand making the gesture for STOP.

Bill knocked on the glass divider. After a moment, it opened halfway.

"Yes, sir?"

"Um, what the heck was that angry voodoo thing?"

"Oh, that? That was one of the three deities who protect the town from evil spirits." The driver glanced back at Bill for a moment. "It appears that you have not burst into flames or suffered an inexplicable heart attack. The gods must like you. Well done, sir."

"Wait, was that actually a possibility?" asked Bill in concern. No answer was forthcoming.

Shortly thereafter, the car pulled over to the side of the road several blocks away from Bill's apartment. The driver walked around to Bill's door and opened it for him. He said in explanation, "Kawaguchi-sama has instructed me to drop you off a safe distance from your apartment. I believe she was concerned that the apartment manager might see you arriving in a Bentley and decide to raise your rent.

Bill nodded. "A wise girl."

"Indeed, sir. Although I fear it may be too late for such precautions."

"Why is that?"

The driver handed him a newspaper. It was one of the more

lax sorts of papers — the sort that might occasionally neglect to check facts from time to time. On the cover, there was the title "Prince William Visits Tokyo on Secret Getaway." He cursed the waitress at Kirin City for ratting him out and then looked at his picture on the cover. He had to admit that he did sort of resemble the Prince, with his sandy hair, blue-gray eyes, and a face that was equal parts handsome and homely.

He held the paper up and asked, "Mind if I keep this?"

"As you wish, sir."

"Great, thanks. Well, this certainly explains a few things that happened today," he said while reflecting on the fuss at the Irish pub. He then thought about the vending machine again, and winced. "I suspect I'm going to be on the cover again tomorrow."

"Yes sir, most probably. But as I said, sir, I would not worry unduly about the vending machine."

"Yes, I suppose not," agreed Bill. "They will probably bronze it, or erect a statue of Prince William with a plaque on the vending machine saying something like 'Prince William, Duke of Cambridge, savaged this machine in April of blah blah blah.'"

The driver laughed. "A good one, sir. Yes, I expect you are correct." He placed Bill's luggage on the ground in front of him. "Well, it has been a pleasure to meet you but I must be off now... more business to attend to... you know how it is."

"OK, well, thanks for the ride." He paused and added hesitantly, "Do I...uh...owe you anything?"

"Oh no sir, this was on the house, as it were — compliments of Kawaguchi-sama."

"OK, well, thank you just the same. Stay well, my friend."

The driver tipped his cap. "And you, sir." He then dropped smoothly into the driver's seat of the Bentley and drove off, leaving Bill once again alone and confused.

"He never told me where my apartment was," he said to the world in general.

He pulled out his phone and used Google Maps and his memory to locate the apartment. It was only three streets away, which he walked with enjoyment as he explored his new surroundings. He was on a narrow street with no sidewalks. There were fields on both sides of it. The field to the right side was somewhat wild and untamed with nothing in it except perhaps a house some way off in the distance. The field on the left side was more cared for, freshly cut, and contained some playground equipment. Up ahead he could see several buildings.

He walked on and started passing homes and nondescript businesses, most of which had very little front lawn (although some appeared to have communal back yards, which they shared with their neighbors both next door and from the next block over).

There were no shoulders to the road and no sidewalks either. The landscape went straight from road to house, with little more than some foot-high stone curbs to keep the cars from bouncing off of the houses. It was certainly nothing like Texas.

He made a left onto his street. He felt he was beginning to get a handle on Japanese addresses, which started out broad and worked their way to defining smaller and smaller areas. Unfortunately, the last few levels of the address scheme were impossible to decipher without a map — and even then it was tricky. Street names were rare. His address was now Fukushima-ken, Tamura-shi, Funehiki-machi Tobudai 3-Chome-### (where ### was the building number assigned sequentially at the time of construction for any building on any street in the 3-Chome area, which was several blocks in all directions).[3]

Despite these hardships, Bill soon found his apartment building, which was a nice clean building that was painted in a color that Bill guessed to be 'coral', but a case could also have been made that it was in fact 'flesh'. A bold choice, thought Bill as he surveyed the building.

"Who are you, then?" asked a serious-looking young Asian girl in casual (and slightly rude) Japanese.

Bill flinched from the sudden burst of Japanese, which jolted him out of his private world of exploration. It took him a few seconds to replay her words in his mind and translate them, at the end of which he was still unsure of what she had said. He asked her to repeat it.

"I said, who are you? I know everyone in this town, and I don't know you."

"I am Bill Brabham. Nice to meet you," hazarded Bill in Japanese.

"Ha-ha, your name is Beer. Where are you from, Beer-san?"

"I am from America."

---

3   Bill's exact location is being withheld for fear that if it were disclosed, then someone would soon put up a plaque on the building stating "Prince William, Duke of Cambridge, resided here in April of..."

The girl looked Bill up and down. "You can't be; you're not fat."

"Hey," replied Bill indignantly, "I thought the Japanese were all very polite."

"Yeah, well I thought the Americans were all very fat."

Bill burst out laughing. The girl smirked. Bill said, "Well, I guess we both learned something today, huh? If it makes you feel better, most people here think I am from England."

"Ah, yes," said the girl while nodding, "That's it. You must be from England. What are you doing here, Beer-san? Are you a pimp?"

"A pimp? No. Why?"

"No reason," answered the girl with a shrug.

Bill continued, "Anyway, to answer your first question, I just moved here." He pointed to the apartment building.

The girl said excitedly, "Oh! We are going to be neighbors. I live upstairs over there." She pointed to the corner of the building furthest from the street. "Where are you?"

"I don't know yet; I've only just arrived. Is the apartment manager around?"

"Yes, he's here. Watch out for him though, he steals your underwear when you are not at home."

This confused Bill on several levels. One of which was that the Japanese word 'pantsu' sounded like 'pants' but meant underwear. He gestured to his trouser leg and said, "Pants?"

The girl shook her head. She thought for a moment and then said, "Panties," in English.

"Oh," said Bill. "Why?"

"Because he is a pervert."

Bill nodded. "Aren't you afraid of him?"

"Oh no, he just likes underwear. He is nice otherwise. I buy extra underwear every week. I leave the ones that I do not like or the ones that are getting old on top of all the others in my drawer. He only takes from the top."

"Doesn't that bother you?"

"Oh no. I look at it as part of my rent. It is still one of the cheapest places around."

"That is a pretty casual way of looking at it. So, he doesn't take anything else?"

"No, just underwear," she replied with a shrug.

"And you think he might want mine too?" asked Bill, doubtfully.

"Oh yes," answered the girl simply.

"Why?"

She thought for a moment and then said, "Because you are foreign."

This seemed to be a good enough reason for the girl so he decided not to question her further and instead made a mental note to buy some extra underwear on his next shopping trip.

He then asked, "Do you think I can sort of slip the underwear through his letter slot? It kind of bothers me to think of him creeping around my apartment."

The girl shook her head and said, "No, I expect that the creeping around is part of the enjoyment for him."

Bill decided to leave it at that and asked, "So, what is your name?"

This was the first time that Bill had seen the girl look the least bit timid. She hesitated, but finally answered in a small voice, "I'm Ōguchi Sakura."

Bill could not see what all the fuss was about. He answered, "Nice to meet you, Ōguchi-san."

The girl winced. "Please call me Sakura. I hate my family name."

"OK, Sakura-san, but what is so wrong with your name?" asked Bill.

She scowled. "If you don't know, then I'm not telling you."

Bill was annoyed at the answer but let it be. He was at a loss as to what else to say to this girl and was about to break away when she asked him where he worked at.

Bill answered, "I'm not working yet, but I am trying to get a job at Fukushima Daiichi." He expected her to looked shocked, and she did, but not for the reason he suspected.

"I work at Daiichi! My uncle used to work there too. I'm a secretary. I answer the phones and say, 'Everything is going great with the cleanup. No problems.'" She made the OK sign with her hand.

Bill was unsure if this was meant as sarcasm or not. "And is everything OK over there?" he asked hesitantly.

Sakura gave him a look that said, "What do you think?" but without needing the words.

"Oh, I see," said Bill. "Well, I was sort of expecting that. Hopefully I can help."

"No problem, Beer-san, I'll tell you where not to go. Hey, you want to ride to work together? I get bored by myself. I could use the company. I love to talk."

Bill considered this. On the one hand, it was a free ride to and from work. On the other hand, it meant an hour and a half of mindless banter first thing in the morning — in Japanese, and another hour and a half of mindless banter after a hard day of work — in Japanese. Still, he kind of liked Sakura despite her demeanor — maybe even because of it.

And now that he looked at her, she was very pretty as well, although he had to tell himself not to look too hard because she was on the younger side of indeterminate and he was 35. It was difficult for Bill to guess the age of most Japanese people, who in his mind always looked much younger than they really were. But if he had to guess, he would have said that she was probably still in college or just recently graduated. Getting involved with her would not be considered robbing the cradle, but he would certainly feel like it.

Putting all this aside, he answered, "That would be great, Sakura-san. Thank you very much."

"No problem, Beer-san, and thanks for paying for half the gasoline."

Bill laughed. "Fine, yes, no problem. Let's trade numbers. Give me a ring in the morning when you are ready to leave. I don't know what apartment I'll be in yet. Speaking of which, where does the manager live?"

Sakura pointed to the apartment on the first floor, closest to the street. "The owner lives there."

"Excellent. Nice to meet you, Sakura-san. See you tomorrow."

"OK. Bye-bye." She waved as Bill walked away.

It's a funny old world, thought Bill as he made his way over to the manager's apartment. It just goes to show you that no matter where you go in the world, people are all basically the same — we are all just trying to get by and make a living and do what we can to survive and to be happy.

He knocked on the door to the manager's apartment. It was answered by a distinguished-looking Japanese man wearing a very conservative gray suit, a black necktie, and a pair of pink panties on his head.

OK, thought Bill, we're not all exactly the same.

CHAPTER 16

> I'm turning Japanese
> I think I'm turning Japanese
> I really think so
> Turning Japanese
> I think I'm turning Japanese
> I really think so
> I'm turning Japanese
> I think I'm turning Japanese
> I really...

Bill reached out from under the covers and grabbed his phone, answered it, and said, "Wha?" at it.

"Beer-san? Are you awake?"

"Who's this? What are you saying? You have the wrong number. It's five in the morning for god's sake. Leave me alone." He hung up.

> I'm turning Japanese
> I think I'm turning Japanese
> I really think so
> Turning...

"Wha?!?"

"Beer-san, it's Sakura. Remember? I'm leaving to go to work in half an hour. Do you still want to go?"

"Huh? Oh, yeah, sorry. Um, you know what, let's make it

tomorrow instead. I'm sorry, I'm just not prepared right now. I guess I didn't think that you would be leaving so early."

"Oh, OK Beer-san," said Sakura dejectedly. "I'll call you after work. You better go with me tomorrow or I'm going to come over and jump on your head until you wake up."

"Uh-huh. Fine. Tomorrow... mumble mumble zzzzzzzz."

Sakura shook her head and hung up. "Slacker," she said to the phone in mock disappointment.

Bill woke some hours later at the more sensible time of nine o'clock. After spending another hour or so getting showered, shaved, and caffeinated, he ventured out for some more exploring. He was wearing tan slacks and a black short-sleeved shirt because he felt that walking around in a suit would likely draw unwanted princely attention to himself.

He felt bad for backing out of his ride with Sakura today, but he really wanted to make a good first impression and that was unlikely to occur with only four hours of sleep and thirty minutes of preparation. He vowed to go to bed earlier tonight and set his alarm for the ungodly time of 4:30 in the morning.

Bill left his apartment and walked east for a block or two in order to get onto the main highway. He figured the highway would be the best place to find things like grocery stores and maybe a place to buy some cheap underwear.

He took the highway north passed the usual collection of gas stations, grocery stores, and car dealerships that are found the world over along these sorts of roads. There was little else interesting as he walked on — perhaps a dental clinic and a medical center, if that was what you were into.

He walked another few kilometers without seeing anything that interested him. He was just about to give up and head west into the neighborhood when there it was, out in the middle of nowhere, the Yummy Plastics factory.

Bill could hardly believe his luck. He had really wanted to visit the factory ever since he had read about it the other day. He wondered if they gave tours. Well, there was only one way to find out.

As Bill was approaching the factory, a truck backed up to the side of it and some men started to hurriedly unload the truck. Bill walked over to talk to one of the men, but before he could, another man, a very angry sort of man, rushed up to him from inside the warehouse and started yelling at him in Japanese that came so fast and thick that Bill had no idea what it meant, but judging by the pointing he was doing, he guessed that the man expected him to help unload the truck. Bill bowed and scurried over to the back of the truck, grabbed a box, and then followed after one of the other laborers.

He noticed that the men unloading the truck were also wearing tan slacks and a black shirt, perhaps a uniform of the shipping company. Well, at least I get to see inside the factory, he thought to himself.

The factory floor was filled with rows of stainless tables. Several workers were busy at their stations, doing some sort of bulk assembly work. Behind each of the rows of tables were rows of stoves with pots of various colored melted plastics or waxes in them.

He watched as one of the workers poured a small amount of a raspberry-colored liquid from one of the pots into the bottom of a clear plastic cup. She then used some sort of powered caulk gun to swirl a creamy, white substance into the cup. It was probably just that, caulk, but it looked very much like vanilla ice cream and raspberry sauce. The worker finished it off with replica blueberries and raspberries. It looked delicious.

Bill was about to set down the box and talk to the worker when the angry man walked up to him and started to yell and point again. Bill bowed apologetically and scurried off to the back room that the man had pointed toward. He stacked his box neatly where he thought it belonged, and looked around. No one else was around.

He noticed that one of the boxes was partially opened. He quietly opened it the rest of the way and took a peek inside.

The box was filled with stacks of rectangular bricks wrapped in brown paper. Bill pulled a brick out and carefully unwrapped it. It was some sort of modeling clay. Well, that isn't very interesting, thought Bill as he carefully re-wrapped it.

And that's when he noticed what was written on the wrapping in big bold letters: **C4**. There was other writing too, lot numbers and manufacturing dates and such, but it was the C4 that really captured his attention. Bill very, very gently replaced the brick and quickly but carefully closed the box.

Just as he was turning to leave, another man, a different one from last time but equally angry, started to do the pointing and yelling thing.

Bill, in his nervousness, knocked over another box on his way out of the door. The box crashed to the ground and out spilled hundreds of very realistic rubber fingers of mixed lengths, styles, and tints.

Bill reflexively knelt down and started picking them up, even as a small part of his brain was trying to work out why anyone would want a box of fake fingers.

The angry man, now bordering on rage, looked as if he were about to kick him. Seeing this, Bill stood up quickly and started backing his way out of the door.

He could hardly make out what the man was saying as he yelled, but he could not help noticing that it sounded an awful lot like the slangy accent that was used in anime when the creators wanted to portray a tough guy — like a member of the Yakuza for instance.

Although most of it was gibberish, a couple of familiar words entered Bill's ears and lodged directly in his hind brain, bypassing the rational part of his mind and causing him to run away seriously fast without further thought. The words were 'baka' and 'korosu', meaning 'idiot' and 'kill' respectively.

Bill ran for several blocks through the back streets of the neighborhood, making random lefts and rights along the way. Eventually he stopped when he convinced himself that no one was pursuing him.

His side started to cramp, which made it uncomfortable to move, but he felt safer to keep walking. As he did so, he looked around him. He was next to some sort of prison — at least that is what he thought it was. The ground sloped up steeply toward the prison, and at the top there was a serious-looking fence. But unlike a normal prison fence, there was no razor wire on the top of it. And now that he was studying it more closely, it looked more like it was designed to keep people out than in.

He walked along the perimeter to investigate. A group of high school girls were heading toward him, but when they saw him, sweaty and limping as he was, they crossed to the opposite side of the street and tried very hard not to look at him as they passed.

Eventually, the hill subsided and so did the fence. Behind it was a perfectly ordinary high school. Well, another mystery solved, thought Bill. I think I'm going back home now and hiding under the covers for at least a week.

He walked back in the general direction of the apartment, but this time along the western side of town. He ended up on a slightly bigger road with two separate lanes. On a whim he made a right and continued down the road and toward a mountain that he could easily see off in the distance.

He continued down this small highway, which now featured sidewalks, for a few blocks. This part of town was still very much a residential area but the homes and apartment buildings were spaced further apart with more property around them, although much of the property was hard to see because of the high walls, fences, and shrubbery that bordered it.

Another block down, he saw a decent-sized park on the left and decided to check it out. The park was really nothing more than a big patch of flat grass, a few trees, a few benches, and a walkway going around the perimeter. It was certainly nothing compared to the parks he had seen in Tokyo, but it still had a certain appeal to him.

Bill followed the trail around the park and stumbled onto an ornate red shrine nestled inside a small cluster of trees. He made his way to the shrine grounds and looked around. It seemed deserted. He walked up to the shrine and stopped at a large box in front of it.

The box was waist high and had a metal grate over the top of it. Dangling in front of the box was a giant rope as thick as Bill's arm. At the top of the rope were two large bells, each the size of his head.

Bill knew that he was supposed to pray to the spirit of whatever the hell was enshrined there, but he was having trouble remembering the proper order for all the rituals. From his Catholic upbringing, he knew the importance of getting the rituals correct, and he half suspected that religion had been invented to give obsessive-compulsive people something to do.

He started to mutter to himself as he worked out the order. "OK, let's see. I'm pretty sure the first thing the spirit wants from me is my money." He knew that he had no change on him and so he opened his wallet and shifted through the bills. Damn, the smallest bill he had was a ¥5000 note, worth about $50.

"Oh well," he said as he pulled it out and held it above the box, "I better get my money's worth out of this." He tucked the bill down between the grates.

"Excellent. Great. OK. Let's see, I think I bow twice like this, and then clap my hands twice like this, and then I make my prayer."

Dear... random deity of this shrine, please hear my prayer. I would be most grateful if you could turn my bad luck around.

Please, please send me some good fortune. Thank you in advance. Oh, and please keep the Yakuza guys from killing me. Thanks again. Eh, over and out.

"And now I bow one more time and... Crap! I forgot to ring the bell. I suppose I'll just have to start over. But listen, I'm not giving you any more money, OK?" said Bill while waggling his finger toward the shrine. He grabbed the large rope with both hands and started to shake it vigorously.

"Oh wait, damn, I was supposed to purify myself with holy water first, wasn't I? I probably just desecrated the sanctity of..."

And then everything went black.

CHAPTER 17

Bill regained consciousness several hours later. He sat up slowly and looked around him. His vision was blurry, but he could easily see the two golden bells, both dented, beside him. Also, the bulk of the rope was draped on top of him. He pushed it off in annoyance.

There was a dull hum in his ears, almost as if he were standing too close to a large power transformer. He felt the top of his head and discovered it to be very, very tender and his hair was clumpy and matted with blood.

He took a closer look at the bells. One of them had a streak of blood on it. He didn't know whether to laugh or be angry. "I should have used the holy water first," he mumbled to himself.

He stood up hesitantly but was steady once he was upright. He walked over to the little fountain of holy water and used the ladle that was hanging next to it to dump water over his head to rinse off the blood, being very careful not to bloody up the fountain in the process.

He then shook his head dry and nearly fell over from dizziness. He smoothed his hair back with his hands and turned his attention back to the bells. He used some more water to rinse them off. Unfortunately, there was nothing he could do about the dents. He looked up to where they had been hanging and decided that he was unable to hang them back, either. Instead, he placed them carefully on the offering box and coiled the rope up next to them.

He had no paper and no pen, so leaving a note was not an

option. He walked out of the cluster of trees and walked around the park to see if he could find someone to tell. The only person he found was an astonishingly old woman. She was hobbling along the trail and smiled at Bill as he approached.

"Good evening, young man," she croaked in passable English.

"Good evening..." he almost said "old woman" but managed to swap it for "dear lady" before it left his mouth. He continued, "I'm sorry to bother you, but I think I accidentally pulled the bells down at the shrine over there." He pointed to the cluster of trees.

"Oh dear."

"Yes, I know. Do you know who I should tell about it?"

The woman shook her head. "Sorry, no. Leave a note?"

"I'd like to but — hey, do you have a pen and some paper I can borrow?"

"Maybe," answered the woman, who then proceeded to fiddle with her purse for what seemed like five minutes. "Here you go, young man." She handed him a pen and a notepad.

"Thank you." He bowed and took the items. He then scribbled a note as follows (translated from Bill's Japanese):

I broke your goats. I am sorry. There is ¥5000 in the cereal box. If this is not good, I will return yesterday to give more.

Bill tore off the note and handed the pen and the notepad back to the old woman and thanked her once again, bowed, and excused himself.

He walked back to the shrine, only to find that the bells and the rope were back in place. He peered at the bells incredulously from multiple angles. They looked new and undamaged.

"OK," said Bill as he looked around for a camera, "Ha-ha, very good. You got me. This is one of those crazy Japanese TV shows, right? Right? Hello?"

There was no answer, at least not one that he could hear. Although he was right about the cameras — well, partially right.

Deep below the shrine sat two monks inside a clean, white room filled with weird looking equipment and chemicals. They were both watching Bill on a video screen.

The senior monk turned to his junior and said very calmly, "I know you were just being keen, boy, but sometimes you don't take the time to think."

The junior monk answered sheepishly, "I am sorry, Master, I did not expect him to return so soon. Shall I fetch the Cane of

Discipline, Master?"

"No, no. No need for the cane today. Just reflect on this incident and search for the wisdom within it."

"Yes, Master."

They turned back to the video screen. Bill was still stomping around the shrine grounds and calling out, "Hello?"

Bill returned to the shrine and took one last look at the bells. He shook his head. He looked at the offering box in annoyance and contemplated breaking into it to get his money back but then thought the better of it. Instead, he just gave up on the whole thing and decided to resume his earlier plan, which was to go to bed and hide under the covers for a week.

As he made his way out of the wooded area, he caught sight of a piece of paper that was being propelled across his path by a light breeze. He picked it up as it fluttered by, thinking that it was probably just litter. Imagine his surprise when it turned out to be a ¥5000 note.

"What the hell?" he mumbled as he turned around, fully expecting there to be cameras and laughing Japanese men behind him this time. Only there were not.

He shook his head again, which still hurt quite a lot. Now completely spooked, Bill made his way back through the park in the direction of his apartment. He noticed the old woman some ways off and called out to her and waved.

The old woman waved back, lost her footing while stepping off of the curb, and fell in front of a passing bicyclist, who narrowly avoided her but not her groceries.

Bill ran over and helped the old woman up. She was covered in eggs and milk.

"I'm so sorry," said Bill frantically. "Are you OK?"

The old woman laughed. "OK, young man. OK, yes."

"Here," he said while holding out the ¥5000 he had just found, "I am responsible for this. Please, use this to replace your groceries."

The old woman shook her head. "I can't take your money, young man."

Bill was unsure what the custom was in Japan under these circumstances. Was he offending her by offering the money? He was unsure, but he did feel responsible and so he put it to her in a way that he hoped would make her feel comfortable about taking the money. "Please, I just found this money only a minute ago near the shrine. I can only assume that..." What the heck was the deity that was supposed to be enshrined there, anyway? "... the shrine god left it for me so that I would have it to give to you. Please, it would make me feel better if you took it."

The old woman took it graciously. "Thank you, young man. You are a prince."

Bill chuckled. "Yes, I get that a lot." He then said his goodbyes and once again resumed his increasingly difficult quest of returning to his apartment and hiding under his covers for a week.

The old woman made her way home as well. She cleaned the egg and milk off of herself and then went back out to buy her groceries once again. Unfortunately, when she went to pay for her items, she was annoyed to find that the ¥5000 note was missing. It must have fallen out of the torn pocket of her dress. Damn her luck today.

CHAPTER 18

"So, do you like my car? It's a Nissan Tiida. They call it a Versa in America. It was in Heroes. Have you seen Heroes? I loved Heroes. What power would you want? Sometimes I think I would like to time travel, but I'm afraid I would mess things up. I think I would like rapid regeneration like Claire. She is very sexy. I like Claire. Did you know I like girls? I like boys too, but I like girls better. So, do you like my car?"

"Yes."

"I know, right? It's a great car. Lots of room and good gas mileage. Plus it was in Heroes. How about I turn on the radio? I listen to J-pop. Do you like J-pop? I wanted to be an Idol, but I can't sing. Idols are so pretty. Do you like Idols? Let's listen to J-pop. Do you want to listen to J-pop?"

"Sure."

"You don't talk much in the morning, do you Beer-san?"

Bill waited for the usual flood of tangential topics, but nothing followed. Seeing the opening in the conversation he answered, "Sorry, Sakura-san. My Japanese is not that good yet. It's hard for me to keep up with you when you talk so fast. Also, I am not good at mornings."

"Oh, sorry Beer-san. I will try to slow down. Let's see... you never answered me about superpowers. What kind of power would you have?"

Bill thought about this. It was such a deep philosophical question for so early in the morning. "I'm not sure. I think maybe you are on to something with Claire's power — and by the way I think she's cute too. Anyway, I think most superpowers are just going to get you in trouble sooner or later, so a power that protects you from damage seems like a smart one to ask for. For instance, I would love to fly; that would be a great power. But then I think about maybe having a bad landing or hitting a building in the fog or even just flying too high and passing out due to lack of oxygen. No, I think regeneration would be the way to go."

"You seem to have thought this out well, Beer-san. Would you be a bad guy or a good guy?"

Another deep philosophical question. "There is a certain appeal to being a bad guy — living without rules, a cool lair on the side of a mountain, blowing stuff up. But all things considered, I think I would just lie low. Why should I pick a side?"

Sakura frowned. "You mean you wouldn't help people with your powers, Beer-san?"

Bill saw the disappointment on her face and began to back peddle. "Oh, well, certainly I'd help people if the opportunity presented itself — you know, like if someone were about to get hit by a car or something. I'm just not sure that I would wake up every morning and actually look for people to save, or for crime to fight. I mean, that sounds like a pretty demanding job. I'm not sure that I'm cut out to be a hero. I love accounting, and I used to trade in stocks and bonds. If I could maybe be a super stock-picker, that would suit me just fine. That would help people a lot, right?"

Sakura looked unconvinced. Bill asked, "Well, what would you do, then?"

Sakura answered, "I'd help people, Beer-san. I would wake up every morning and try to help people. I'd wake up early, too."

Bill looked unconvinced. "Do you do that now?"

Sakura looked confused. "I don't have superpowers now."

"If you don't wake up early every morning and try to help people now, what makes you think that having a superpower is going to turn you into a better person?"

Sakura frowned. "Well, I have to work. If I had a superpower, then I would have more free time."

"Why is that?" questioned Bill, "Do you think you won't have to eat or pay your bills as a superhero? Do you think there is some sort of superhero fund that you get to draw from once you are in the superhero club? Now, see, if I were a super stock-picker, then I could make a living and help others to make money too."

"That's not very heroic, though, Beer-san."

"Yes, but it's practical."

"You are a strange man, Beer-san. But I like you anyway. I don't think anybody else would have answered me like that."

Bill shrugged.

"It looks like we are almost to work, Beer-san. I'll take you to my supervisor and put in a good word for you. Do you remember what I told you to say if they tell you that an area is safe and you don't need a suit?"

"Fuck you?"

"Yes, that's it," said Sakura approvingly.

After another five minutes of driving, they made it to the plant. Sakura showed her badge to the security guard, who opened the motorized gate for them after recording the particulars of Bill's passport and issuing him a visitor's pass.

Bill was shown to the manager's office. He found that the plant was much different from what he had thought it would be. He had half expected the whole place to be a smoldering pile of rubble, but most of the place — and it was a very large place — was intact and quite tidy. Although he was sure that he would be seeing the untidy parts soon enough.

And speaking of untidy parts, it was clear to Bill that the power station was built solely for function and accessibility, and not at all for aesthetics or comfort.

The entire trip to the office had been a maze of steel: steel framing, steel rails, steel fences, steel stairs, and steel pipes — even the floor was made from steel grating. When he did finally enter something that resembled a more traditional building, it consisted of narrow and never-ending hallways that branched off in random directions. The walls were a light green color, and exposed piping ran along the corners of the ceiling.

The place was truly stark and completely lacked any standard office items such as pictures, potted plants, coat racks, and water coolers. Not even an annoying motivational poster could be seen. It was cold, disorientating, and clearly a place designed for making power and not for people to inhabit. Bill felt as if he were a mouse in the middle of a car engine. He was also starting to have flashbacks of his time in jail and he really hoped that no one was going to feed him a baloney sandwich.

CHAPTER 19

"How was your day, Beer-san? Mine was great. I answered forty-seven phone calls today from the press and government agencies. I told them everything is fantastic, no problems!"

"But, there was another leak from storage tank A5 today," argued Bill.

"No problems," repeated Sakura sternly, "You are a company man now. You must learn the slogan. No problems." She held up her hand and made the OK symbol in demonstration. "Everything is OK, Beer-san."

"Doesn't it bother you to keep things from the public?" asked Bill.

"Why? It would only worry them. What could they do even if they knew?"

"Move?" suggested Bill.

Sakura made a "pssst" sound at this. "To where, Beer-san? Mars? No, it's better that we tell them what the truth should be, and then we work really, really hard to make it actually happen. Did you work really, really hard today, Beer-san?"

"Uh, not really. I guess we will have to live in denial for one more day."

Sakura frowned and said nothing, which was unusual for her.

"It's not like I was lazy," explained Bill. "It's just that I spent the day filling out paperwork and listening to hours and hours of safety lectures. And they made me pee in a cup. I guess to check for drugs... possibly for isotopes... I don't know. I think tomorrow I start actually cleaning up."

"Sounds boring," suggested Sakura.

"It was, although all kinds of things kept going wrong. The supervisor gave me his divorce papers instead of the job application; I had them halfway filled out before I even noticed something was wrong. My reading and writing is not so great, you know. Then the safety guy tripped over the cord to the projector and sprained his wrist. After that, the lady at the lab dropped my cup after I had, uh, filled it up. What a mess. At least I was able to sit and drink tea for about an hour until I could pee again. They should forget about the urine test and screen for clumsiness. It's no wonder that..." he stopped abruptly when he saw Sakura hold up a cautionary finger, "...everything is OK. No problems."

"That's it, Beer-san. You learned the most important lesson. Good job."

Bill shook his head.

CHAPTER 20

On Bill's second day of work, he realized something. Actually, he realized several somethings that added up to one bigger something. He realized that he was not spoken to very often because his Japanese was not great, and it took him a long time to put sentences together. He realized that he was probably paid less than everyone else. He realized that they immediately gave him the crappiest jobs. In short, he realized that he was "The Mexican". It was...humbling.

However, despite this feeling of inequality, everything seemed to go just fine. He was allowed to play with a gigantic indoor crane, and when they saw that he was surprisingly skilled at it, they told him to very, very carefully use it to pick up one of the rods that were piled up chaotically at the bottom of a pool that was located below the crane. He was to keep the rod under water at all times, and load it into a massive steel chamber that was also in the pool.

The rods were some 4.5 meters (15 feet) long and weighed 300kg (660 pounds) each. He was told that the chamber would weigh close to 90 tonnes (99 tons) when filled with rods.

Bill asked what would happen if he broke a rod and was told, "That would be unacceptable." He asked what would happen if one of the rods were exposed to the air and was told, "That would be most unacceptable." He asked what would happen if he bumped the side of the pool and caused a leak and was told, "That would be catastrophically unacceptable."

He looked at his co-workers. They were calling out things

like, "You can do it, big man!" and giving him the thumbs up. Bill shook his head. Damn, he thought, I really am the Mexican.

"OK," agreed Bill, "I'll give it a shot."

Everyone looked really happy and patted him on the back, and then they all left the room and sealed the door and watched him from behind a thick, leaded-glass window. He could just make out the silhouette of his supervisor with his hand hovering over a big, red button. He shook his head and mumbled, "OK... So it's like that, is it?"

And so Bill began his second day at work doing one of the most delicate and dangerous jobs in the world. He was removing spent fuel rods that had been jostled out of place during the earthquake and preparing them to be moved to a more stable environment. He had been told that the rods were somewhat delicate, and that they may have become even more brittle due to salt water corrosion (because the fresh water of the pool had been replenished by the salt water of the ocean during the meltdown).

If the rods were exposed to air, they would overheat and irradiate the atmosphere in a most "catastrophically unacceptable" manner. If he broke one, pretty much the same thing would happen. It was a delicate and dangerous thing to try.

As Bill sat at the controls with his hands sweating and several expectant faces watching him with nervous apprehension, he really wondered if it might be a good time to admit that he had stretched the truth on his application. He had put down that he had been a crane operator for 10 years (because Sakura had hinted to him that they were looking for crane operators). What he had not put on the application was that the cranes were the little ones at the arcade. A bead of sweat dripped off of his nose, and his suit's visor was starting to fog.

He looked over at the window. Some of his co-workers gave him the thumbs up again. Bill looked back at the pool and mumbled, "Peer pressure," while shaking his head.

And so, ever so gently, he began to nudge a rod here, and pull a rod there. It was like trying to remove a cigarette from a crumpled pack using only a pair of tweezers and without spilling any tobacco.

After about twenty minutes of work, he was able to get a rod into a removable position, which he did while humming the theme to Mission Impossible. This was done subconsciously but had the bonus effect of drowning out the sudden gasps and intakes of breath that he would have otherwise heard over the headset every time he had pulled off a particularly lucky maneuver. Of course, it also meant that everyone in the control room was listening to him hum Mission Impossible and trying not to laugh distractingly.

It took him another ten minutes to do it, but he finally moved the rod over to the transportation chamber and loaded it inside.

He heard cheering over his headset. He waved his hand toward the window and gave them the company hand signal — the OK sign.

Well, thought Bill, that wasn't so bad. It only took me a half hour to get the easiest rod in the entire pool. One down, 1499 to go. I guess I have job security for as long as I don't irradiate the atmosphere. Sweet.

The second rod was also relatively easy to remove from the pile, but as he was moving it to the chamber, it slipped out of the crane's grippers and came within two inches of hitting the bottom of the pool before he somehow managed to catch it again with the crane. He was lucky that it had happened under water because the water had marginally slowed the fall. Even still, it was a tense moment for everyone. Bill was not sure what would have happened if it had hit the bottom of the pool, but he guessed that the word 'catastrophic' would have been mentioned in relation to it.

He looked at the window again. His supervisor was gone. Bill found out later that he had fainted. After the supervisor revived, he told Bill to break for lunch.

While on lunch, his supervisor asked him what he thought of the job. Bill said, "Eh, I've had worse," which was such a line of bull that everyone laughed.

Bill was relieved by the laughter, and that they had not given him a baloney sandwich to eat.

After lunch, he was back on the crane. He was really starting to get the feel for the controls, and he removed eight more rods by the end of the day without incident — catastrophic or otherwise.

After work, Bill was invited to go out drinking with some of the guys to welcome him to the company and to celebrate his success with the crane. Sakura invited herself along because she said that it was her duty to chaperone him since she was the one who introduced him to the company. It wasn't at all to do with the free food and drinks.

Everyone was very nice to Bill, and he was the center of attention for much of the night. He mused that he was no longer "The Mexican" and had now been elevated to "The Cool Mexican".

His workmates feasted on sushi and sashimi, both variations on the theme of raw fish — something that Bill humbly excused himself from eating. Instead, he was served some sort of fried noodle dish with vegetables. Sakura ate this too because she thought it was fun to steal Bill's food when he was not looking. It was a game of skill, and only Sakura knew the rules. Bill noticed her doing it, of course, but he did not have the heart to call her out on it — she looked like she was having too much fun.

In fact, it was a fun night for Bill as well, and he was able to successfully bond a little with his new coworkers. However, there were a few uncomfortable moments. Periodically throughout the night, several of his coworkers had pulled him aside individually and ask him where they could find a woman. They would usually accompany this with a nudge or a wink.

To the first man that asked him, Bill had simply told him that he did not know, which had left the man very unsatisfied and feeling as if Bill was holding back information. Bill had noticed this, and so the next several times when he was asked a similar question, he looked around conspiratorially, pulled in close to the men, and whispered to them that there was a really nice girl named Tina at Club Essex in Tokyo who would show them a very good time if they told her that Bill had sent them. He also told them that she had never been to Disneyland and would probably love to be taken there.

CHAPTER 21

Bill's third day at work was much less stressful, although as it turned out, it was still fraught with danger. He was doing cleanup work along the outside of reactor two, and he was working with a completely different work crew. When he asked why, he was told that everyone else from his old crew had called out sick with food poisoning. Only he and Sakura had escaped unscathed, apparently.

His new crew proved to be just as unlucky. One man was trapped in a trench when the earth collapsed and buried him up to his waist. He was fortunate not to have been buried alive and the other men were able to dig him out unharmed.

A second man got his arm pinned between some shifting rubble and was trapped for almost an hour while the others worked to free him.

A third man hurt his hand when he took a swing at Bill for something that he had said. Bill had thought that he had told the man that he was slipping out to use the restroom, but because of the noise, and because Bill had mixed up some words, what the man had heard was that Bill was sleeping with his wife. As the man took a swing at him, Bill slipped on some debris, which caused the man to miss Bill's head and instead hit the steel beam behind him with considerable force. Even wearing work gloves, the man had broken several bones in his hand.

A fourth man received a random text message from his girlfriend telling him that she was dumping him. He was so distraught that he absentmindedly walked into an open pit and broke his leg.

A fifth man was nearly crushed by falling concrete debris when the cable connecting the concrete to the crane above it had snapped. The debris spilled down exactly where Bill had been not two minutes prior, just before he had asked the man to cover for him while he used the toilet.

Sadly, all of this happened in just the short hours before lunch, and after lunch, things failed to get better. By four o'clock, Bill was the only man in the crew still able to work.

CHAPTER 22

"How was your day, Beer-san? My day was great. I was promoted to public relations manager today. I am so excited. They gave me a nice raise, too. I can even afford a better apartment if I wanted to move, but I like it where I'm at so I think I will stay."

Sakura's wave of positivity was met with an equal but opposite wave coming from Bill. "I was fired. I didn't do anything wrong, and I was really good at working the crane, but they fired me anyway. I don't get it. They said I was unlucky. Can you really fire someone for being unlucky?"

Sakura changed the gears of the car while she mentally changed gears as well. Finally, she replied, "Oh, I'm so sorry to hear that, Beer-san. And here I was bragging about getting a raise. I'm sorry."

Bill shrugged. "It's fine. It's not your fault."

"Did they really fire you for being unlucky? I've never heard of that."

"Me neither, agreed Bill. "And the worst thing was that after the manager fired me, he asked me if I knew any women that would show him a good time. Why the hell does everyone think that I'm a pimp?"

"Well, not to sound stereotypical," replied Sakura, "but you are white after all. White and black guys are always involved in that sort of stuff. At least that's what I hear."

"Are we?" asked Bill rhetorically, "I never knew." He shook his head in mock disbelief.

They sat there in silence for a few minutes as Sakura

continued to drive them home. Suddenly, as if she had been pondering it the whole time, Sakura blurted out, "It still doesn't make sense. I don't get why they fired you. You told me about how you were really good with the crane over the storage pool. I can't imagine an unlucky person would be able to do that successfully."

"That's just it," said Bill, "They told me that while I was great at the crane and that I am very lucky for myself, somehow I am a jinx to those around me."

"Like that old lady you were telling me about?"

"Exactly," agreed Bill, "That old lady is a perfect example. I find some money, and she falls and her groceries get ruined by a passing bicycle. I give her some money that I found, and she loses it. Then I see her the next evening, and we talk as we walk around the park. I found a watch, and she gets shit on by a passing bird. It seems like coincidence, and maybe it is, but when you look at it in conjunction with the events at the plant over the last few days, maybe they have a point about me. I keep getting lucky while those around me keep having accidents. I'm actually starting to think that maybe you should stay away from me for a while. I don't want you to get hurt too."

"That's nice of you, Beer-san, but don't worry about me. I'm always lucky. No problem."

"Oh, well, that's good then," said Bill. "I'd miss my little Big Mouth."

Sakura gave him a playful scowl. "You looked it up, Beer-san. Now you see why I don't like my name? I talk a lot and my name is Big Mouth. That's just not funny."

"Depends on your point of view," said Bill. "I find it hysterical."

"Ha-ha, Beer-san. Can we go back to talking about your getting fired? I don't like to talk about my name."

Bill shrugged again. "OK, Big..." Sakura cut him short by once again holding up her finger in warning, and so he quickly corrected himself, "...Sakura-chan."

Sakura nodded. "So, did they tell you anything else before they let you go, Beer-san?"

"Yes, they did. When I argued with them that it seemed extreme to fire someone for being unlucky, they told me that I was too much like Kurokawa-san for them to take a chance on. Apparently, this guy Kurokawa-san had been like me and brought misfortune to those around him. At least, that's what my supervisor told me. I asked him what happened to Kurokawa-san, but he didn't know. The only thing he knew was that Kurokawa-san quit the day before the disaster.

"I tried to look him up out of curiosity while I waited for you to finish work, but there are too many people called Kurokawa Yoshi, and the few I called did not seem to be the right one. I don't know how I can ever find him."

"Wait," said Sakura in astonishment, "did you just say Kurokawa Yoshi? That's my uncle! Remember I said that my uncle used to work at the plant too? That's him!"

"Get out of here," protested Bill. "That's a lucky coincidence, don't you think? I mean, what are the odds?"

"Yes, Beer-san. But you forget that we are Mister and Misses Lucky."

"Hmm," said Bill, "Yes, I guess you're right." He paused for a moment of thought and then added, "So, do you think we can go visit Uncle Lucky? Maybe he knows something."

Sakura nodded happily. "OK, Beer-san. We will go. I'll take us there now. But I have to warn you that he is a bit weird."

"Weirder than the panty guy who owns our apartment complex?"

"Well," considered Sakura, "maybe not as weird as that. Or maybe just as weird but a different type of weird. He is a recluse now. He's been this way ever since he left the power company. He actually won the lottery the day before he quit, but he lives in a crappy, little house in the middle of nowhere.

"Most of the family has nothing to do with him. Or maybe, he has nothing to do with the rest of the family. Either way, I'm pretty much the only one who visits him now, and only because I was persistent about it because he is my favorite uncle."

This was intriguing information for Bill. The man had obviously been very lucky to win the lottery, and also to avoid being at the plant during the disaster. And now he is hiding away from everyone else as if he were afraid that he might cause them misfortune. It is as if he were lucky, but at the expense of those around him — just like me. Very odd. I wonder what happens when we meet? Do we steal each other's luck at the same time and get stuck in some weird recursive loop that leaves us paralyzed? Do sparks shoot off of us? Do we rip a hole in the fabric of the universe? Do we cancel each other out and suddenly return to normal? Or do we both just figure out that we are reading too much into things and are both just being stupid? My money is on the last one.

Suddenly the Nissan began to buck and sputter. Bill snapped out of his contemplations and asked, "What's wrong?"

Sakura looked at the dash and said, "Oh."

"What?"

"Um, we're out of gas."

"Great," said Bill. He looked around. "Hey, there's a gas station right there. Try to coast over to it."

Sakura tried this and was successful. While the car was refilling with gas, Bill took the opportunity to stretch his legs. As he was walking around near the street, he saw something shiny buried in the grass. He picked it up. It was a key.

He examined the key closely. It looked very special because it was made from silver and was decorated with a red gemstone. The stone looked like a ruby, but it just as easily could have been glass. Either way, Bill thought that it looked valuable, and so he added it to his keyring.

He then meandered back to the car and got back inside just as the pump was shutting off. Sakura held out her hand.

Bill looked at it for a second and then said, "Oh, right!" He pulled out his wallet and gave Sakura a little over half the money for the gas.

Sakura nodded. "Good boy."

As they pulled away from the gas station, Sakura said, "Wasn't that lucky of us to have run out of gas right in front of a gas station?"

Bill sniggered. "Yeah, lucky. Imagine that."

After they were a half mile from the station, it burst into flames.

CHAPTER 23

"Who's there?" grumbled a voice from behind the door.

"It's me, Uncle, Sakura."

There was the sound of several locks being opened, and then the door cracked open. A man peered out from the crack to confirm Sakura's identity. Then the door closed and a chain was unhooked from the door. Finally, the door was opened all the way.

"Hello, Uncle," greeted Sakura.

"Hello... Who is that?" asked Kurokawa while backing away from them, as if getting ready to dart back inside the house and slam the door shut.

"This is my friend, Beer... Bill-san. We live in the same apartment building and work together at the power plant."

"Oh no," exclaimed Kurokawa, "I told you that I did not want to see anyone — especially from the power plant. I do not want to cause any more trouble. Please, no offense, but go away." He backed up further into his house.

"No, wait," cried Sakura to her uncle before he could slam the door. "He doesn't work there anymore. Listen, Uncle, he is just like you. He has been causing problems at work. They just fired him. He's like you, and he wants to talk."

Kurokawa stopped his retreat and slowly made his way back outside. He stared at Bill for an uncomfortably long time. Kurokawa was an older Japanese man and was well dressed for a hermit, except for his wild, gray hair. His face was very creased and very animated. When Kurokawa frowned at someone, they knew it. He was doing it to Bill right now.

Bill shifted under the glare. "Hello," he said while waving a hand at Kurokawa.

Kurokawa stared for a few more seconds, and then suddenly spoke. He said, "OK, come inside, please. At your own risk, of course." He had said this in English and with a smile.

The two men then sat on opposite sides of a small kitchen table while Sakura prepared some tea at a nearby counter.

There were a few minutes of banter between the two that Bill called handshaking. The conversation flowed back and forth between Japanese and English while they worked out the best mode of communication in much the same way that two computers will try different communication protocols with each other until they can agree on the speediest one. For the two men, this turned out to be English, much to Sakura's annoyance. She had learned English in school but she had no practical experience with it and therefore could not meaningfully communicate in it more than simple sentences.

Kurokawa spoke in a slow and measured manner. Bill found him stately, as if he were a high government official who was weighing every word before using it.

He looked at Bill and said, "I am sure that Sakura-chan told you about me, she is an Ōguchi after all. Please tell me why you think you are like me."

In answer to this, Bill told him all about the events of the last few days, which was difficult to do with Sakura in the background ranting in Japanese about how she does not talk too much and that she really hates her name.

Kurokawa listened politely but occasionally interrupted to ask for clarification. Every once in a while, one or the other of the men would use Japanese, either because the Japanese word was a better fit, or in the case of Kurokawa, simply because he did not know the English version.

After Bill had finished, Kurokawa said, "Thank you. Now let me return the favor and tell you my story. This story starts a few weeks before the disaster. I am sure you know the one I mean. I went to Tamura to visit my niece." He pointed toward Sakura, who looked annoyed at being the subject of a conversation that she could not understand. "Thank you, by the way, for being her friend. She is a good girl, and I hope you will continue to watch out for her."

He cleared his throat and took a sip of the tea that Sakura

had just deposited in front of him. Bill tried it as well and thought that it was quite good.

Kurokawa continued, "After I visited Sakura, I went for a walk to enjoy the nice weather. I found a small park on the other side of town, and inside the park was a small shrine. I went to the shrine to pray for good fortune for Sakura and myself because both of us had been having some troubles at the time. But before I could pray, do you know what happened?"

Bill had his suspicions, but merely shrugged.

"I forgot to ring the bells. When I did, they fell and hit me on the head. I was knocked unconscious. When I awoke some hours later, I had the curse. And a low hum in my ears."

Bill almost jumped out of his seat. "You mean the small park on the west side of Funehiki?"

"Yes."

"I swear to you on my life that the exact same thing happened to me at that very same shrine. It has to be the cause of all this."

"Very likely, Mr. Bill," agreed Kurokawa without excitement. I have often speculated about it. I have made several more trips to that shrine, but I can never find any answers, and no one in town has heard of anything strange happening there. It is an aggravating dead end, I'm afraid."

Bill told him about the new bell being put up just after he had left the shrine. Kurokawa then said, "That is very interesting, Mr. Bill. Very interesting. I returned the next day, and I also saw new bells. That seems to indicate that someone is monitoring the premises closely, yet prefers to remain anonymous. Very Interesting."

"What's interesting?" asked Sakura excitedly after hearing a word that she understood. Bill took a moment to translate everything for her while Kurokawa sipped his tea and contemplated the information that he had received thus far. Occasionally, he would also correct Bill's awkward Japanese. Bill started to wonder why he was the one doing the translating.

The two men decided to switch to Japanese in order to avoid the wrath of Sakura, although to her credit, she had remained silent without interrupting up until that point.

Kurokawa continued his story, "To continue, after I regained consciousness, I noticed many of the same occurrences that you have, Mr. Bill."

Bill interrupted, "Sorry, but do you mind not calling me Mr.

Bill? I keep thinking of a clay cartoon character every time I hear it, and it's distracting. Just Bill, or even Bill-san would be fine."

"Of course, Bill-san. Sorry about that, I did not know."

"No problem."

Kurokawa gave him a small nod. "Getting back to the story, I started noticing that I was having the most extraordinary luck. I was winning at *pachinko* all the time, enough that they accused me of cheating. At work, I would always get a front spot in the parking lot. The elevators would always be waiting for me. They would always have my favorite foods in the cafeteria. You get the point.

"But those around me were not so fortunate. Many accidents happened to people around me, and even the equipment seemed to break down more often. It distressed me greatly because I was in charge of maintenance for my area."

"What area was that?" asked Bill.

Kurokawa took a deep, slow breath while looking down at the table. Softly, almost shamefully, he answered, "The cooling systems, including the backup generators."

"Oh," said Bill flatly.

"Yes," agreed Kurokawa. "It is as you suspect. I won the lottery two days before the disaster. I quit my job the day before the disaster. On the day of the disaster, I was not there to organize my men. I was not there to fix the generators. I was not there to help."

Kurokawa's eyes were starting to tear. His elastic face was forming a deep frown. Bill thought he looked like a sad clown, and then cursed himself for thinking like that at a time like this.

Bill said, "I understand why you feel that way, but logically it was better for you not to have been there. You surely could not have fixed the generators by yourself, and anyone who tried to help you would have suffered from bad luck. I'm not sure how this works, but the generators themselves could have been affected by you, as weird as that sounds. Hell, this whole thing is weird. But if it is true, then I say you should be happy you were not there."

Kurokawa blew his nose and considered this. He was not someone to make a quick decision, and so his consideration took a few minutes.

Bill was worried about the silence and started to apologize, but Sakura told him not to worry — her uncle was always like that. Finally, Kurokawa spoke. He said, "Thank you."

Bill said, "You're welcome," for lack of anything better to say.

Kurokawa looked as if he had made an important internal decision. His demeanor changed to being one of a college professor, which was not much different from his normal demeanor, all things considered. "I would like to tell you some more things, Bill-san, important things. I feel you are a decent man, and I want to help you as much as possible. I had promised myself that I would not tell anyone what I am about to share, but then again, I did not expect to meet someone else with the same curse."

Bill did not know what to say to this, and so he simply nodded.

Kurokawa then turned to Sakura and said, "You might as well listen too, child. I know I would have to chain you down to prevent it, and I'm too old to chase you around and try to do that."

Sakura laughed.

"Just promise me that you will not tell anyone about Bill-san and I, or anything about what I'm about to say. It might endanger our lives if people learn about us."

Sakura promised and bowed, which was so unlike her that Bill was caught off guard.

Kurokawa noticed Bill's reaction and said, "She can be very reliable, Bill-san, despite how she appears. She is a good girl. She will keep her word."

Bill believed him. There was something about Sakura that made Bill trust her completely. It was odd. It was almost as if she had a serious side to her that was hiding behind a giant mask of...Sakura-ness.

"No, I get that," replied Bill. "I'm quite fond of her too. She is like the little sister I never had."

Sakura smiled at this, as did Kurokawa. "Excellent," said Kurokawa, "Then let's begin, shall we? As you know, I have been living a secluded life ever since the disaster. But I have not just been watching TV and eating instant ramen. No, I have been diligently and scientifically studying my curse. And while I do not profess to know everything about it — like how I came to acquire it in the first place — I have been able to string together a list of working theories that seem to model the curse to a high degree of accuracy."

"So, you figured out the power?" asked Bill.

"Yes, that is what I just said," scowled Kurokawa, "Please pay attention."

"Sorry," replied Bill, "It is just that I do not know half of the words that you just used. My Japanese is on a 4th or 5th grade level."

Kurokawa considered this. "Well, try to keep up just the same. This is important. I will tell you in English if you miss something."

"Thank you. So, does this mean that you are able to... What? Control your luck or something?"

"Yes, Bill-san, something like that. Let me explain the nature of our curse, and then I will teach you how to control it."

"That would be great. Thank you."

"Our curse, or power as you call it, is the ability to redirect the flow of luck. By that, I mean that life is made up of all kinds of chance events. These events can be counted as good or bad depending on whether they ultimately help or harm us. Notice that I did not say whether they make us happy or not. Sometimes luck comes to us in disguise. Have you ever heard the story of Saiou's horse?"

Bill shook his head. Sakura had heard it before, but she sat quietly and listened with her arms folded on the table and her chin resting on top of them.

Kurokawa explained, "One day, Saiou's horse got loose and ran away into enemy territory. Saiou cursed his misfortune. But then the next day, the horse returned with two other horses, and so Saiou realized this was good fortune after all. Now that there were several horses around, Saiou's son decided to learn to ride them. One day while he was learning, the horse bucked him off and he broke his leg. Saiou was downcast and cursed his misfortune once again. Then, the war escalated and many young people from the area died in battle, but Saiou's son survived because he was home with a broken leg. Saiou once again felt that all of this had actually been good fortune."

After listening to this, Bill said, "So basically, life is a big ball of random crap and we can never be sure if something is good luck or bad luck?"

"Ha," replied Kurokawa, "Funny, Bill-san, but not quite right. The lesson here is that sometimes things will happen that may look like good or bad luck at first, but may turn out to be just the opposite later on."

"Isn't that what I just said?" questioned Bill.

Sakura laughed and said, "I think he has a point, Uncle."

Kurokawa looked flustered, and his mouth did the sad clown thing again. "Maybe. But the point I was trying to make is that it was very hard for me to test my curse knowing this story. I had to monitor the subjects for long periods after I came in contact with them. I also kept a log of out-of-the-ordinary events that happened to me, and I tried to correlate them with what happened to the other subjects."

"Subjects?" asked Bill, now a little worried.

"Yes, subjects. People whom I tested my power on."

Bill stared at him.

Don't look at me like that — it's not as if I dissected them, Bill-san. And besides, I limited my exposure to people who probably deserved a little bad luck — like bankers and lawyers."

Bill nodded in agreement. "Oh, that's alright then."

"To continue, after careful observation of the subjects and myself, I learned a few things about my curse. For one, I learned that it has a lot to do with probabilities, or the odds of an event occurring or not.

"Let's say that life consists of a series of events, each with their own probability of happening to us. The probability that the sun will rise is nearly 1:1. If we flip a coin, the probability that it will land on heads is nearly 1:2 (scientifically, we must consider the option to land on the edge). If you are married, you have about the same 1:2 odds of getting a divorce. A role of a die gets you a 1:6 shot at any one of the numbers. These are about the same odds that a person between 45 and 64 will visit a physician during the year. These are all in the realm of common occurrences.

"Then, we move on to less common occurrences, but ones that will not surprise us unduly if they happen. The odds that an astronaut will be killed during a mission is about 1:50. The odds that a man between 25 and 44 has had no female sexual partners is close to the same.

"By the way, you will note that the way a person leads his life has a lot to do with these odds. If you are an accountant, then the odds of dying from your job are a lot less likely than if you were an astronaut. Some of our choices raise or lower the odds of some things happening, but there will always be an element of randomness involved.

"At any rate, after the less common occurrences, we move on to the ones that we would deem improbable: the odds of being struck by lightning in the span of a year is 1:1 million, which is about the same odds of winning an average Pick-6 lottery in that same year if you had bought one ticket each month.

"Of course, there are all sorts of other events that happen, whether it is getting cancer or getting a raise — all of which have a probability to them. I find it easier to think about them if I flip the ratio for these events and call the result 'lucky points', so winning something with the roll of a die is six lucky points. Winning an average Pick-6 lottery with one ticket is about 14 million lucky points. Bad events are negative lucky points.

"Picture your life as a blank piece of paper with a horizontal line drawn across the middle. The beginning of the line would represent your birth, and the end of the line would represent your death. We will use the western convention and say that we go from left to right. You can imagine the events of your life as dots being plotted above or below the line as you move from left to right. Positive events go above the line, negative events go below. The line would represent even odds. The farther away from the line in either direction, the more unlikely the event. Obviously, the dots will be more heavily concentrated around the line because they are more likely, and they will thin out as they move away from the line because they are increasingly unlikely. Are you following OK, Bill-san?"

Bill nodded. "Yes, I think I've got it."

"Good. Now we will assign a scale to this graph. We will use lucky points. The line is one lucky point, which simply means 1:1 odds. Above the line, the points increase to the positive. Below the line, the points decrease to the negative. So obviously, a positive event with the probability of 1:40 will go above the line at the 40 mark. A bad event with the probability of 1:200 will go below the line at 200. Easy.

"Here is how I see our curse working: we are able to skew someone's lucky points by a certain negative amount while we simultaneously skew our own to the positive. I like to envision it as an invisible umbilical cord being attached between us and our victims with which we constantly siphon off a certain amount of luck."

Both Bill and Sakura wrinkled there noses at this explanation. Kurokawa continued, "So let us say that we are siphoning off 10 lucky points from someone. If we looked at their chart, suddenly the cloud of dots will be centered around the -10 mark. In other words, bad things that would normally happen to a person only 1 in 10 times are now almost certain to happen. Bad things that were likely to happen 1 in 50 times will now happen 1 in 40.

"You will note that good things can still happen to the person too, but if they had a 1 in 20 chance of happening, then they now have a 1 in 30 chance of happening. It is as if all events get a 10 point penalty added to them.

"On our side of the umbilical cord, we get a 10 point bonus added to all events in our life. So suddenly good events that would normally only happen 1 in 10 times start happening all the time.

"From observation, I noted that the default amount that I stole from others was only about 0.5 lucky points. In other words, about 1:1.5 odds. However, I noticed that in times of stress I somehow stole more. Tell me, Bill-san, do you have a ringing in your ears? Or maybe more like a hum, or a throb?"

Bill, surprised, answered, "Yes! Ever since that stupid bell hit me...in...the...head. Oh, I see. It has something to do with our power, doesn't it?"

Kurokawa nodded. "Yes, Bill-san, it does. It seems the hum is an indicator of the amount of luck we are taking from the surrounding people. No, that is not quite right. It is more like this: if you hear a low hum and then you look at Sakura, you will form a bond with her and start draining a small amount of her luck. And if you look at me while still hearing that same low hum, then you will start to draw that same amount of luck from me. However, afterwords, the hum will not increase. It is not an indicator of the total amount of luck you are drawing in, but an indicator of the amount of luck you will draw from someone when that initial bond is formed."

Bill interrupted, "Does that mean that you know how to change the hum? To change the amount of luck we draw from someone? Can we shut it off?"

"Yes, Bill, I do. Unfortunately, it does not appear that we can shut it off entirely without some concentration. But we can turn it off on a temporary basis. And we can turn it up quite high. I have even found that we can reassign the good fortune to someone other than ourselves."

"Really? How's that all work, then?"

"Well, if you concentrate on the hum and then hum to yourself in the same frequency and then..." he broke off and quickly held his palm up at Bill and said, "Do not do this now,

Bill-san. This is very dangerous and you could potentially kill me or Sakura if you did it while looking at us. If you stole enough of our luck, then we could even get hit by an asteroid or a crashing plane. I think we should both be immune to you, but just to be safe, please do not do this now.

"Anyway, you can raise the hum by matching it and then humming in an increasingly higher pitch. You can lower it or even turn it off by matching it and then humming in a lower and lower pitch until it is too deep for you to even make a sound. You may try this now if you would like, but please face that wall just in case."

Bill shrugged and turned his chair around and faced the wall. Then he made a hum that sounded close to the hum of an electrical transformer. He slowly made it deeper and deeper until it ended in a strangled, airy sound. Then he turned back around and said, "Yes, the hum is pretty much gone."

"Well done, Bill-san. For me, the hum tends to work its way back during the course of about an hour. That is, unless I get worried or frightened about something — then it comes back almost instantly and is usually even higher pitched. It appears to be a self-defense mechanism, I think. Some animals will spray you with a bad scent, others will sting you with poison, but we will suck out your good fortune. Pretty scary, this curse."

"Yes, if what you say is true, then it sounds... Well, I guess the way you described it is correct; it is like a curse. We can have good luck, but it comes at the expense of those around us. Do you think it is possible to lead a normal life if we just keep lowering the hum every so often?"

"Maybe, Bill-san. But if you forget to lower it, it comes back. And it happens so gradually that sometimes you do not notice. Even worse, like I said, when we get panicked, it seems like it spikes higher on its own. We can immediately bring it back down, of course, but if we were looking at someone (or something), then they (or it) will feel the effects of our curse."

Bill suddenly had a flood of questions at this point. He blurted out two. "Wait, hold on. Something? What do you mean by that? Also, can we sever a bond once we form it?"

"Ah, very perceptive, Bill-san. Yes, it appears objects are affected too. Imagine me as I worked at the power plant: every day looking at the people around me, and looking at all the cooling equipment. All the time with that cursed hum in my head. When you consider the fact that I had absorbed enough luck to win a multi-million yen lottery, I must have formed a bond with thousands of things around me to accumulate that many lucky points. Remember, our baseline seems to be 1.5 lucky points per victim. But I had a stressful job, so there is every reason to believe I could have stolen 2...3...4... maybe even 10 lucky points from some victims. In your case, being the first few days of a new job, it could have even been more."

Bill offered, "They had me working the crane over the storage pool, remember."

"Exactly," responded Kurokawa with his exaggerated frown, "Very stressful."

"Well, I guess that explains why all of my first crew got food poisoning. And all of my second crew had some sort of accident. I keep thinking of all the stress I was under while looking at the spent fuel rods. That's not good."

Kurokawa shook his head. "No, I think you are OK with that, Bill-san. I think you probably subconsciously transferred some luck to the rods. You were concentrating on them and wanted them to be safe. In fact, their safety was vital to your safety, so you can think of it like another aspect of the self-defense mechanism."

Bill pointed at Sakura and asked, "What about Sakura-chan? She seems to be impervious to bad luck." He then turned his head to her and asked in confirmation, "You haven't had any bad luck lately, have you Sakura-chan?"

The girl shook her head. "No, life's been pretty good. I even got a raise today, remember?"

Kurokawa said, "That is because I gave her some of my luck. Or maybe I should say that I gave her someone else's luck. Not a lot, mind you. But I found that once you transfer luck to someone, then they are no longer vulnerable to the curse. It is as if people and things can only have one bond at a time. You and I, Bill-san, are obviously the exception to this."

"OK, that makes a sort of sense I guess. But going back to my earlier question, can we sever a bond altogether? If I start sucking out someone's luck, can I remove the straw?"

"Yes, it seems that we can. I found that if I looked at a victim and then I did the trick with the humming, I could adjust the flow of luck coming from that person. And if I brought the hum down to silence while I looked at them, then it would break the bond."

"That's good news."

"Yes, also, I found that if I transferred luck to someone, and by that I mean I made them the beneficiary of someone else's luck instead of me, then it would sever any previous bonds I had with them."

"Huh?" asked Bill, totally confused.

"OK," said Kurokawa patiently, "Let's say that Sakura and I are just normal people. Now you look at Sakura and put the curse on her. Now there is a bond between you two, and you are draining her luck. So she becomes unluckier and you become luckier. Now you can look at me and transfer the bond to me. Then you are no longer part of the bond. Sakura would still be unluckier, but I would now be luckier instead of you. I would be getting her luck, not you."

"OK, I get that much. Now explain the other thing about breaking a bond with a new one or whatever."

"OK, let's start over again. And again, Sakura and I are normal people."

Bill interrupted, "I'm having a hard time visualizing Sakura as normal."

"Ha-ha," replied Sakura and then stuck out her tongue at him.

Kurokawa made a deep frown. Bill said, "Sorry. Please continue."

"As I was saying, Sakura and I are normal. You look at her and form a bond, so her luck is flowing to you. You then look at me and form a bond, so my luck is also flowing to you. If you transfer my bond to Sakura, then it breaks the bond she already had with you. So you end up in this case without any bonds, and Sakura would end up getting my good luck. You see, she can only have one bond at a time, so when you gave her the good end of my bond, it broke the bond from her to you. I think this must be a way of preventing some sort of cosmic short circuit. Or maybe it is just so that us stupid mortals can keep track, otherwise we could get ourselves tangled up in a spiderweb of lucky bonds."

"I'm amazed that you were able to figure all this out," said Bill.

Kurokawa replied, "It was nothing. I am a patient man with a lot of free time. That is all."

"You are being modest, Kurokawa-san. By the way, speaking of modest, if you won the lottery, then why is your house so modest?"

Kurokawa frowned again, but only slightly. He then said, "I

felt very bad for the trouble that I caused at the power plant and, by extension, to Japan. I donated most of my winnings to help relocate the families in the area and to pay for medical treatment to anyone who needed it."

"That is very admirable," said Bill solemnly. "I heard that even one of the main Yakuza clans had sent hundreds of trucks filled with food, water, blankets, and sanitary accessories to help the people who were affected by the disaster. It is nice to see that when times are rough, even gangsters will lend a hand — not that I'm calling you a gangster. Sorry, that didn't come out how I had meant it."

"It is OK, Bill-san, I think I know what you meant. That group has done some other good things in the past. But it is important to remember that normally they do a lot of bad things. In fact, the rumor is that the entire relief effort was organized by an underling without the knowledge of the boss. She was supposed to use the trucks and a large amount of cash to buy and transport contraband, but instead she used the money to buy supplies and the trucks to haul them to the disaster victims."

"Wow, really?" asked Bill.

"As I said," explained Kurokawa, "it is only a rumor."

"Does the rumor say what happened to her?"

"No. I expect she was punished in the traditional way, and perhaps even exiled from the clan. She was well respected, so it is doubtful that she was killed."

"What is the traditional way?" asked Bill.

Kurokawa held up his hand and then pretended to slice off a finger with his other hand.

Bill cringed, as did Sakura. Seeing her cringe, Bill took note of Sakura and asked her, "So, what do you think of all this, Sakura-chan?"

Sakura pretended to think deeply for a few seconds and then said, "Well, Beer-san, you could probably become a super stock-picker now if you wanted to."

CHAPTER 24

Kurokawa shook his head at Bill and gave him a very large frown. He looked around randomly at the hustle and bustle of the streets of Tokyo and said, "I still do not think this is a good idea."

Bill answered as reassuringly as he could, "Don't worry, big guy. This will work — I'm sure of it. Look, we will start small and progress very carefully and scientifically. This is a great chance to do some good. And you are here to guide us every step of the way."

"I would like to guide us home, then."

"Now, now — that's just your agoraphobia talking. You've been locked away by yourself for months now. It will take some time for you to get used to people again."

Kurokawa shook his head. "I just think that no good can come from using our curse."

Bill answered quickly, "That's why we are here, to see if we can use our power to do some good."

"And who is the judge of what is good and what is bad?" asked Kurokawa.

Bill looked confused. He answered, "Well, us of course. You're a good judge of character, aren't you?"

Kurokawa looked at Bill, frowned, and answered, "I used to think so."

It was Bill's turn to frown this time. "Now, come on. Let's just give this a try. Think of us as very timid and careful superheros, fighting crime and helping the needy — from the sidelines. And listen, I've been working on a code of conduct so don't worry about that. We can discuss it tonight at HQ."

Kurokawa wrinkled his brow. "What is HQ?"

"Headquarters," answered Bill simply.

"And where is headquarters?" asked Kurokawa, not sure he wanted to know.

Bill hesitated. "Well, for now it's my apartment — at least until we can afford to carve a hideout on the side of Mt. Fuji... Don't frown at me like that. And listen, we are moving you into our apartment complex so we can all be close together to save on gas."

Kurokawa then motioned to Sakura and asked, "And how does Sakura-chan fit into all of this?"

Bill inspected his hand for a moment and answered sheepishly, "Well, she is our cheery sidekick, of course."

Sakura, who was wearing a pretty little sundress, did a twirl in demonstration.

Kurokawa stared at Bill and frowned for an uncomfortably long time until Bill finally cracked and added, "OK, yes, and also because she has a car."

Sakura said enthusiastically, "It's a Nissan Tiida. They call it a Versa in America. It was in Heroes. Have you seen Heroes? I loved Heroes."

Bill then said, "See, there you go. A genuine superhero car."

Kurokawa considered this and said, "So, if I understand you correctly, you want us to become cowardly superheroes who fight crime from a safe distance away, and we will be dashing around the city in a small Nissan hatchback driven by a teenage girl."

Bill said, "Um, yes, I think that about sums it up."

Sakura added, "It's a good car. It was in Heroes."

CHAPTER 25

Now back at HQ (Bill's apartment), the three superheroes sat around the Pillar of Justice (Bill's small dining room table) and reviewed the day's events.

Kurokawa lead with, "I believe we learned some important lessons today. And by 'we' I mean you, Bill-san."

"Look, I'm new at this, alright. I'm sure that lady's hair will grow back... eventually," explained Bill.

"And what did you learn from that?" asked Kurokawa.

Bill mumbled softly, "That the power does not necessarily manifest immediately."

Kurokawa nodded and then asked, "And what don't we do if it seems like nothing is happening?"

Bill continued to stare down at the table and said, "We don't keep turning it up until something does happen."

Kurokawa nodded again. He then turned to Sakura and asked, "And what don't we say to Bill-san when he suggests that he use his power unnecessarily?"

Sakura replied studiously, "We don't say, 'Yeah, yeah, teach that chick a lesson.'"

Kurokawa said, "Good," and then he turned back to face Bill and continued, "I think it might be prudent now for us to discuss the code of ethics you were working on." He took a deep breath, as if steadying himself against an expected wave of stupidity, and continued, "So, what did you have in mind?"

Bill cleared his throat and made a show of straitening his paperwork. "OK, now these are the rules I came up with so far —

and mind you, this is a work in progress. Nothing is written in stone yet. Please, take a look at them and tell me what you think."

Bill handed out copies of his proposed code of ethics, which read as follows:

1. Definition of "bad person / bad people": A bad person shall be defined as someone who meets any or all of the following descriptions:
   a) Someone who uses violence, or the threat of violence, for any reason other than self defense.
   b) Someone who attempts to fake reality, such as the case with lying or forgery.
   c) Someone who seeks the unearned or undeserved, such as the case with robbery or begging.
   d) Someone who attempts to justify their actions by saying that they are for the good of society, the will of god, or any other unknowable or irrational reason.
2. We shall attempt to punish individuals that we identify as "bad people" as defined above by removing some of their good fortune. Conversely, we shall attempt to donate the collected good fortune to "good people" who appear to be in a difficult situation in life — not from their own doing, but from a twist of fate. In other words, we shall donate the good fortune to "good people" who are down on their luck. "Good people" shall be defined as: People who do not appear to meet the criteria for a "bad person" as defined above.
3. We shall accomplish #2 while avoiding at all costs becoming "bad people" ourselves.

After it appeared that everyone had finished reading, Bill asked, "So, what does everyone think of it?"

Sakura shrugged. "Sounds good to me."

Kurokawa looked thoughtful, as always. "I will have to consider this at length, but on first blush, I have to say that the rules seem simple yet well thought out. If anything, perhaps we should add a sub-clause somewhere that states that excessive use of our power constitutes an act of violence because it could lead to injury or death, and is therefore subject to section 1-a."

Bill tapped the table restlessly with his fingertips while he thought about this. Finally, he said, "I'm seeing some problems with this, already. I don't see how we can accomplish #2 without violating #3. I mean, technically speaking, any use of our power is increasing the risk, by definition, of something bad happening to someone. So we would immediately become bad people under 1-a. And I can imagine several scenarios where telling a bad guy the truth would be a really stupid idea, so there goes 1-b. Not to mention that we will be stealing good fortune from others — a benefit to ourselves that could be seen as unearned or undeserved. So that's bye-bye 1-c."

At this point Sakura interrupted and said cheerily, "I think it is OK, Beer-san, if we bend the rules a little because we are doing it for the good of society."

Bill laughed and said, "And there goes 1-d down the drain." He turned back to Kurokawa and asked, "So, do you see our dilemma?"

The much anticipated frown appeared once again, and Kurokawa said, "So, if I understand you correctly, by the standard of our own ethics, if we wish to do good, we must become bad people."

Bill said, "Um, yes, I think that about sums it up."

Sakura asked, "Do we get costumes?"

Bill ignored her and said, "OK, so a show of hands, all in favor of abolishing #3 raise their hands."

Neither one of the other two raised their hands. Sakura saw the opportunity and said, "I'll raise my hand if we can wear costumes."

Bill said, "I don't think Kurokawa-san or I are into that, but you can wear one if you'd like. How's that?"

Sakura quickly answered, "Deal," and then raised her hand.

Bill said, "OK, majority rules. #3 is stricken from the books."

Kurokawa shook his head and said, "This will not end well."

CHAPTER 26

A few days later the three stooges were back in Tokyo with the main goal of accumulating some luck from petty criminals. However, one of their side goals was to remain anonymous as they worked, and it was becoming increasingly evident that this was not going to be possible because everyone who passed by — everyone — looked at Sakura at least once.

Bill was looking at her too. As he did so, he said, "OK, so I know I told you that you could wear a costume, and as promised I'm even letting you try it out. But as you can see from the looks we are getting, it does not fit well with our goal of remaining anonymous."

Sakura said, "But, Beer-san, I'm dressed as a lucky cat," and then she raised one hand up in demonstration and said, "*Nyan, nyan.*"

For those who are from a Western culture, some explanations are in order. What Sakura was referring to was a *maneki-neko*, which literally means 'beckoning cat'. It is a common Japanese figurine and is seen as a lucky charm. The figurine is of a cat sitting up with one paw raised in a manner that appears to Westerners as asking for a high-five, but in Japan is the gesture for "come here." It is frequently displayed in the front window or entrance of shops, restaurants, and other businesses as a charm to draw in customers.

The other thing to explain is that "*nyan*" is the Japanese version of "meow", the sound that a cat makes.

Sakura's rendition of a *maneki-neko* was covered in gold

sequins. She was wearing a red collar with a gold-colored bell on it that jingled loudly with every movement she made. It was certainly not subtle, and it would have been too much even for the most flamboyant drag queen to wear.

Bill had, of course, argued with her about wearing it long before they had left for Tokyo, but arguing with Sakura was like trying to punch fog. She had a way of leaking around any argument from multiple angles at once. For instance, when Bill had first raised concerns about the costume, Sakura had barraged him with, "But, Beer-san, you said I could wear a costume and you didn't say what kind and I worked hard on this for several days and you promised me that I could wear one if I raised my hand and if you say that I can't then that means that my hand-raising would be void which means that you would have to abide by rule #3 and be a good person and good people don't lie or break promises so that means that either way you have to let me wear my costume."

It had taken Bill several seconds to mentally catch up with translating Sakura's rant, both in terms of Japanese-to-English and also in terms of Gibberish-to-Reason. He had been linguistically ill-equipped to verbally spar with her, so all he had been able to say was, "I just think it will draw unwanted attention."

But Sakura had merely replied with, "Pleeeeease, Beer-san," and had raised a fluffy, paw-shaped hand up as if begging for food.

So, of course, Bill had caved in — his logic had been no match for her cuteness.

Now, it was time to argue with her once again. He turned to Kurokawa for help, but he just shook his head at Bill and frowned disapprovingly.

Bill turned back to Sakura and said plainly, "Look, it's very cute, and I'm sure there will be occasions where it will be needed, but I'm afraid now is not the time. I'm sorry, but you understand, right?"

Sakura put her paws on her hips and said, "No, I don't. Aren't superheroes supposed to be noticed?"

"Ah," said Bill, "but we aren't superheroes. We are just three people trying to fight crime and help...the...unfortunate." Even as he said it, he realized his mistake.

"And you have powers too, Beer-san. So that makes you superheroes — stands to reason," replied Sakura, victoriously.

Bill frowned almost as deeply as Kurokawa. He tried another approach. "Sakura-chan, listen, even superheroes go plain-clothes sometimes. Think of us as being undercover right now. There will be plenty of time later on to bust out the costume. But for now, it is important that we are not noticed."

Sakura sensed that all the fun was draining out of the situation and so, with reluctance, she took a suitcase out of the trunk of her car and went and changed in the bathroom of a nearby business. She emerged sometime later wearing jeans and a pink Hello Kitty t-shirt.

She walked up to Bill and said, "OK, Beer-san, now I am a lucky cat in disguise." She raised her hand up and added, "*Nyan, nyan.*"

Bill patted her on the head and said, "That's a good kitty. Now, let's see if we can give some bad people a bad day."

He turned to Kurokawa and asked, "What do you say, Kurokawa-san — how about we start with jaywalkers and... I don't know... how about those jerks that don't use their turn signals? That always bothers me. I find it very rude and dangerous."

Kurokawa's attention had not fully been on Bill. He stopped watching the flow of people in the streets and answered, "Oh, yes, that sounds like a good start. Just remember to go easy on them. Maybe keep the curse down to a two or three."

"Two or three?" questioned Bill.

"Yes," replied Kurokawa, "If you think of the default hum that you hear as a number one, then a number two would be a doubling of that pitch. A number four would be a doubling of a number two. A number three would, of course, be halfway between a number two and a number four. And so on. I found that anything over number twenty became hazardous to the person's health. I never tried it, but I expect that a number one hundred would be instant, random death. So I suggest we stick with two or three, and only use the higher settings if someone is being aggressive."

Bill pointed at Kurokawa and said, "Good information, Kurokawa-san. Thanks. I'll keep it low, then."

And just then, Bill spotted his first victim of the day — or rather victims. He recognized them as the "rebels" from the other day. They were crossing a busy street on the red light, so Bill let them have a taste of number two.

The group made it to the other side of the street safely,

where they did their rebel yell again. Bill shrugged. Then he saw a car turn onto their street without signaling. Kurokawa had seen it too. Bill said to him, "Go ahead, K-san, that one is yours. Maybe a number three?"

Kurokawa really disliked the impertinence of drivers like that — it was as if they could not be bothered to extend the basic courtesy of signaling to others. In his annoyance, he absent-mindedly zapped the female driver of the car with a number ten.

Shortly after, the driver's purse tipped over and started spilling its contents all over the floor of the car. The driver instinctively grabbed for the purse. As she did, the car swerved onto the sidewalk and struck a fire hydrant in the vicinity of the jaywalkers. One of them even had to jump out of the way to avoid being struck. As he did, he lost hold of a piece of paper and it fluttered away on the breeze.

The fire hydrant was now shooting water into the air and drenching the jaywalkers. Two of them got mad and gave the car a few kicks, then all of them scampered off together.

A few kind passersby alerted the authorities and attended to the driver, who was very shaken but fortunately not physically harmed.

Bill slid his palms together repeatedly in the gesture of someone who was cleaning his hands and said, "And there's a job well done." He grabbed Kurokawa's hand and shook it vigorously. Kurokawa was not keen on this but went along with it all the same. Bill then said, "Well done, K-san. Didn't that feel good? It was like watching instant karma, wasn't it? And now we are both charged up with luck that we can give to someone else. Speaking of which, how do we do that?"

Kurokawa considered this and asked, "How good is your memory, Bill-san?"

Bill answered proudly, "Excellent. I have a great memory — it was one of the things that helped me become a successful trader. You never know when a particular fact will come in handy. Take for instance the fact that Russia controls a large percentage of the palladium market. Palladium is a lower cost alternative to platinum in catalytic converters. So when tensions between the US and Russia started heating up again, I remembered about Russia, the palladium market, and catalytic converters so I dumped my General Motors stock and bought palladium. That proved to be a most excellent trade."

Kurokawa had hoped for a simple "yes" or "no". He gave Bill a warning look and continued, "That is good, Bill-san. That will help with the transfer. You see, you transfer luck by first shutting off the hum, and then you must look at the person and mentally picture the person you want to transfer luck from. If you think about luck being transferred from one to the other, then it will happen. So you see, the key is to be able to remember who you have already stolen luck from, and what setting you used at the time. This way you will have a mental catalog of available luck to give to someone else. Myself, I have to keep a notebook to keep track. I also try not to keep too many people in my so-called catalog at once, not only because it gets hard to remember them all, but also because the accumulated luck can become very noticeable and quite embarrassing. I used to like *pachinko*, but now I am banned from most of the parlors because they think that I was somehow cheating — which in a way, I was."

"OK, I think I get it," said Bill. He looked around. "Hey, where's Sakura-chan?"

Kurokawa scanned the street and said, "She is over there, playing in the hydrant water."

Bill laughed. "She's so funny. It's kind of refreshing to see someone enjoy life so much. Just having her around always raises my spirits."

Kurokawa nodded. "I agree. She is very lively. Sometimes she can be tiring, but I do enjoy her company. What makes her even more remarkable is that not long ago she lost both of her parents to a violent mugging in Spain. The two of them were on vacation there. Neither one spoke Spanish very well. They probably were not even sure what was happening or what the mugger wanted from them. They ended up getting stabbed several times and died before making it to the hospital. It was probably for the best that Sakura-chan was not with them, or she too could have been killed. I have been watching over her ever since. She is my favorite niece and is very special to me."

They looked at Sakura again. She was being shooed away by the tow truck driver, who was keen to remove the car and be on his way.

She came back to join the other two. She then shook herself like a wet cat, shaking water on the other two. After that, she wiped her face dry with her arm — also in a cat-like fashion.

Bill laughed at the show. Kurokawa removed a handkerchief

from his pocket and dabbed his face dry with it. He replaced the handkerchief and said, "She certainly is a joy."

Bill noticed a piece of paper flitting down the road toward them, and intercepted it. He then looked at it and said, "It's just a deposit slip from Tamiya Bank." He looked around for a trash can but could not spot one, so he put the paper in his pocket.

Kurokawa said, "That was my bank, once. I had been with them for decades. They were always very happy to take my deposits and use my money for their own investments. But when I approached them a few years ago for a loan to open up a ramen shop, they denied me without explanation. I have good credit, and I had been at my job for a very long time. Tell me, how is this country's economy supposed to improve if the banks will not lend money?"

"That's disgraceful," sympathized Bill. "I think it has something to do with central banks holding down interest rates. Because of these low rates, banks feel that they do not make enough money from loans, so they instead gamble their money on stocks, bonds, and risky derivatives like mortgage-backed securities. You would think that after the financial crisis of 2008, the central banks would have more sense, but they don't seem to make the connection. So here they are, not only repeating the same mistakes that caused the problem, but doubling-down on the same failed policies. Sometimes I think that it would be much more preferable if the bankers just left us all alone."

Kurokawa had been nodding in agreement the whole time. He said, "If you are looking for criminals, Bill-san, you only have to pick any banker at random."

Sakura interjected, "So why don't we go after some bankers?"

Bill said, "Hmm, that's a good idea. But how do we find some dirt on them? I mean, it's funny to say that they are all guilty, but it's not exactly fair of us to punish them all indiscriminately. It would help if we could audit their books or something like that. Surely we could find some wrong-doing if we did that. But how do we go about it?"

He looked at Kurokawa, who merely shrugged. He then turned to Sakura who held up a finger, as if to ask for a moment of silence. Bill waited.

Finally, Sakura said, "I've got it. Beer-san, call your girlfriend and ask her to meet us at HQ tonight."

Bill squinted at her. "My girlfriend?"

Sakura rolled her eyes. "Yes, Beer-san — that Natsuko-san woman you've told me about."

Bill protested. "We aren't dating. We just hang out sometimes, and she has been helping me with my Japanese."

Sakura rolled her eyes again and said, "Come on, Beer-san, you just hang out? Like just hang out and eat dinner together and go to the movies and stuff like that?"

"Yes..." answered Bill, reluctantly.

"That's called dating, Beer-san. Anyway, please ask Natsuko-san to come over tonight. I have a plan."

CHAPTER 27

Natsuko entered Bill's apartment feeling once again as if she were a gazelle that had been invited over to the lion's house for dinner. And this time there were three lions.

Bill introduced Natsuko to the members of his crew. He had anticipated that there might be some tension or jealousy between Sakura and Natsuko, at least coming from Sakura, but he was happily wrong about that. Sakura had no love interest in Bill — she saw him as more of a big brother or perhaps an interesting playmate. Furthermore, Sakura could certainly act childishly, but she could also behave like an adult and was surprisingly astute at knowing which was appropriate at any given time.

In fact, Sakura's strong personality made her the official mood-setter for the group. This evening she was in a mood for serious planning and so she was dressed in business attire.

Sakura served tea and snacks to the others and then began to set up an easel that she had brought from her place — something she normally used for painting water colors. Today, however, she was using it as a make-shift whiteboard.

She paced back and forth in front of it several times with her hands clasped behind her back, as if she were deep in thought. The other three followed her with their eyes until Sakura suddenly stopped and pointed to Natsuko with a marker and barked, "Natsuko-san."

Natsuko jumped to attention and almost saluted. She answered back, "Yes?"

Sakura continued, "Your job is to pose as a member of the British embassy. Beer-san will be playing the role of Prince William. Kurokawa-san will be playing an accountant." She turned and wrote down the names and their associated roles on the whiteboard.

Bill protested, "Oh, come on now. Really?"

Sakura answered levelly, "Please save all comments and questions for the end of the presentation." She then turned to Natsuko and asked, "Are you able to retain the services of that driver and his Bentley again? The one that you hired to take Bill to his apartment."

Natsuko answered, "Yes, that should not be a problem."

"Good," said Sakura, "Now let me tell you the plan. We will be targeting Tamiya Bank because they suck for not giving Kurokawa-san a loan. First, Natsuko-san will call the bank posing as a British consul. She will arrange a meeting with the bank manager. At that meeting, she will explain that Prince William is looking to set up a second home near Tokyo and wishes to transfer substantial financial assets to a solid bank in Japan..."

Sakura's presentation was concise and was over in a mere fifteen minutes. At the end of it, the three sitting at the table all looked at each other for some sort of confirmation that they were not all crazy for wanting to go along with the plan.

Kurokawa, surprisingly, was the first to speak. "Sakura-chan, that was a wonderful presentation, child. You must be the envy of all your office mates. And the plan, well, the plan is very interesting. And I dare say it may even work. I think, however, we should add one thing to the beginning of the plan to ensure its success."

Bill and Natsuko watched Kurokawa for the answer while Sakura asked, "What is that?"

He answered, "Bill-san and I should first collect substantial luck, and then we should share it with Natsuko-san and you. I believe that we have the skills needed to pull this off, but it does not hurt to have luck on our side."

Bill patted Kurokawa on the shoulder and said, "I'm proud of you, K-san. I was starting to think that you might be a stick-in-the-mud, but you're actually OK with this, huh?"

Kurokawa answered, "I like to be careful, that is all. But those bankers really make me angry. All I wanted was a small little noodle shop, but they brushed me off like I was the dirt on their shoes."

Bill patted him on the shoulder one more time and said, "That's the spirit, tiger. Let's kick some banker butt."

CHAPTER 28

The assistant bank manager showed Natsuko to the main office and gestured toward the small conference table. "Right this way, Kobayashi-sama."

Natsuko had, of course, supplied the bank manager with an assumed name. She had even procured replica business cards from the British Embassy that featured this new name.

The cards were very well done and, if compared with an original, were quite a bit more elaborate. Natsuko knew enough about scamming people to give them what they expected, not what was accurate. People would expect the business card of a British consul to be gold-laced with pictures of crowns and such. The truth is that they are rather dull apart from the British seal. Her version was much more convincing. After all, what are the odds that the bank manager would have ever seen the real thing before? It was better to give him a show.

The assistant manager took one last look at the card before placing it carefully in his shirt pocket. He then said, "Impressive card, Kobayashi-sama. My friend used to work at the embassy, and his card was surprisingly dull."

Natsuko said without missing a beat, "I am fairly new at the embassy. I believe this is a new style being phased in. I've seen the older ones and I agree — they are rather boring."

The assistant manager took a seat and gestured for Natsuko to do the same. He then asked, "So, how may I assist the British government?"

Natsuko leaned forward slightly and said, "As you may be

aware from the unfortunate coverage in the papers recently, Prince William, Duke of Cambridge, is in Japan for a holiday. It seems that he has taken a liking to your country and is interested in establishing a vacation home in or around Tokyo."

"That is interesting news," said the assistant manager, "I believe that Japan is a wonderful country and I am happy that the Prince also finds it to his liking. But, how may the bank help in this matter?"

Natsuko answered, "The Prince will, of course, need a bank account established here in Japan. It is my understanding that he wishes to transfer a substantial sum to a reputable bank in Japan. The Prince has hired a local accountant to pick the bank and to handle the transfer. The Prince, himself, will have the final say, of course. Your bank was identified as one of the leading candidates."

The assistant manager beamed with pride. "That is very gratifying. It would be an honor for us to handle the account."

Natsuko sat back again, her body language getting slightly colder in the process. She then said, "That is very good to hear. All that is needed now is for the Prince's accountant to audit your books and then we can open the account."

This time the assistant manager sat forward. "Excuse me, but did I understand that properly? The Prince wishes to audit our books? That seems highly irregular and unnecessary. Surely if you have asked around, you would have heard that we are one of the most trusted banks in Japan."

Natsuko was ready for this. "I believe I mentioned that the transfer was to be substantial. It could very easily double your deposits overnight. It would be careless to entrust that much money to any entity without first ensuring their solvency. Surely you can understand that."

This was quickly getting too serious for the assistant manager to handle. This was a really big deal and he did not want to mess it up. He felt that the best thing he could do now would be to push the decision off onto the manager, and so he said to Natsuko, "Yes, of course. I completely understand your situation. I do not think it would be a problem to open our books to the accountant as long as he can be trusted not to divulge our information to our competitors. However, this is not my decision to make. The manager is out of town but will be back in about two weeks. I have every confidence that he will be able to assist you upon his return."

Natsuko already knew about the manager's absence through her own information channels and was banking on his absence, if you will pardon the pun. Now was the time for her to play hardball.

Natsuko stood up from the table and bowed to the assistant manager. She then said, "Thank you so much for your time. It is unfortunate that you are not able to help in this situation. I am afraid that the Prince wishes to move quickly on this matter. In fact, he and the accountant are waiting in the limo right now and I should not keep them waiting any further. Good day to you."

She bowed one last time and started walking toward the door. The poor assistant manager watched in horror as a potential fortune was about to walk out of the door. He thought about how mad the manager would be if he found out that he had lost such a high-end account. He then thought about how thrilled the manager would be if he returned to find that Prince William was now a customer of the bank. He almost knocked over his chair as he chased after Natsuko.

"Please, Kobayashi-sama, I did not realize that time was of the essence. I think... No, I am sure that I can help you. Please, it would be my honor to open the bank's books for the Prince and his accountant to examine."

Natsuko stopped and faced the assistant manager. She bowed to him and said, "That is wonderful to hear. I am sure that the Prince will be most grateful. If it is agreeable with you, I would like to invite him in now, along with his accountant."

"Of course. Please, please," said the poor assistant manager. "Do not keep him waiting."

Natsuko walked to the limo and gave the crew the good news. Shortly after, Bill entered the bank. He was flanked on one side by Natsuko and by Kurokawa on the other. Following about three paces behind was Sakura.

Sakura's original plan had been to dress up as a member of the Queen's Guard, complete with red blazer and giant, fuzzy, black hat, but Bill had managed to convince her that that was a palace guard, not a body guard, and they never traveled along with the royalty.

And so she was dressed as her version of a body guard, which bore an uncanny resemblance to a 1980's Secret Service man, complete with sunglasses and an earpiece tethered by a coiled wire that traveled down into the collar of her dark-gray suit.

She was scanning the room, left and right, looking at the other customers in the lobby suspiciously and pretending to talk to her collar.

There were murmurings in the lobby of "It's the Prince of England!" and "Look, it's that prince guy who was kicking the vending machine."

Bill was cordial to the other customers and waved to them as he walked, but he remained silent the whole time.

A man took out his cellphone with the intent of taking a picture. Sakura snapped her fingers and pointed at the man while shaking her head. He was so scared that he actually dropped his phone and was afraid to pick it back up.

The retinue swept briskly through the lobby and was shown to a larger conference room at the back of the bank. Once they had all been seated, the assistant manager welcomed the Prince to the bank. Natsuko acted as his interpreter.

Once the welcome was interpreted into English, Bill responded, "Thank you, sir — it's smashing to be here. I think we are all going to be jolly good friends. Well now, shall we get cracking?"

This was apparently Bill's idea of how a British person talked. Of course, Bill's main exposure to British culture had been from watching Benny Hill and Monty Python as a child.

Natsuko almost laughed but held it together. She translated, "Thank you good sir for your hospitality. I look forward to a profitable relationship with you and your bank. I would like to get started as soon as possible if that is agreeable with you."

Kurokawa was then introduced as the accountant. The assistant manager fetched a laptop and set it up in front of Kurokawa and Bill while saying, "I have logged you in under my account, which grants you full access. You are of course free to look at anything you like, but I must insist that you are careful not to make any changes. All changes are logged, and I would have a lot of explaining to do if that were to happen."

Kurokawa fielded this one. "We appreciate the extreme courtesy and trust that you are extending to us. We will treat your system with the utmost care. The Prince is already impressed with your level of hospitality and openness. I am sure that this process will not take more than a few hours. Now, if you will excuse us, we would like to get started."

The assistant manager looked confused. He asked, "Are you suggesting that I not be present for this audit? Surely I can be helpful if there are any questions."

Kurokawa answered, "Your assistance will be most welcome. However, the Prince and I need to be able to speak in confidence as we audit the books. Frankly, he is a bit of a dolt when it comes to finance and he would be embarrassed to ask questions in front of you."

The assistant manager looked shocked and quickly looked at Bill, who showed no sign of outrage, let alone understanding. Kurokawa said, "Do not worry; he does not know Japanese. Now, if you would excuse us, I am sure the Prince would like to get started."

The assistant manager bowed and excused himself from the room. Sakura, who was guarding the door, looked at him menacingly and whispered code words into her collar as he walked by.

Bill said cheerfully, "Jolly good chap, that one."

Natsuko playfully smacked him on the arm. They then proceeded to audit the books, being careful not to say anything out of character because they had all seen enough movies to know that the bad guys always had listening devices set up for just such occasions. They instead wrote on paper that Kurokawa had supplied from his briefcase. Bill took the lead on the computer because, despite what Kurokawa had said about him, Bill was by and large the best man for the job.

Watching Bill work was like watching a sculptor chip away at a slab of granite as it slowly takes the form of a graceful human body. He saw things in the numbers that spoke to him. He saw patterns that most people would have dismissed. He could almost visualize the ebb and flow of the money as it made its way through the bank. And·what he was noticing was that an awful lot of it was flowing from just a handful of accounts over to another handful of accounts.

Sure, the money sloshed around here and there, swishing around the ledger like a meandering river, flowing in and out of other accounts and companies, but at the end of the day, Bill could see the endpoints clearly. He wrote down his findings on a piece of paper as two lists of names under the headings of "From:" and "To:".

Kurokawa and Natsuko scanned the lists. Kurokawa took the pen from Bill and wrote "Politicians" next to the "To:" column. Natsuko then took the pen from Kurokawa and wrote "Gangsters" next to the "From:" column.

Bill said, "Bloody hell." He then took the pen from Natsuko and wrote down "Take a lot of pictures of the screens I am about to display." Natsuko nodded.

After collecting the evidence, the group stuffed all the writing paper and Natsuko's camera back into Kurokawa's briefcase and locked it. Kurokawa then left the room to fetch the assistant manager, who had clearly been sweating but was nevertheless contriving to nonchalantly read a magazine behind his desk. Kurokawa brought him back into the room. Sakura eyeballed him again as he passed. Bill immediately stood up from the table, walked over to the assistant manager, and shook his hand firmly while saying, "You've got an ace of a bank and no mistake, governor. I'd be chuffed to open an account here."

The assistant manager smiled blankly as he shook Bill's hand. He turned his head questioningly to Natsuko for the translation. Natsuko said, "The Prince said he is highly impressed with your bank and he would be delighted to open an account here."

After the handshaking was finished, the assistant manager bowed deeply to them all in turn and rattled on and on about what a great honor it was to do business with the Prince.

Kurokawa told him that he will contact him within the next few days to open the account and to arrange for the wire transfer from England. The four of them then excused themselves and walked back out through the lobby in the same formation as they had arrived.

The number of people in the lobby had quadrupled since they had first arrived. Many of the people were just milling around and pretending to fill out deposit slips and other such things.

As the group approached the thickest part of the crowd, Natsuko leaned forward ahead of Bill and spoke across him to Kurokawa in a not-so-quiet whisper that got everyone's attention. "I sure am glad that we checked the books before banking here. Who would have thought that Tamiya Bank was in financial ruins?"

Kurokawa looked around nervously and said, "Shh — not so loud. We promised the manager that we would not tell anyone that they are broke."

Immediately they heard snippets of conversations from the crowd — things like "Oh my god, did you hear that?" and "We should get our money out of here as quickly as possible, don't you think?"

And then, just to drive the point home, Sakura spoke into her collar saying, "Abort mission. I repeat, abort mission. Code word: insolvent. Code word: insolvent. All members report back to HQ."

The group made their way back inside the Bentley. The driver pulled away gracefully. Now inside the darkened-glass privacy of the limo, the group began to laugh and slap hands. Bill hugged all three of them — even Kurokawa. He then said, "That poor assistant is going to have a really bad week. I hit him with a number four — I was going to hit him harder but I think he is just a clueless flunky. At any rate, I'm pretty sure that we just started a bank run."

He chuckled and turned to Sakura. "And you — good job, Sakura-chan. Your plan worked flawlessly. How did you ever think of it?"

Sakura said, "Oh, that's easy, Beer-san, I used to get all kinds of emails from a man claiming to be the Prince of Nigeria. He was always trying to get my bank account information. I thought maybe we could try the same trick."

CHAPTER 29

Bill and Natsuko were at the beach, enjoying time together in a completely "not dating" capacity. Natsuko was dressed in a modest two-piece bathing suit, if one can call any two-piece bathing suit modest.

Bill had built up a fantasy in his mind that Natsuko was a former member of a Yakuza group, and so he had half expected her to be covered in dragon tattoos but, thankfully for Bill, he had once again totally misjudged one of his new friends.

Natsuko's skin was completely virgin, which came as a relief to Bill in more ways than one. She looked very attractive in the suit, but Bill was wondering why she was wearing sneakers. He could have understood her wearing sandals or flip-flops, but sneakers? They completely spoiled the look.

Bill smiled at her and said, "You look wonderful, Natsuko-san. Thanks for meeting me here. I love the beach, but I would have felt silly coming here alone." He looked down at her shoes and added, "I have to ask; wouldn't you be more comfortable in sandals or perhaps just going barefoot? Those shoes look hot."

Natsuko looked down at the shoes, slightly embarrassed. "No, I prefer these. I do not like the feeling of sand on my feet. I hate when it gets between my toes."

Bill replied, "Oh, OK. I can see that." He reached out and took her hand. "Let's walk, shall we?"

Natsuko nodded and they started walking along the water's edge. Bill took in his surroundings. It was a clear and sunny day, the breeze was gentle and refreshing, the air smelt great, the little birdies were cheeping away pleasantly, and Natsuko was smiling at him as they walked together. This was one of those rare days when Bill felt that he was a very, very fortunate man.

CHAPTER 30

The floundering four were at HQ to discuss their next move. Bill said, "So let me get this straight — the bank manager and the head of the loan department are both in the hospital? That was quick work, Natsuko-san, well done."

"No, no, no," argued Natsuko, "It was not me. Those two were already in the hospital before we had even decided to go after the bank. Do you remember when the assistant manager said that his boss was out of town? Well he is — he is in an out-of-town hospital. It is the same with the senior loan officer. My contacts tell me that members of the Yasei-kai are responsible. Do you remember the names on the 'from' list? They are all members of the Yasei-kai. Clearly the Yasei-kai must be forcing the bank officials into laundering money for them."

Bill said, "OK, I'm getting it now — this is all starting to make sense."

Kurokawa asked, "So what do we do now? We probably have sufficient evidence against the bank to get them in serious legal trouble. However, with so many politicians on the bank's 'to' list, I'm afraid that the whole thing will likely be swept under the rug."

Natsuko said, "I agree with Kurokawa-san. I believe that if we want justice in this case, then we will have to see it through ourselves."

Sakura said, "Yeah, let's get them!"

Bill nodded. "OK, then I say the next logical step is to investigate this Yasei-kai group. I noticed that the bank had recently extended a very large unsecured loan to a company called Yummy Plastics, which is actually just around the corner from here. They make those plastic replicas of food that you see in so many of the restaurants around town.

"I know from personal experience that something odd is going on in that factory. When I first came to town, I stumbled on the factory and went inside to see if I could get a tour. I swear that they were unloading boxes of plastic explosives in the back warehouse. I mean, I could be wrong, but the wrappers said 'C4' on them, and I can't imagine that C4 means something different in Japanese.

"Also, I remember that Kurokawa-san told me that Yakuza groups sometimes require underlings to cut off part of their fingers as a penance for failure. Well, along with that C4, I also found a box of very realistic fake fingers. I didn't see the connection at the time, but if you look at it alongside the evidence from the bank, I think Yummy Plastics could be a front for the Yasei-kai. What do you guys think?"

Natsuko said, "The removal of parts of the finger for the purpose of atonement is a real thing. And I'm certain that anything marked 'C4' cannot be good. If that corrupt bank is funding them, then I agree that we need to investigate Yummy Plastics."

Bill nodded and could not help but stare at Natsuko's fingers, searching for any irregularities. No, he told himself, you have to stop thinking like that about the poor girl. Besides, I've held her hands often enough to know that all of her fingers are present and accounted for.

Kurokawa said, "I agree as well. I know that I was reluctant to get involved in your superhero fantasies, Bill-san, but now that I know this information, it would be impossible for me to forget it and return to my life as a hermit. As long as we proceed with caution, you can count me in."

They all looked at Sakura for her input. She held her hands open and said, "You know me — I'm up for anything. Just remember that, unlike you bums, I have a job so we need to limit our outings to nights and weekends."

Natsuko said, "I too have a job."

Sakura corrected herself, "Yes, sorry, no offense. I was referring to those two. Some people have all the luck, if you know what I mean." She sniggered.

"Ha-ha," said Bill. "I don't suppose you have another hair-brained plan for us, do you?"

Sakura shook her head. "Not really, Beer-san." She stared blankly at the wall for a second and then said, "Maybe we can put a mole inside the factory. Natsuko-san and I already have jobs, so it has to be one of you two. Beer-san has already been seen at the factory, so the only person left is Kurokawa-san."

They all turned to Kurokawa. He rubbed his fingers subconsciously and said, "This does not sound like proceeding with caution."

CHAPTER 31

Bill and Natsuko went for a walk while Sakura worked to nag Kurokawa incessantly until he agreed with the plan.

They approached the small park that contained the infamous shrine. Bill pointed toward the shrine and said to Natsuko, "That's the shrine that put the voodoo curse on Kurokawa-san and I just over there. Care to take a stab at it? Are you feeling lucky?"

Natsuko said, "No, that is quite alright, Bill-san. It would probably not be good for me to have such a power."

Bill said, "You're kidding, right? You are one of the nicest people I know."

Natsuko shook her head. "No, I am both good and evil — just like anybody else. I used to be more evil than good, but I am trying to mend my ways."

Bill said, "I guess I can understand that. I suppose we all have those dark thoughts sometimes. Still, I can't imagine you as evil."

"Thank you, Bill."

Bill shrugged. He then saw the astonishingly old woman walking the path around the park. He shouted over to her, "Hello, dear lady! How are you today?"

The old woman flinched and turned around to see Bill waving to her some ways off in the distance. She screamed, "You stay the fuck away from me!" and then turned back around and tried to hobble a little faster away from Bill.

Natsuko burst out laughing and said between laughing fits, "I guess you must be pretty evil too, Bill, to scare a little old lady like that."

Bill looked up at the sky, sighed deeply, and said, "Just a simple misunderstanding, I assure you." He looked down again and spotted the old woman. He then hummed and gradually lowered the pitch until it turned to silence. Then he visualized the assistant bank manager and pictured his luck flowing into the old woman. In his mind, luck looked like a cloud of four-leaf clovers.

He called out to the old woman, "I'm sorry for the bad luck lately. I promise that everything will be better from now on."

The old woman ignored him and continued her high-speed hobble.

Natsuko laughed again and said, "It is certainly never boring with you around, Bill."

She nuzzled up closer to him as they walked. Bill thought, hey, this is not bad at all. He wondered if he should press his luck by asking her out again, and then he thought, hell, I seem to have plenty of it to press. He therefore asked her, "What are you doing tomorrow, Natsuko-san? Are you free?"

To this she replied, "Bill."

"Yes?"

"Natsuko is fine."

It took Bill a second to understand this. She had been calling him Bill this whole time and he had not noticed. He smiled. "OK then. What are you doing tomorrow, Natsuko?"

She smiled and said, "Spending it with you."

CHAPTER 32

The assistant bank manager was having a really bad day. In fact, the last several days had been bad too, but this one was shaping up to be a real doozy.

Ever since that Prince William fellow had visited, everything had started to go terribly wrong for him. For some reason, more and more of the bank's customers had been demanding to withdraw their money. At first, this had only been a handful of people, but as rumors of the bank's insolvency spread, panic started to breed more panic, and now the lobby was packed full of angry customers demanding to withdraw their money.

The assistant manager marched into the center of the lobby to put an end to all of this once and for all. Addressing the crowd, he said loudly, "Valued customers, please calm down. I know that you all have heard the completely unfounded rumor that our bank in not on a sound financial footing. I assure you that these rumors are false, and you have nothing to worry about."

Someone from the front of the line shouted, "Then why is the teller saying that she cannot honor my request for withdrawal? If you have the money, then let me have it."

The bank manager scoffed at the man and said snootily, "Sir, everyone knows that banks do not retain one hundred percent of deposits — it is simply not done. Most of that money gets loaned out or otherwise invested."

The crowd looked stunned. "What?" said the guy, panicked. "You don't have my money? I want my money."

The lobby erupted with the sound of angry customers. The assistant manager fled to his office and locked the door. He tried to call the bank manager but there was no answer, as had been the case for the last several days.

Then he thought to himself, OK, relax, this will all work out when the Prince deposits his money. Then I will have plenty of money to return to the customers. And once things have calmed down and news that even the Prince of England banks here, then the other customers will surely return and re-deposit their funds. No problem.

He had forgotten to take a business card from Prince William's accountant, but he did still have one for the lady from the embassy, and she could surely put him in touch with the accountant.

He hastily grabbed the card from his desk drawer and dialed the number. A voice answered, "You have reached the suicide prevention hotline. This is Suzuki speaking. I'm here to help. Please, what is your name?"

The assistant manager quickly hung up. He looked at the card. He must have miss-dialed. He tried again. "You have reached the suicide prevention hotline. This is Suzuki. I'm here to help. May I ask your name?"

He slammed the phone down in agitation. He then put his face in his hand as he slowly realized that the whole Prince thing had been a scam. He could hear the voices of dozens of angry customers in the lobby. His own employees were banging on his door and shouting at him to tell them what to do. The bank had no free funds left. The Prince was not going to be depositing any money. Everyone was shouting at him, and no one was around to help him.

Sweating with panic and on the verge of a nervous breakdown, the assistant manager looked at the card and once again dialed the number.

CHAPTER 33

Bill woke up in his bed and saw something odd sticking out from the covers at the foot of the bed. He counted: 1,2...3,4. He blinked and pinched the bridge of his nose to combat the fuzziness of sleep. He counted again: 1,2...3,4. He looked at the other thing poking out from the covers and counted: 1,2,3,4,5. He then looked back at the first one. Only four, he thought. And then all sorts of little facts and suppositions started to connect in his brain, causing him to say, "Oh."

Natsuko woke up from the sound of his voice. She saw him staring at her feet and quickly pulled them under the covers. Before she could say anything, Bill said, "I think it would take A LOT of sand to fit between those two toes."

"That's not funny, Bill," she snapped.

He saw the mixed emotions building up on her face and said, "Relax — it's OK. It seems we are about to have one of those serious conversations. But before we do, let me just make us some coffee and breakfast. Everything is better with caffeine and food."

Natsuko nodded and pulled the covers over her face.

Bill made breakfast while Natsuko got dressed. She made sure to put on socks and then ventured out of the bedroom. She then sat down at the small island that separated the living room from the kitchen.

Bill was just finishing up making some omelets. He placed a plate of them in front of Natsuko along with a cup of coffee. He then walked around and sat beside her on the island, pausing to give her a hug as he passed. He said, "OK, if you still want to talk, I'm here to listen."

Natsuko tried the omelet. "Wow, this is good."

"Thanks," answered Bill, "I'm not a great cook, but I am learning."

Natsuko replied, "You are a quick learner. I can tell that you are good at putting things together — you're sharp."

Bill shrugged.

Natsuko continued, "You... I might as well tell you about myself. I'm sure that you will piece it together one way or another."

"Hold it," said Bill.

"What?" asked Natsuko, worried.

"If you tell me," asked Bill, "are you going to have to kill me afterward? Because, honestly, it's not all that important if that's going to be the case."

She pushed him jokingly and said, "No, I definitely won't kill you." She paused for a moment and added, "I'm not so sure about my family, though."

Now Bill started to look genuinely worried. He asked, "Are we talking family, or are we talking family?"

Natsuko answered, "Both, I'm afraid. I am the granddaughter of Okane Noboru, head of the Ishiku-gumi, the most powerful Yakuza group in Japan."

Bill thumped the table and said, "I knew it."

Natsuko jumped.

Bill quickly said, "Sorry. It's just that I had a feeling about you this whole time. In fact — and I'm a little embarrassed to admit this — I expected you to be covered in tattoos when I saw you at the beach."

Natsuko said, "Well, I did give you some hints. I think maybe I wanted you to know. Anyway, do you like tattoos?"

Bill shook his head. Natsuko said, "Me neither. They fade and they look ugly. I would not get them."

Bill looked at her feet and said, "Um..."

Natsuko said, "I also like my fingers. I told you that I made a big mistake, yes?"

Bill nodded.

"Well, to atone for it, I cut off one of my toes and gave it to my grandfather."

Bill said, "And this is normal behavior in your family, is it? Maybe just a bit extreme, no?"

Natsuko said, "I cost my family several hundred million yen and, at the same time, insulted one of our biggest business partners. One little toe is hardly sufficient to pay for that."

Bill wanted to argue, but put into context, he had to admit that she had a point. He said, "O...K... I guess I can see where you're coming from. So, what's the deal now? Are you out of the family?"

Natsuko said, "I guess you could say that I am still in the family, but not the clan. I no longer do business for the clan except for minding the shop for my father."

Bill said, "Oh. I see. So, your father is...part of the clan."

Natsuko looked at him like he was stupid. "Of course, he is next in line to run the clan."

Bill nodded and wondered if maybe, just maybe, he had pushed his luck a bit too far. I mean, a man could start losing digits by getting tangled up with a girl like this. And then he thought about what other parts of himself could get cut off if he were to leave her, and scrunched up his face.

Natsuko saw this and said, "Bill, I understand that this is asking a lot of you. If you are having second thoughts about being with me, well, I can't say that I would be happy about it, but please know that no harm will come to you if you wanted to leave. I want you to be with me because you like me, not because you are afraid of me or my family."

Bill now felt ashamed, and looked it. "Sorry, I think my imagination was starting to get the better of me. Listen, I do like you, and I'm not going anywhere." He paused for a second and then corrected himself, "Actually, that's a lie."

Natsuko looked shocked. "What do you mean?"

Bill smiled. "I'm going to Disneyland. Right now. And you're coming with me."

CHAPTER 34

Kurokawa was not doing well. Somehow, despite all the talk about being cowardly heroes who fight crime at a safe distance, he was now sitting across a workbench from three men who could probably make him disappear from the Earth with very little fuss.

And where were the others while he was risking his life? He knew that Sakura was at work having a good time building a campaign of plausible deniability, and that Bill and Natsuko were probably off somewhere being lovey-dovey. But here he was on a job interview for the Yakuza. Clearly he has not been keeping enough luck for himself lately.

He looked at the rough-looking men sitting across from him and frowned. He was wearing a white smock and standing in front of one of the workbenches in the Yummy Plastics factory. His nervousness was causing the humming in his head to increase to a high whine.

The men were staring at him while they waited for him to start crafting a masterpiece in plastic. He had, of course, never done anything like this before. His closest experience had been with his passion for model trains. He thought about how he used to craft his own scenery elements, and he really hoped that he would be able to draw from that experience now.

While he was contemplating all of this, the men were getting impatient. One of them said, "Come on, old man, show us what you can do."

And so Kurokawa took a deep breath and started to work. He

took a handful of brown plasticine and started molding and shaping it with the various tools available on the bench. He added some texture and some darker color here and there. He did a similar process with the green plasticine. This took a good ten minutes of work, but they turned out nice. He then mixed some red and orange plasticine and molded something else. He took a paintbrush and meticulously painted on details, and then used an airbrush to coat various parts of the work with a clear coating to make them look wet. The last thing that he did was to ladle on some thick, brown resin from a hot pot. The brown stuff solidified in under a minute as it cooled.

Kurokawa gave his creation one last look with an appraising eye and slid it over to the others for their inspection.

As meals go, the dish was fairly uninteresting. It consisted of Salisbury steak smothered in gravy, accompanied by broccoli on one side and tomato slices on the other. But as a work of art, well, it was actually making the head man salivate. Fortunately for Kurokawa, this happened to be the man's favorite meal.

The three men all studied the dish and then looked at each other with little nods and grunts of approval. Finally, the leader said, "Well done. You may start tomorrow."

Kurokawa bowed deeply and thanked him. The men then excused themselves and turned to leave, but as they did, one of them knocked over the pot of hot, brown resin. The artificial sauce spilled down onto his groin and started to instantly bond his trousers to some of his very private parts. He screamed.

Kurokawa quickly pushed some rags over to the man, who snatched them up greedily and used them to pat down his trousers. Unfortunately for him, the rags first absorbed some of the liquid plastic and then bonded themselves to the front of his trousers as the plastic cooled and hardened.

The end result of all this was that he had not only scalded his private parts and encased them in plastic, but the addition of the plastic-soaked rags made it look as if a turkey had crashed into his groin.

The other men laughed at him and called him "turkey crotch" as he ran away screaming. Kurokawa remained silent and concentrated on removing his apron.

The other two men wiped tears from their eyes and resumed walking toward the door that lead outside. As they did, they motioned to Kurokawa to follow them out.

Once outside, one of the men got into a generic looking van

and started it up while the second man began to load a few boxes into the back. One box was a little too heavy and awkward for him, so he called to the driver to give him a hand. The driver was annoyed by this and hastily exited the van, slamming the door behind him.

Kurokawa was walking toward the van and was about to ask the driver what time work started, but the man looked so upset that Kurokawa thought the better of it.

The driver helped the second man lift the box, and as they placed it into the back of the van, the van started to roll forward.

The driver quickly ran to the driver's-side door and managed to open it while jogging along. The van was now on the steepest part of the driveway and was gaining speed rapidly. The driver kept trying to jump into the van, but it was starting to get away from him. At this point the second man ran and jumped into the back of the van in hopes of saving the day.

Things were getting serious now as the van was approaching the end of the driveway, or if you prefer, the beginning of the busy highway. The van bounced over a pothole, which flicked the door closed and trapped the driver's tie inside.

The man inside the van was now trying to maneuver into the driver's seat. He saw his partner running along beside the van as it entered the busy highway. The man, now seated, slammed on the brakes just in time.

Of course, just in time could mean a lot of things. It could mean "just in time to prevent an accident," but in this case, it does not. No, in this case, it means "just in time to stop in front of a very large truck."

Still, if you want to look on the bright side of things, then you could say that they had been lucky that it was rush hour, and therefore no one had been going very fast at all. You could also say that they had been lucky that the van was struck in the rear, and therefore had avoided direct contact with the man being drug along by his necktie. You could say that they had been lucky about a lot of things, but it is doubtful that they would agree with you.

Kurokawa, who had watched all of this transpire, said to himself, "So what time do I start work?"

CHAPTER 35

Bill and Natsuko were walking around Disneyland with linked arms. Bill was feeding Natsuko some *takoyaki*, which were fried balls of dough about the size of a golf ball and, much to Bill's horror, filled with a little piece of octopus.

The couple were discussing which ride to try next when Bill stopped abruptly, thus causing Natsuko to stop abruptly as well. Bill's mouth hung open for a second, and then he started to laugh like a super villain.

Tina of Club Essex, who had been the cause of Bill's outburst, turned to see who was laughing like an idiot. When she saw Bill, she too stopped short, causing her client to stop a few paces past her.

This allowed Bill to see who she had been escorting — his old supervisor from the power plant. Bill redoubled his laughter, which ultimately ended in a coughing fit and watery eyes.

"What is it? What's so funny?" asked Natsuko.

Bill could only shake his head while he caught his breath. In the meantime, Tina had sent her client to go fetch some snacks, allowing her some time alone to talk to Bill. She hurried over to him.

"Bill! Who is that you're here with? You're not cheating on me, are you? So, how much does this one charge, anyway? Professional interest, you understand." blurted Tina in rapid succession.

Bill was thrown by Tina's remarks and he suddenly worried about what Natsuko might be thinking. He stammered, "Um, hey, yeah, I think maybe she might charge me a finger or two if you don't cut it out."

Tina waved her hand at him while saying, "Oh, come on. You're no fun when you're not near to death on gin." She turned her attention to Natsuko and said, "I'm sorry. I was only joking with Bill, but I was being rude to you. Please accept my apologies. My name is Tina. I work at a host club in Kabukichō. Your boyfriend stumbled in there some time ago when he first came to Japan. He's quite a character, that one."

Before Natsuko could answer, Tina turned back to Bill and said, "Thanks for all the business you've been sending me, by the way. They are the most unlucky group of misfits, though. Where the heck did you scrounge them up from?"

Bill answered, "Ah, yeah, no problem. Scarily enough, those unlucky bastards are all from the power plant."

Tina nodded. "Oh, well, that makes sense. No wonder things are so chaotic over there."

Bill shook his head and channeled his inner Sakura. "Oh, no. Everything is fantastic there — no problems," he said with a smirk while giving her the OK sign.

Tina looked unconvinced. She nodded in the direction of the returning client and asked, "So, who is this guy, then? I'm guessing he is not the VP of Sony like he says."

Bill laughed and shook his head. "No, he's actually the ass that fired me from the power plant. He's just a cleanup supervisor."

Tina nodded again. "I see. Well, I have to go back to my wonderful first date at Disneyland. Bill, nice to see you again. And you, Miss, nice to meet you too. Take care of this goofball, OK?"

She gave them a quick wave and scurried off to rejoin her client who was heading back with two handfuls of snacks.

On an impulse, Bill canceled his former boss's bad luck and channeled some good fortune his way. He hoped that maybe it would help to improve conditions at the power plant.

Natsuko, who had been earning herself the title of the world's best girlfriend by not exploding in a fit of jealousy and questions, said to Bill placidly, "OK, now we are going to go sit down and have a nice lunch while you explain to me who that was and why it was very silly of me to have contemplated throwing her off the top of the Ferris wheel."

"Ah," said Bill, "So this is that evil side you hinted at then, is it?"

Natsuko replied, "Oh no, Bill, my evil side would not have stopped at contemplation. This is me being very, very good."

Bill looked at his fingers nervously and subconsciously slid them into his pockets to protect them.

Natsuko relaxed her posture and giggled. She then said with a smile, "I'm just messing with you, Bill. I do want to get some lunch, however." She gave him a quick hug and led him in the direction of the food stalls.

Bill said, "OK, but no finger food, OK?"

CHAPTER 36

The bank manager and senior loan officer of Tamiya Bank were finally being released from the hospital after their rather violent reeducation at the hands of Sakamoto's henchmen. The bank manager was still on crutches, and the loan officer was wearing a sling around his arm. They were in the middle of discussing whether they could somehow regain control of the bank from the Yasei-kai when they suddenly saw the very same gangsters that had assaulted them before.

The gangsters were being pushed through the corridor of the hospital on three separate stretchers and, thankfully, were in too much pain to notice the bank personnel. One of the gangsters was wearing a neck brace, another had his chest wrapped in bandages, and the third was, well, it was hard to tell. His body was covered with a sheet, but there was a strange sort of bulge around the area of his nether regions.

The bank manager turned to the loan officer and asked, "Hey, is that what happens when you take too many Viagra?"

The loan officer, who had the sense of humor of...a loan officer, only shrugged and continued walking.

CHAPTER 37

"Master," said the junior monk, "What is your take on all of this? To me, it appears that our Divine Devotion serum is not working how we anticipated, but it does still seem to have had a remarkable effect."

The senior monk nodded. "Yes, my boy, I think there is wisdom in what you say. Indeed, the serum does not appear to make the subjects any more devoted to religious pursuits; however, as you say, it does appear to have manifested in the most remarkable way."

"But Master," argued the junior monk, "do you suppose that such a thing is possible? Can those two really manipulate the fortunes of men? Have we not overstepped our bounds by unleashing this upon the world? Should we not end the experiment immediately? Surely no man is meant to have such godlike powers."

The senior monk stroked his beard for a few seconds while he wrestled with the ineffable. Finally, he answered, "I think that if such a thing were not meant to happen, then it would not be allowed to happen. The two men and their friends seem to be using the power for good; therefore, I see no harm in allowing the experiment to continue while we further study the effects of the serum. If the serum proves to be safe, it could be of inestimable value to our order. Think about the good we could do with hundreds of men all working in unison to redirect good fortune to those that are most deserving of it. But before we can do that, I'd like to make sure that it does not turn us all green, or blind us, or make our heads explode, or some such thing."

"Very wise, Master. Speaking of which, I have installed the surveillance camera as you requested. Now we can gain further knowledge by studying their strategy meetings."

"Excellent, boy. Let's have a look, shall we?"

CHAPTER 38

Bill and his group of do-gooders were gathering around the Pillar of Justice for another secret meeting — and also for supper. Bill was just putting the final touches on the meal as Sakura set the table. Natsuko and Kurokawa were already seated at the table and were discussing the panty-stealing building manager and what they thought would drive a man to behave in such a way.

After dinner had been fully prepared, Bill and Sakura joined the other two at the table, and all four began to eat. After they had a chance to get settled, Bill began the meeting by addressing Kurokawa.

"So, K-san, you've been working at the factory for over a week now. What have you learned?"

Kurokawa finished chewing and answered thoughtfully, "Well, I learned a lot of things. I can make a very realistic-looking cheesecake with some sand and..."

"I meant about the Yasei-kai," interrupted Bill.

"Oh," said Kurokawa, a little disappointed. "Well, I have been able to sneak around most easily because the three main men are in the hospital. I was especially lucky today because I was finally able to piece together what has been going on over there for the last several months. You really will not believe it."

The other three looked at him with interest. Bill said, "Good work, K-san. What did you learn?"

Kurokawa continued, "You really will not believe it. I found out what they have been doing with the C4 — they have been sculpting it inside of the plastic replicas along with remote detonators."

Natsuko gasped.

"Exactly," said Kurokawa. "They have been secretly switching all the plastic replicas throughout Tokyo with their own explosive versions. I, myself, had to recreate a replica of cheesecake. You see, I found the trick was to use sand to..."

"Kurokawa-san," said Bill, interrupting.

"Yes?"

"While I am very interested in hearing about your modeling techniques, perhaps now is not the best time. Would you tell us more about the explosives? Do you have any idea of the group's motives?"

Kurokawa looked a little ashamed, as if he did not realize until just then that he had been going off on a tangent. He cleared his throat and said, "Of course, sorry. From what I could overhear from the others, it appears that they are after control of Tokyo. Tell me, Bill, have you ever heard of the Ishiku-gumi?"

Bill flashed a look at Natsuko (who showed no reaction to the name) and answered, "Uh, yes. Aren't they the biggest criminal organization in Japan?"

"Quite right," affirmed Kurokawa. "It seems that the Yasei-kai think of themselves as challengers to the Ishiku-gumi and are going to use the bombs as leverage to force them to relinquish their interests in Tokyo.

Bill glanced again at Natsuko's deadpan face and replied, "That cannot end well."

"No," agreed Kurokawa, "I expect not."

"Everyone," said Natsuko softly, "I think I need to disclose something to you right now before we continue. I apologize for not telling you sooner, but up until now I felt it to be irrelevant. You see, I am the granddaughter of Okane Noboru, leader of the Ishiku-gumi. For reasons I do not wish to discuss, I am no longer a member of the clan, but many of them are, quite literally, my family."

Sakura said, "Oh, I knew that, Natsuko-san. Just because you are using an assumed name doesn't mean that your face has changed. You are sort of famous, after all. I mean, you were even in my Heroes of the Yakuza coloring book that I had as a kid. I always thought of you as the most valuable member of the clan — I can't believe they kicked you out. They're stupid."

Natsuko looked at Kurokawa, who simply nodded at her. She then looked at Bill, who shrugged.

Bill then turned to Sakura and asked, "Did you really have a Yakuza coloring book as a child?"

Sakura nodded and smiled.

Bill said, "That somehow explains a lot."

Natsuko cleared her throat to reassert control of the conversation. She then looked around at all of them and said, "I did not realize that I was that well known, Sakura-chan. At any rate, I would consider it a personal favor if you would help me stop the Yasei-kai, not only for my family but for the citizens of Tokyo. A clan war is an ugly thing, and many innocent people will get hurt if we do not stop this right away."

Bill looked at Sakura and Kurokawa, who were nodding in agreement and said, "I think we are all in agreement here. Even without your family's involvement, this is something we would have to address. I'm sorry that it had to be your clan that was involved, but maybe it is for the best because now we can ask for their help with our plan to stop the Yasei-kai." He turned to Sakura and asked, "So, what is our plan to stop the Yasei-kai?"

Sakura smiled. "I've got a plan all right, Beer-san. I call it 'Instant Karma'. Here is what we are going to do..."

CHAPTER 39

"Everyone, this is my father, Okane Gin. Father, this is my boyfriend, Bill Brabham, and my friends, Kurokawa Yoshi and Ōguchi Sakura."

Everyone bowed in turn and paid their respects to her father. Bill was particularly nervous, a condition made even worse after he had heard her father's name. Although it probably was not spelled the same way, the way it sounded could be translated as "Silver Money" in English, which sounded like a rap star name to Bill. He thought about how awkward it would be right now to start laughing, which made him start to sweat instead.

Okane noticed Bill's discomfort and walked over to talk to him directly. "So, you are the mysterious man that my daughter has told me about." He looked Bill up and down and said in English, "You seem like a reliable man, Bill. Natsuko certainly speaks highly of you. Welcome to the family." He reached out to shake Bill's hand, which Bill recognized as a very gracious gesture.

Bill first shook his hand, and then bowed to him. He said in Japanese (trying to show off), "Thank you, Okane-san. I believe myself to be a reliable person, and I will certainly look after Natsuko with all of my strength." This seemed to Bill to be a rational thing to say to someone's father, and he hoped that it did not sound as corny in Japanese as it did in English.

Okane seemed to be OK with it and nodded approvingly. He then said, "I am grateful for that, Bill." He then added with a smile, "I am sure that we will get along well. Just remember: if you make her cry, then I make you cry."

"Uh, yes sir," stammered Bill. "Of course, sir."

Natsuko laughed and said, "Forgive my father. He loves to tease my boyfriends. I am sure that he knows that I am old enough to look after myself, don't you father?"

Okane said, "Of course, dear. Sorry, Bill — just having a little fun. You don't have to worry about me. I'm well aware that if you make Natsuko cry, then she will be the one to make you cry in return. And god help you if that happens."

"Father!"

"Kidding, kidding," said Okane with his hands up. However, to Bill's dismay, he caught Bill's eye and slightly shook his head.

Okane then moved the conversation along by introducing his men, who were standing some distance off in the mostly empty warehouse. "Everyone, these are the men that will be helping you with your plan. Allow me to introduce them." He then rattled off their nicknames, which approximately translated into English as follows: Meat Cleaver, Left Eye, The Wrath of Kahn, Sally, Six Pints, The Fisherman, Rock, Bone Crusher, Tank, and Mr. Slick.

Natsuko nodded approvingly. She said, "All very good men. Oh, and Sally too, of course. Thank you, Father."

Her father shook his head. "No, thank you all for bringing this to my attention. Those Yasei-kai are real scum, and they bring shame to the rest of us. We need to rid the town of their kind. And I am very impressed with the plan that you came up with to do it."

He turned to Sakura and continued, "Natsuko tells me that this amazing plan was your idea. You have a truly remarkable brain, young lady. Tell me, how would you feel about joining the Ishiku-gumi?"

Sakura beamed. "Oh wow, could I? I'll join if I can wear a costume. Bill hardly lets me wear one anymore. I want a nickname too — something like Miss Sparkles or Glittering Sunbeam or Dragon's Fire. I'd also like a company car. And at least six weeks of paid vacation. Do you have a retirement package? Stock options? I'll need to review your employee handbook before I make my final decision..."

Okane's eyes were getting wide. He looked at Bill and the others for confirmation that this was normal behavior for Sakura. Bill smiled and shrugged. He then grabbed Sakura gently by the shoulders and interrupted her, saying, "I'm sure we can all work out the details another time. But for now, since time is of the essence, how about we focus on getting Meat Cleaver, The Wrath of Kahn, and these other fine gentlemen up to speed. Oh, and Sally of course."

Sakura said, "OK, Beer-san. That will give me some time to draw up a contract."

Okane laughed and said, "Yes, and that will give me time to find the best lawyer in Tokyo to review that contract — something tells me that you drive a hard bargain, young lady."

"You bet," said Sakura, proudly and with a toothy grin.

Bill motioned to Kurokawa and said, "Kurokawa-san here is the brave man who has infiltrated the Yummy Plastics factory. He is also something of a master craftsman and has learned many extraordinary techniques for reproducing food in plastic and other materials. You should see his sandy cheesecake — it's superb."

Okane turned to inspect Kurokawa, who looked embarrassed at the fuss. Okane said, "Well done, Kurokawa-san. My clan owes you a debt. You have my word that we will repay you in any way we can."

Kurokawa nodded in silence and then Bill continued, "Sakura's plan is to have Kurokawa teach your men his techniques while the rest of us scour Tokyo for the explosive replicas. We will take several pictures of them, marked with their location, and bring them back here. Kurokawa and his pupils will then replicate the replica replicas."

All fourteen of the others said, "Huh?" to this last sentence. Bill rephrased it, "You will make copies of the explosive plastic food replicas in the pictures. When you've finished, then we will secretly swap the explosive replicas with your harmless ones."

One of the men, perhaps it was The Fisherman, asked, "What are we going to do with the explosives?"

Bill said, "A good question. Tell me, have you ever heard of the phrase 'instant karma?'"

CHAPTER 40

Kurokawa was not doing well at all. Somehow, despite all the talk about being cowardly heroes who fight crime at a safe distance, he was now standing in the middle of a cluster of workbenches populated by ten men who could probably make him disappear from the Earth with very little fuss. And he was tired because he had been working full days at the Yummy Plastics factory and then spending his evenings here, teaching gangsters words like 'delicacy' and 'patience'.

And where were the others while he was risking his life yet again? They were off visiting the restaurants of Tokyo, taking pictures, and probably stuffing their faces at each one. He could not help but think that maybe, just maybe, he was somehow getting the raw end of the deal once again.

He sighed inwardly as he surveyed his students. Bill had been collecting luck from petty criminals throughout Tokyo and secretly diverting it to Okane's men (and Sally). But even still, they were very rough diamonds indeed, and no amount of luck was a substitute for skill.

He looked at Sally, which he had incorrectly assumed to be the least troublesome of the bunch. She was clearly frustrated and was taking it out on her model by stabbing it repeatedly with a #2 pick.

A hand twice the size of hers gently reached over to stop her. Six Pints, the owner of the hand, said to her in a slow, simple tone, "That's not how you do it, Sally. You have to scratch it real gentle-like with the #1 pick, just like Kurokawa-san showed us."

Sally sized the man up, as if trying to work out which bit to stab, but instead carefully set down the #2 pick (which was now badly bent) and then picked up the #1 pick while Six Pints nodded to her encouragingly. She used the pick to gently scrape delicate flakes into what was supposed to be a replica of shrimp *tempura*[4].

Six Pints said, "That's it, Sally — that's the way," and patted her on the shoulder in congratulations, which jostled her arm and caused her to destroy some of the flakes that she had just so carefully carved. She screamed in frustration and started stabbing her work again and again.

Kurokawa pretended not to see this and walked to the other side of the work area to help some of the more sedate students. There he found that The Wrath of Kahn had created a very realistic replica of the Starship Enterprise and was inexplicably crashing it into a mountain of replica mashed potatoes. Kurokawa felt like crying.

---

4   Battered and deep fried shrimp.

CHAPTER 41

"What do you suppose they are doing, Master?" asked the junior monk.

"Well, boy," answered the senior monk, "if you had done a better job of installing the camera, then we would know for sure, would we not?"

"Yes, Master. Shall I fetch the Cane of Discipline, Master?"

"No, but please contemplate that it might be wise next time to not place the camera over the rice cooker. Steam rises, boy, remember it."

"Yes, Master."

"As for your question about what those four are up to, I really do not know. It seems like they have recruited some gangsters to swap the plastic food models throughout Tokyo with exact copies. Where is the sense in that? I surely do not know."

"Shall I replace the damaged camera so we may find out, Master?" asked the junior monk.

"No, never mind about the camera. I think we need to see things firsthand."

"Yes, Master."

CHAPTER 42

The manager of Tamiya Bank was reading the newspaper while riding the train to work. He glanced at the cover story — apparently the Prince of England was in town and was allegedly having an affair with one of the local girls. The manager shook his head and wondered what the world was coming to.

His stop came a few minutes later. He set down the paper, gathered up his crutches, and hobbled his way toward the bank.

The bank manager had been in the hospital for weeks without being able to communicate with his staff. When he had finally been stable enough to talk on the phone, he had decided against it because he was curious to see how well his men could handle the pressure without him. This would be a sort of test — a surprise inspection.

He was thinking about his employees as he rounded the corner of the block and was immediately enveloped in an angry mob, which seemed to be centered in front of his bank.

He hobbled a few steps backward on his crutches and demanded of a person on the fringe of the mob, "Tell me, what is all this about?"

"Why? Who are you?" asked the agitated youth.

"I happen to run this bank," said the manager while trying to stand as tall as he possibly could while on crutches. "Now tell me, what is all this about?"

"Hey, everybody! This guy is the bank manager," shouted the youth toward the crowd. This caused an immediate chant of, "Where is our money? We want our money! Where is our money?

We want our money..."

The bank manager, who was now scared and flustered, instinctively leapt for the haven of the bank. He held one crutch in front of him to serve as a make-shift jousting lance and hobbled his way heroically through the mob.

Had this been New York City, he would have, of course, been instantly beaten with his own crutches. But because this was Tokyo, he was able to make it to the security of the bank with only a few wrinkles in his suit and the word *baka* (idiot) written on his back with a black felt tip.

He quickly locked the door behind him, which the mob allowed him to do because this was Japan, where even mobs knew how to behave. One of the men outside banged a crutch against the window of the bank menacingly, but not so menacingly as to break the glass.

The manager was instantly aided by a few of the brave tellers who had continued to show up for work — mainly for the easy paycheck.

The paycheck was easy because, apart from getting through the initial mob, there was not actually a lot of banking going on inside the bank. In fact, the tellers had turned the lobby into an ad hoc beauty parlor. He glared at the head teller, who shrank down in her seat from the weight of his scrutiny. She was getting a pedicure, and now with the bank manager here, she suddenly felt a little foolish about it.

"What's been going on here? Someone tell me this instant!"

And so, they told him — about the Prince, about the bank run, and about the assistant manager going a little funny in the head.

After hearing about the assistant manager, the manager immediately hobbled to the back of the bank on his one remaining crutch and proceeded cautiously into the assistant's office. He cleared his throat.

The assistant manager looked up from a newspaper. He appeared to have been showered and shaved, and in no way crazy. He looked just fine.

"So...I'm finally out of the hospital. Sorry to leave you here all this time without help. So...um...is everything alright? Any problems?" asked the manager, gingerly, as if testing the waters.

"Everything is superb, sir — couldn't be better," replied the assistant manager, who then went back to reading the paper, which he held in front of his face like a shield.

The manager pressed on. "It's just that it seems like there is an angry mob outside the bank. You wouldn't know anything about that, would you?"

The assistant manager moved the paper aside and said with a shocked face, "Mob, sir? No, I'm sure it is nothing to do with us."

"But they are chanting that they want their money," argued the manager.

The assistant gave a half shrug. "Probably just some people who forgot to record a few checks and then went into overdraft by mistake — happens all the time. Don't let it worry you. I'm sure it will sort itself out."

"But there has to be forty or fifty of them out there. They say we are out of money. Is that true?" asked the manager, determined to get a straight answer.

The assistant shook his head. "A vicious lie, sir. Think nothing of it."

The manager gave him an angry look. Seeing it, the assistant felt his resolve slip a little and he said, "Well, maybe we are a little low on deposits, but that is no cause for concern. I have it on good authority that the Prince of England is due to make a very large deposit very soon."

"Ah," said the manager, "About the Prince... Wasn't he supposed to have made his deposit weeks ago?"

"I'm sure he is very busy — lots of princely duties to perform — you know how it is," said the assistant, dismissively.

"Yes, I'm sure, it's just that I saw his picture in the paper today and I'm not sure that he is a reliable type of fellow. Perhaps it might be wise not to count on his business."

The assistant manager placed the paper down on the desk in a gesture that hinted at a loss of patience and said, "Everything is fine, sir. You are worrying over nothing. You are going to make yourself ill if you keep fussing over every little detail. Sure, we had a few hiccups while you were gone, but everything is sorted out now. No problems."

The manager wanted to get angry, but something in the back of his mind told him that it was best not to upset someone who was so clearly delusional. Instead, he decided to continue his assault using facts. He said, "The bank is closed — it's the middle of a work day and the bank is closed. The head teller is getting a pedicure. There is, in fact, no business happening at all. This is a problem."

"Problem, sir?" said the assistant, questioningly. "It has been great — nice and quiet. Plenty of time for everyone to catch up on things like personal hygiene or reading the newspaper. Speaking of which, sir, if you don't mind, I was in the middle of a very interesting article about salmon fishing. It's been nice talking with you, sir — glad to have you back." And with that, he picked up the newspaper and continued reading.

The manager had a brief daydream of himself ripping the paper out of the man's grip, rolling it up, and swatting him with it. But then he suspected that if he went down that route, the assistant would only make him angrier by answering with injured innocence.

The manager instead exhaled loudly while swiveling around on his single crutch. He then hobbled out of the office as indignantly as he could muster. He felt that his best course of action now was to hobble over to his own office and seek refuge in his drinks cabinet. Perhaps the world will look better when viewed through the bottom of a bottle of *sake*.

CHAPTER 43

Sakamoto, head of the Yasei-kai, was on the phone with his underlings at the Yummy Plastics factory. He was being extra cautious with this group because this was such an important mission and it was now being manned by little brothers, or lower-tier members, because the three big brothers who were meant to be in charge were still in the hospital.

In fact, Sakamoto was quite worried about those three in the hospital. He had heard that one man had arrived at the hospital with a case of whiplash, but has since had his leg amputated due to a mix-up with his chart. Another man had contracted a rare skin disease from his roommate. And the third man will never have children again — or even be able to attempt it. Those three were really running into some bad luck lately; it was almost as if they were cursed.

But for the time being, Sakamoto pushed his worries of the three men aside and continued to address the underlings at Yummy Plastics. The call was brief, and the last few things he said to them were: "Yes, that's right...What did you say?...Did you just question me?...I didn't think so. We'll do it tomorrow evening. Be here tomorrow at six. Bring the box. Make sure that you bring the box. Repeat that...Good."

CHAPTER 44

"So tell me again, why are we heading to the power plant?" asked Bill.

Sakura took her eyes off the road for moment to glance at Bill and answered, "I told you, Beer-san, because I want to ask to be reduced to part-time. I'm in the Ishiku-gumi now. I need to free up time for them."

"Why not just quit, then?"

Sakura flashed him a stern look. "Don't you have any sense, Beer-san? The power plant is a sure thing, but the Ishiku-gumi is not. If things don't turn out well, then I still want to have a foot in the door at the power plant. Besides, they will likely struggle in my absence, so I can probably bargain for a raise if I decide to return to full-time."

"You are one shrewd girl, Sakura-chan." Bill looked around the interior of the car and said, "Nice car, by the way. I can't believe the Ishiku-gumi actually gave you a company car — a 370Z for that matter. How did you pull that off?"

Sakura shrugged. "Easy, Beer-san. Simple psychology. I asked for a new Porsche first. That was so unrealistic that when I said that I would settle for a used 370Z, it seemed reasonable to them. No problem, Beer-san. You want one too?"

"I don't even have a license," argued Bill.

"No problem, Beer-san. I can get you one of those."

"Ummm... Sure. Why not. So anyway, why am I coming with you to the power plant? I thought they hated me there."

"Oh no, Beer-san, that's all forgotten about now," answered

Sakura, reassuringly. "Since things have still been going wrong, strictly off the record of course, they have come to realize that it was really not your fault, even though we know that it was. That's why you are coming. You will walk around the plant and say hello to all your old pals while you secretly turn off their bad luck and send them some good luck."

"I did send some good luck to my old boss the other day," offered Bill.

"Yes, I already guessed that. He's been blabbing on about how happy he has been lately. He met some bimbo the other day and now he is in love." Sakura hugged herself and made a kissy face in mock demonstration.

"Really?" asked Bill with little enthusiasm. "Well, good for him."

Bill then caught an astonishing sight out of the window and yelped, "Holy shit — what happened to the gas station?"

"Oh," said Sakura unconcerned, "Didn't you know? It burned down the same day that we stopped for gas — you remember, the time we coasted in on fumes."

Bill considered this. He then asked, "Do you think it was my fault?"

"Maybe yes, maybe no," answered Sakura, unhelpfully. She then added, "You were certainly wound up that day, and that was before you knew how to control your power."

Bill sighed. "I suppose I better hunt down the owner and try to help him, then."

Sakura smirked and said, "If he is still alive."

Before Bill could comment on this dark thought, Sakura's cellphone suddenly rang to the tune of Chopin's "Funeral March." She sighed wearily and answered it while pulling over to the side of the road.

Bill noticed something dangling from the bottom of the phone. It was a little figurine of the grim reaper. Bill knew that phone charms like these were popular in Japan, but they were usually in the form of something much cuter than the anthropomorphic personification of death. This, coupled with the ring tone, made him feel very uneasy about the purpose of the phone. He listened as Sakura spoke on it:

"You have reached the suicide prevention hotline. This is Suzuki speaking. I'm here to help. Please, what is your name?... Oh, hello again, sir, how may I help you today?...I see...hmm...uh huh...yes...uh huh...ah, OK. Do not worry about it, sir, your boss will leave you alone soon enough. I suggest that you continue to follow my advice, which I will explain one last time. The first thing is to make sure that everyone else is convinced that everything is OK. You must always restate any situation given to you in a positive light. You must radiate an air of confidence and control...OK, yes, if you want to be crass about it, you could say that you must lie to everyone. But here is the amazing part — after a while, you will also believe that everything is OK...Yes, yes, fine — you will also believe the lie. But you see, that is just it — if everyone believes the same lie, then does it not become the de facto truth? See, no problem, sir — just keep saying that and it will eventually be true. Good day, and thank you for using the suicide hotline."

She hung up the phone and put it away, then eased the car back onto the motorway. Bill asked, "What the hell was that?"

Sakura frowned at him and said, "That is the stupid hotline number that you set up as a joke on the banker — only the joke is on me because he keeps calling. It's very annoying. People should learn how to handle their own problems."

"So why don't you just stop answering it?" suggested Bill.

Sakura looked shocked. "Oh no, Beer-san — it's a suicide hotline. You can't not answer a suicide hotline. That would be wrong."

Bill knew the futility of arguing logically with Sakura, so he let it go at that.

A few minutes later, they arrived at the power plant and were admitted without hindrance. They split up once they were inside the gate. Sakura went to see her supervisor while Bill made his way through the maze of steel framework and dull corridors to see his own former supervisor.

Bill was shocked to be greeted with a deep bow from his former boss, who then said to him, "Bill-san, great to see you again. I have to thank you from the bottom of my heart for recommending Tina the other night at the party. At first I was skeptical and things did not seem to be going well with her, but then while we were at Disneyland, things suddenly just clicked."

Before Bill could respond, or even properly absorb this information, the supervisor gave a short, forced laugh and said, "Get this, Bill-san: do you know Tina's actually been to Disneyland dozens of times?"

"No!" exclaimed Bill in mock surprise.

"Yes!" affirmed the supervisor. "When I had first met her, I had lied and had acted like a big-shot corporate businessman. However, for some reason, I later came clean about my occupation, and then she gave me a hug and said, 'Thank you for respecting me enough to tell me the truth.' Then she laughed and told me about her Disneyland racket. We had a good laugh about it together and by the end of the day we just sort of felt at home with each other. But anyway, thanks again, Bill-san. I owe you one. How can I repay you? Would you like your old job back? We still need someone skillful to man the crane over the spent fuel rods."

Bill was surprised by the offer, but he thought quickly and replied, "Actually, yes, that would be great. I could come back part-time, say three days a week. But since I have experience now, I will have to insist on double the salary."

"Bill-san, come on, be reasonable. I cannot agree to that."

Bill made a show of being disappointed. He then said, "Oh, OK. I'll settle for a fifty percent raise."

The supervisor, who felt like he had just won, said, "You've got a deal, Bill-san."

Bill thanked Sakura in the privacy of his own mind. He then excused himself from the supervisor's office in order to visit his former coworkers.

As he mingled amongst them, some of his former coworkers were still leery of him, while others were genuinely glad to see him — especially the current crane operator who was ecstatic to hear that Bill was returning. Bill spread good fortune to all of them indiscriminately.

Meanwhile, on the other side of the power plant, Sakura was also having a conversation with her supervisor.

"Please reconsider, Sakura-san. We need you here full-time. You are so skillful with the press. What are we to say to them in your absence?"

Sakura put a reassuring hand on her boss's shoulder and said, "No problem, boss. Everything will be fine. You just stall the press on days that I am not here. If they are insistent, then I have a list of things to say." She handed over the list.

The supervisor took it and read it aloud, "Things are on schedule, everything is fine. It was a minor setback, but we are working hard to make it right. The leaks are not serious and have not reached the ocean. The radiation reading was just a transient spike. We have a bold plan to deal with the ground water. We are securing the site as fast as we can, but funding is tight and government assistance in this area would speed things up greatly. We are in control of the situation. Cleanup of the surrounding areas is nearly complete..."

After the supervisor finished, Sakura added, "These are just templates to give you an idea of what to say. Just stick to the following themes and you will be fine: anything bad is just temporary, things are getting better, we are in control, and there is nothing to worry about."

The supervisor looked panicked. He asked, "And what if they ask us what sort of bold plan we had in mind to stop the contaminated groundwater from reaching the sea?"

Sakura looked at him like he was an idiot and answered, "Just make something up. Make it sound futuristic and scientific. No problem. For instance, you could say that we are designing a giant, underground ice-wall or something like that. Never mind the cost or the logistics, just as long as it sounds like we are thinking of something big."

"An ice-wall, you say — interesting," mumbled her supervisor. He then said, "But what of the cost? How do we explain that?"

Sakura shrugged. "You don't. You don't actually do anything, you just claim to be planning it. And if anyone presses you on the lack of progress, you just read them this one here." She pointed to one of the items on the list.

The supervisor read the item, "We are securing the site as fast as we can, but funding is tight and government assistance in this area would speed things up greatly."

The supervisor shook his head slowly. "Sakura-san, you are a genius."

CHAPTER 45

Kurokawa was not doing well at all, which was a shame because just five minutes ago he had been having the time of his life. He had just perfected a newer, cheaper, faster way of recreating salmon sashimi when two men suddenly appeared on either side of him and informed him that the boss (actually, the acting boss) wanted to see him immediately.

Now he was sitting on a stool in the middle of a back room of the Yummy Plastics factory. Three men were pacing around him, sizing him up. Kurokawa thought, well, it was a nice life.

Finally, the head man said, "Kurokawa-san, we know what you've been up to. We've been following you this whole time."

Kurokawa thought, it was a nice life, but I really want it to last longer. This is not good. I need to do something.

The head man said sharply, "Why are you humming? Stop that and pay attention!"

"Sorry", muttered Kurokawa, who stopped the humming.

The head man continued as he paced back and forth in front of Kurokawa, "We've seen you at that other warehouse. We've seen you training those men. Do you deny it?"

Kurokawa looked down and shook his head. There was a high-pitched whine in his head that was making it hard to concentrate.

The head man nodded. "Thank you for not insulting me by lying."

Kurokawa nodded and remained silent. He braced for the inevitable punch to the face, but it never came.

Luckily for Kurokawa, these men were underlings, relative newbies, and also not very bright or perceptive. They therefore had spotted that Kurokawa had been teaching men how to replicate Yummy Plastics' dishes, but were too thick to notice who the men were, or more to the point, what group they belonged too.

To give Meat Cleaver and his associates their due, they had been doing a good job of remaining in disguise in order to avoid this very situation. But all the same, their faces were known to many. Fortunately for Kurokawa, the underlings running the Yummy Plastics factory never had the same coloring books as Sakura.

Kurokawa was, of course, well aware that he was lucky, but he was also well aware that being lucky still did not guarantee his safety, and so he began to sweat.

The head man nodded to one of the other men, who in-turn went over to a nearby table to fetch a briefcase. Kurokawa imagined it to be full of torture implements — pliers, thumbscrews, and the like. The man handed it to the head man.

The head man held it flat, pointing it away from himself and toward Kurokawa. He opened it slowly while Kurokawa stared at it nervously.

It was full of money.

Kurokawa quickly looked up at the man and gave him a questioning expression.

The head man closed the case and smiled. "We know you've been moonlighting at your own plastic food business and stealing our company secrets. We would normally punish you severely for this, but we are also aware that you have been the one to originate so many of those very same techniques, and you have helped us to maintain our aggressive timetable. We owe you a debt for your service, so we are overlooking your deceit. And the truth is, we are closing shop today — I can't tell you why — but we feel that your talent should not go to waste."

He then handed Kurokawa the briefcase and continued, "Here is some money to get your own business off the ground. Consider it a loan that you may have to repay with a favor in the future. But for now, use it to make your dream flourish."

Kurokawa managed to say, "Thank you," and was then overwhelmed with emotion and unable to speak. He started to tear up.

The men took turns patting him on the shoulder and filing out of the room. Kurokawa returned their kindness by turning off the curses that he had just placed on each of them.

After collecting himself, he went back to HQ and informed the others that it sounded like the Yasei-kai were about to make their move.

CHAPTER 46

The Yasei-kai's headquarters was located on the outskirts of Tokyo in a multifunction building consisting of a first-floor warehouse and several stories of office space. The warehouse portion was used as a storage area for goods, as a training facility, as a general hang-out, and as an armory. The many, many offices above were used for the financial and legal departments.

Bill was in an office on the top floor of the very same building. He was by himself on one side of a large conference table, which itself occupied the center of the room.

On the other side of the conference table sat Sakamoto, who was flanked by One and Two. They remained standing beside him as motionless as gargoyles. There were also two mean-looking men standing in two separate corners of the room. Their job seemed to be to try to make Bill wet himself just by looking at him, and they were nearly successful at it.

Also, on the other side of the conference table was the door, and Bill knew that there would likely be one or two men posted just outside of it, as well as hundreds throughout the rest of the building. After all, this was supposed to be a night of victory and celebration for the Yasei-kai, and therefore all the members were gathered together in the same building.

This made Bill feel quite lonely — he was all by himself on one side of the large conference room while, metaphorically, an entire Yakuza gang populated the other side.

He looked at one of the henchmen, who returned a crotch-wetting stare. Bill looked away.

Bill was not totally unprepared, however. He was wearing brown contacts, and he had dyed his hair black with a temporary colorant and gave it a messy, gelled look with the hope that this was enough to keep them from recognizing him as himself, or perhaps as the Prince of England — either one could have been troublesome.

He also had Sakura's plan. Yes, the plan. I better get to work on the plan, he thought.

Sakamoto was in the middle of addressing him when Bill suddenly interrupted him by waving his hand around in a fanning motion and saying, "Ho, man, hold that thought. I better open a window." He turned around and took a few steps toward the window while continuing, "I'm sorry, but fish really gives me the wind. Fish, fish, fish — all you people ever eat is fish. Even when I think I've found something without fish, it's been cooked in fish oil."

He opened the window and stuck his head out briefly. He looked down and confirmed the presence of something on the ground. He brought his head back inside, turned around, and said, "Sorry about the smell. It should clear out in a minute or two. Now, what were you saying? And can you speak slowly? My Japanese is not so good."

Sakamoto, visibly annoyed, said tersely, "I was asking who you are and where is Okane-san? Are you his second in command? Are you even authorized to bargain on behalf of the family?"

Bill looked shocked. "Oh gosh, no. I'm no lieutenant. I'm not sure why Okane-sama did not come. All I know is that he came barging out of his office muttering something about a no-good, low-life, worm or something like that. He saw me sweeping, and then he came straight up to me and said, 'Hey, you, you want a promotion?' and I was like, 'Yes, sir,' and then he said, 'Good, because you are going to represent me at a meeting tonight. I can't be bothered to waste my time on such trash.' And that was pretty much it. He scribbled down your address on a piece of paper and told me to be here at six."

"You're a janitor? He sent a janitor in his place? This is insulting! This is beyond insulting! I'll teach him to take me lightly." Sakamoto then turned to one of the men in the corner and said, "Get me the box."

The man in the corner answered, "Box?"

Sakamoto almost lost it. Veins were starting to bulge around his temples. He said, forcibly calm, "Yes, the one I asked you to absolutely remember to bring."

"Oh, right," answered the henchman, "That one. I've got it. I'll go get it." He left the room to fetch it.

Sakamoto resumed his ranting, "Where are you from, janitor? You are obviously not from Japan. It is bad enough that he sent a janitor, but a *gaijin* too. Despicable."

Bill said in English, "Oh, I'm from Texas, partner." He then shaped his hands into make-believe guns and pretended to pull them from invisible holsters at his side. He pointed his fingers at the henchmen while going, "Pow...pow...pow...pow."

The henchmen tensed and looked as if they were going to retaliate with lethal force. Bill said in English, "Whoa, partners. Easy there." He then switched back to Japanese. "I'm just teasing. I don't have any guns. I know they wouldn't work on you guys, anyway. I know all about you. You guys are ninjas, right? I've seen enough movies to know that you guys can just swat the bullets out of the air. Gosh, real ninjas right here in front of me. Do you think I can have your autographs? The wife will never believe me. She thinks I'm just a good-for-nothing but I keep telling her, honey..."

"Enough!" exclaimed Sakamoto. Be quiet. What are you doing now? Stop humming! I said be quiet!"

The other henchman came through the door with an ornate silver box encrusted with red gemstones. Something about it looked familiar to Bill. Why did it look so familiar? And then he realized it and smiled at his luck.

The henchman placed the box in front of Sakamoto. Sakamoto turned his attention from the box back to Bill while saying, "So, janitor, you are from America. Funny, I always thought that all Americans were fat and stupid. It seems that I was only half right."

"Hey!" said Bill while covering his stomach with his hands, "I'll have you know that I've lost a lot of weight since I've been here — probably all the fish. Shame it gives me the wind something fierce."

Sakamoto and the henchman looked at each other and shook their heads. Sakamoto continued, "At any rate, your boss..."

"Who are those two?" interrupted Bill while looking at One and Two.

Sakamoto was again agitated. He said, "What? Oh them, never mind about them. They are nothing. They are furniture."

"Nice furniture you got there," said Bill while smiling at the girls. Do they make tea? I'm dying for some tea. All this diplomacy is making me parched."

Sakamoto waved a hand at the girls, who fetched the previously prepared tea from the other side of the room. One slid a cup in front of Bill, while Two placed a cup in front of Sakamoto. Then, they both kissed Sakamoto's cheeks and resumed their motionless stance on either side of him.

Bill took a sip of tea, as did Sakamoto. Bill then said, "I'm impressed. I have got to get myself one of those. Is there a store or something where you get furniture like that? I've never seen any — and I've seen a lot since I've been in town. Of course, I think I'd feel like a loser if I had furniture like that. I mean, I have a nice wife at home who does that stuff for free. Well, I say for free but you know how expensive..."

"Enough!" shouted Sakamoto. "Okane calls me a worm, and now this one — a janitor — calls me a loser. I'll show you who's the loser, janitor." He turned to the henchman nearest him and demanded, "Give me the key." He held out his hand.

"Key, sir? I don't have the key. I thought you had it."

Bill used this moment of confusion to take out his phone and, while keeping it hidden under the table, used it to text Natsuko with "Call me in two minutes." He also attached something to the phone where a phone charm would normally go.

Meanwhile, the two henchmen and Sakamoto were searching their pockets for the key to the box.

Bill interrupted them, saying loudly, "Yes, you are right Sakamoto-san, you are certainly showing me what a loser looks like."

Sakamoto was about to lunge over the table when suddenly:

I'm turning Japanese
I think I'm turning Japanese
I really think so
Turning Japanese
I think I'm turning Japanese
I really think so
I'm turning Japanese
I think I'm turning Japanese
I really...

Bill said hurriedly while holding up his finger, "Be with you in one second, gentlemen. It's the misses — I have to take this."

Bill answered the phone and started to pace back and forth while talking on it, all the while making sure that Sakamoto could see what he had attached to his phone.

"Hey honey, what's up?...Oh, sorry I'm late but I'm in a meeting...No, really...No, I'm not cheating on you, I'm in a meeting for the big boss...Yes, really. I told you I was going to move up the ladder quickly..."

Sakamoto and the others noticed the key dangling from his cellphone. Sakamoto exploded. "Get off the phone, you idiot. I'm going to kill you. I'm going to kill every last one of the Ishiku-gumi, and make you watch. Then I'm going to rape your wife in front of you, kill her, and then torture you to death. Now hand over that key right now!"

Bill continued as if totally oblivious to the hostility, "Honey, I have to go. I think negotiations are just about over, though. Keep dinner warm for me. I love you...No, I love you more...No, I love you more...No, I love you more..."

"Hang up the damn phone, you idiot!" ranted Sakamoto.

Bill did. He then said, "Sorry about that. OK, where were we?"

"Give me that key."

"What key?"

"The one on the phone, and don't play dumb again or I'll have that guy in the corner there cut your balls off."

Bill looked at his phone in surprise, as if noticing the key for the first time. "Oh, what, this thing?" he said as he removed it. What do you want with it?"

"It's mine," demanded Sakamoto.

"Now, hold on just a minute. I found this the other day at a gas station. It's mine. I mean, finders keepers, losers weepers."

Bill quickly held up a hand and added, "Not that I'm calling you a loser, mind you."

"Get him!" shouted Sakamoto.

One of the henchmen began to make his way around the table. Bill quickly slid the key over to Sakamoto and said to the henchmen, "OK, OK. Heel boy. Heel."

Sakamoto motioned for the henchman to stop. Bill looked at the henchman triumphantly. The henchman fixed Bill with another bowel-clenching glare and internally marked him down on his "people to kill" list.

"Before you die, janitor, I want you to witness this," said

Sakamoto, ominously. He inserted the key into the box and turned it.

-CLICK-

The box opened to reveal an ornate control panel containing dozens of switches with little labels under each one.

"Oh cool, what do the switches do?" asked Bill while, to Sakamoto's horror, he reached over the table and flipped a couple of them at random.

Instinctively, Sakamoto jerked the box away from Bill's reach. Then he laughed. "You fool," he said. "Do you know what you've just done?"

"No, what? Did I just turn the lights off in the bathroom? That would be funny."

Sakamoto pushed a few buttons on a different remote. A large screen at the end of the conference room turned on. Sakamoto tuned it to the news channel. He then turned smugly to Bill and said, "In a few minutes, you will see the horror of what you've done."

Bill said, "OK, well, if we're watching a show, can we have popcorn? I always eat popcorn when I watch TV. And no cooking it with fish oil — OK? It gives me wind."

"Silence, janitor. Sit quiet and wait."

And so they sat in awkward silence for a good ten or fifteen minutes. Well, mostly silence. Bill would absent-mindedly hum a show tune now and again until a henchman would glare at him to stop.

Finally, the current news story was interrupted by breaking news — there had been a series of explosions located randomly throughout Tokyo. Bill saw it and said, "Oh my, I hope no one was hurt."

Sakamoto smirked. "Just watch, janitor. Watch and despair."

The coverage started to show video of the various explosion sites, and Sakamoto's face went pale. "No," he said simply.

"Hey!" said Bill cheerily, "That's a nice, big house that got exploded. And a warehouse. And some poor bastard's car, too. I wonder what happened?"

"My house," mumble Sakamoto. "My warehouse. My car. How?"

"You don't look so good, Sakamoto-san. Maybe have some more tea?"

Sakamoto stared at the video and drank some more tea. As he continued to watch, his eyes started to close involuntarily and he had to fight to keep them open.

Bill said, "Well, you certainly know how to throw a party, but I have to be going. Dinner is getting cold and the misses is expecting me any second now."

And with that, he flipped the remaining switches on the control panel and lunged head-first out of the window.

Distant blasts could be heard all around the city. Before the henchmen could react, the two girls nodded to each other, slid over the table, and also dove through the window.

One of the henchmen lumbered around the table and peered out of the window. He could see several fires flaring up throughout the city. He looked down. Bill was already off of the Hollywood-style air bag and one of the girls had just landed on it. When the other girl landed some twenty feet away from her, it caused the first one to be launched up and over the side of the bag. She screamed.

Bill heard the scream and looked up just in time to see One flying through the air towards him. He took a few well-judged steps and caught her. She instantly flung her arms around him and gave him a kiss on the cheek. And then Natsuko walked around the bag and saw them.

Bill quickly put her down and said, "It's not what it looks like, I can explain." He was then interrupted by another scream, this one coming from Two, who was sliding uncontrollably down the side of the bag. Bill ran and caught her as well. She also hugged him and gave him a kiss on the other cheek.

Bill set her down and said to Natsuko, "See...they just keep falling from the sky."

Natsuko smiled and hugged each of the girls. She then said to them, "I'm glad you are both alright. Did everything go according to plan?"

They both nodded. Two said, "Yes, Okane-sama. Sakamoto-san is sleeping soundly in his office. Bill-san was perfect — he was so annoying that even I wanted to punch him."

Natsuko started to reply, but she was interrupted by Sakura, who had just walked up to them. She was dressed as a Hollywood movie producer, complete with hat and megaphone. She said through the megaphone, "Good comedic ad-libbing, you two. Excellent work. But you, Beer-san..." she shook her head "...you totally forgot to say your lines on the way down. I'm afraid you are going to have to do it again."

Bill and the others removed their fingers from their ears and

Bill said, "Ha-ha."

Sakura smiled a cheesy grin.

Bill said, "Good plan as always, Sakura-chan. It's all up to Natsuko's group now."

Sakura said, "Then that means that I'm on stage now, too." She then ran to a nearby trailer, flung open the door, and darted inside.

Bill looked around and said, "She certainly went all-out, didn't she?"

Natsuko answered, "Yes, I would swear that this was a real movie set."

The area around the building had been roped off in yellow tape and was guarded by security. There were genuine camera crews filming. There were also a number of trailers for the stars and the props. Sakura even had some people acting out real movie scenes on the street not far from them.

"And she set these up at every one of the bomb sites?" asked Bill, amazed.

Natsuko said, "Yes, all of them were roped off and cleared of people under the pretense of shooting a movie. I really have no words to describe this. She had all of this stuff waiting on standby and was able to mobilize and coordinate the entire project in less than a day."

Bill shook his head. "I feel like such a proud parent right now."

The door to Sakura's trailer flung open again. The trailer was pink and had a giant golden star on it with 'SAKURA' written in golden letters underneath it.

Sakura emerged wearing her golden lucky cat costume. Bill buried his head in his hand and said, "OK, I'm not so proud anymore."

Sakura then ran over to the Yasei-kai's headquarters and straight through the front door.

Bill and Natsuko looked at each other. Natsuko said in disbelief, "Did she just..."

Bill nodded. "I think so."

Natsuko said, "Come on, let's go!"

As they ran toward the front of the building, they passed a couple of monks in white robes, who were probably part of Sakura's make-believe movie. The two monks studied Bill as he ran past. After a moment, one of them said to the other, "He is an idiot, Master, but a lucky one. And he has yet to turn green, go blind, or explode."

The other monk nodded.

Bill and Natsuko ran to the front door and walked cautiously inside. They were in the front reception area and it was clear that the Ishiku-gumi had already stormed through there. No one was around to stop them, well, no one could stop them that was around. They were all lying here and there either injured or worse.

Bill and Natsuko walked on. They followed the sounds of combat, which took them to the warehouse portion of the building. They entered cautiously, and instantly noticed Sakura in her golden suit. She was literally kicking someone's ass. The man stumbled forward and hit his head on a pole, knocking himself out.

They called to her, and she came trotting over as if she were merely taking a break from a basketball game.

"Hey guys, come to help?" asked Sakura.

Bill said hurriedly while looking out for impending doom, "You've got to get out of here; it's dangerous."

Sakura shrugged. "No problem, Beer-san, Kurokawa-san juiced me up this morning — watch."

And with that, she turned and ran back into the fray. Natsuko screamed, "No, Sakura, come back!"

Sakura turned to face them and stood still in the middle of the room. All around her, people were punching, knifing, and smashing each other over the head with bits of furniture.

To Bill and Natsuko's horror, Sakura closed her eyes. The chaos seemed to writhe around her, but never actually touched her. She stretched her neck just as a brick flew passed her head, narrowly avoiding her face. With her eyes still closed, she produced from a pouch on her back several *shuriken*, also known as Chinese stars.

Bill and Natsuko instinctively ducked. Sakura spun around and around, eyes still closed, and threw the stars blindly into the crowd.

Bill and Natsuko were appalled until they realized where the stars had struck, which was in various body parts of the Yasei-kai, and only the Yasei-kai. In fact, this simple act had turned the whole momentum of the fight around and the Ishiku-gumi started to win handily.

Sakura opened her eyes and surveyed her work with satisfaction. She called out, "See, Beer-san, no problem."

Just then, a huge man grabbed her from behind and started to crush her.

Sakura quickly tapped the toe of her shoe on the ground and the man instantly convulsed and fell to the floor. This was not magic, but merely clever usage of a stun gun, a micro-switch, and alternate layers of insulating and conductive clothing. But it was still pretty cool.

Bill and Natsuko clapped. Sakura bowed, narrowly avoiding a throwing knife, which went on to stick in the eyeball of a man that had been sneaking up behind her.

As she stood back up, another man knifed her in the shoulder. She cried out in pain and instinctively activated the stun gun again, but because the knife had breached the insulating barrier of the costume, both Sakura and her assailant convulsed and dropped to the floor.

Bill summed up the situation masterfully by saying, "Shit!" and then he sprinted over to her, scooped her up, and jogged out of the building with her as Natsuko followed just behind.

Meanwhile, somewhere partially hidden in a corner of the room was Kurokawa, who was doing his best to shift the luck from one group to the other. He frowned as he watched his friends running away without him. "This will be discussed at the next meeting," he muttered to himself as they fled.

CHAPTER 47

On one side of a large, square table sat Okane Noboru, Natsuko's grandfather and big boss of the entire Ishiku-gumi clan. Sort of huddled around the other side of the table sat Natsuko, Sakura, Kurokawa, and Bill.

The table was very low — maybe a foot high. The five of them were sitting around it on the floor with their legs crossed and their bottoms on little pillows.

The Japanese spend a lot of time near the ground, Bill observed, with some furniture designed for sitting on the floor, and often beds consisted of "futons", which in Japan were merely thin mattresses that were placed directly on the floor.

That explains the custom of taking off one's shoes at the door, thought Bill. Who wants to sit or sleep on a floor after someone has tracked in dirt from the outside?

Bill's mind quickly came back to the present as Okane Noboru cleared his throat and prepared to speak. "I welcome you four to my home. I have been told of the astonishing feats that you all have performed, and I owe each of you a debt for your efforts in saving my clan and the people we protect. I will start with Kurokawa Yoshi-san."

Kurokawa stood up.

Okane Noboru picked up a briefcase and handed it to an attendant, who in-turn, handed it to Kurokawa.

Okane motioned to the briefcase and said, "Please, open it."

Kurokawa moved his tea and placed the briefcase on the table. He sat back down while Okane continued, "Kurokawa-san, you have shown tremendous bravery and great skill in your infiltration of an enemy stronghold. This is our thanks."

Kurokawa opened the case. He reached inside and pulled out the deed to the Yummy Plastics factory. It showed Kurokawa as the new owner. Attached to the deed were the keys to the building.

Kurokawa said while holding back his tears, "Thank you so much, Okane-sama. This is incredibly generous." His hands were trembling as he held the deed.

Okane said, "Not at all — a skill like yours should be fostered. There is also enough money in that case to hire two dozen good men and new equipment for all of them to use."

Kurokawa lifted up the deed and saw the money below it. Unable to reply verbally, he bowed in thanks.

Okane then focused his eyes on Sakura and said, "And now for our precious new member, Ōguchi Sakura-san. You have already shown your bravery in battle..." he indicated the sling around her arm "...as well as your strategic genius. Tomorrow we will have a celebration in your honor, and you will drink with me and become part of the family. You will become a captain, and you will be in charge of a special group whose job will be to unwind the filthy ventures that were formally controlled by the Yasei-kai. I believe that most of the drugs have been destroyed by the explosions the other night, but you must close the pornography studios and put an end to the forced prostitution. You will return the girls to their homes — those that wish to return — and anonymously provide their parents with compensation as you see fit."

Sakura, who was already standing at attention, bowed sharply and said, "Yes, boss. Thank you, boss." She then daintily sat back at the table and gave Bill a huge, toothy grin. He patted her on the head.

Okane continued, "Next is my precious granddaughter, who has shown me that we must also be compassionate in our undertakings. Although I do not often say it, you have always made me very proud. I humbly ask that you rejoin the clan as a lieutenant. If you accept, you will control a large group, whose function will be to provide disaster relief and public assistance. You will be the charitable face of our clan." He smiled and added, "You have already proven that you are capable of doing such work. So, what do you say, granddaughter, will you join us again?"

Natsuko smiled back and said enthusiastically, "Yes, grandfather, I would love to. Thank you." She bowed and sat back down. She then gave Bill a smile and squeezed his hand under the table.

"And now, lastly, we come to my new American friend, Bill Brabham-san."

Bill stood to attention.

Okane eyed him up and down. "I understand that you are dating my granddaughter, is that correct?" inquired Okane.

"Yes I am, Okane-sama," affirmed Bill, expecting the death threats to start at any moment.

"Very well," said Okane, "Then as compensation for your bravery and leadership, I will allow this to continue."

Bill, happy not to have been threatened, said excitedly, "Yes, Okane-sama. Thank you very much." He bowed twice out of nervousness and sat back down, smiling at Natsuko as he did.

Okane looked surprised. He cleared his throat and said to Bill, "Brabham-san, were you not expecting further compensation?"

Bill stood back up. "Compensation? I do not understand."

Okane looked at him quizzically and said, "Yes, compensation. You have done the clan a great service. You put yourself in immense danger. You were surrounded entirely by the enemy and bravely matched wits with their leader in my stead."

"Oh," said Bill, "I understand now. Truthfully, sir, if I am honest, what I did, I did it because I felt it to be the right thing to do. Although I am very pleased that my actions helped your clan, it was not my main intention." He looked at Natsuko and added, "I therefore feel that no further compensation is needed — I am quite happy with what you have just given me." He sat back down.

Natsuko suppressed the urge to hug Bill because she knew her grandfather well enough to know what he was about to do next.

Okane said kindly but firmly, "Brabham-san, please stand back up."

Bill did so and said, "Yes, Okane-sama?"

"I appreciate your candor, and it does you great credit, but you will not be so rude as to refuse a gift from me, will you?" asked Okane.

"No," said Bill hastily. "That was not my intention. Please

forgive me if I have offended you." He bowed twice and stood there looking panicky.

Okane picked up another suitcase and handed it to his attendant, who brought it over to Bill.

Okane said, "Please have a seat now, and open the case."

Bill nodded and took a seat. He opened the case slowly, half expecting it to release a golden glow as he did.

There was no glow, but there was a driver's license inside it. There was also a car key, and attached to the key was a leather key fob with "370Z" embroidered on it.

Bill smiled and held up the key and the license. He motioned toward Sakura with his head and said to Okane, "I'm guessing this one gave you some suggestions."

Okane smiled in reply.

Bill continued, "Thank you so much — this is fantastic."

He then took out his keyring and flipped through the seemingly endless number of keys, trying to find a suitable spot to add the car key. There was the key to his old office, the one to his apartment, the one to his bicycle lock back in America, the one to... What does that one go to? It was a small key, something that would maybe be used to open a locker.

Before Bill could contemplate it further, Okane said, "There is more, please continue Brabham-san."

Bill put his keys back in his pocket and reached into the briefcase, pulling out a Japanese passport with his name and picture in it. Bill held it up and said, "I don't even know what to say. Thank you so much, Okane-sama. Does this make me a Japanese citizen now?"

Okane became uncharacteristically coy. He scrunched up his face and wiggled his hand saying, "Eh, more or less."

Bill dug in the briefcase again and pulled out a file folder that was fat with documentation. Bill flipped through it randomly and came across his court settlement paperwork from Miss Trezzor's lawsuit.

Confused, Bill held it up as if it were a hair that he had found in some soup. "What? I don't understand? Why do you have a copy of my settlement paperwork?"

Okane cleared his throat again and said, "Brabham-san, our legal staff has been diligently cataloging the records kept by the Yasei-kai. As incredible as it sounds, one of our clerks stumbled on this information about you and brought it to my attention. After further investigation, we discovered that the Yasei-kai have organized a group of con-artists in America known as COUGARS."

He switched to English temporarily and said, "The Coalition of Urban Girls Against Repressive Sexuality."

Switching back to Japanese, he continued, "They are, apparently, a group of attractive, middle-aged woman who all have a grudge against men. Each member recruits new members into the group to form a profit-sharing pyramid scheme, with the Yasei-kai sitting at the top of the pyramid. The members help each other to set up elaborate traps for men, catching them in awkward-looking situations and then suing them for sexual harassment."

Okane pointed to the briefcase and added, "That file contains everything you need to prove your innocence to your former wife, if that is something you wish to do. There should also be enough to provide a case against Trezzor-san."

Bill, not able to process all of this, held his hand up to his head and said, "This is a lot to take in. Um, thank you very much. This was very unexpected."

Okane said, "There is still more to see, Brabham-san, will you please continue?"

Bill shook his head, not to say no but to try to clear it. He then hesitantly reached into the briefcase and pulled out another file folder. He took a deep breath and opened it. Among the documents were some photographs. Bill picked a few at random and studied them. Each one was a picture of two monks in white robes, although they were clearly taken at different locations.

Bill held one up. "Monks?" he asked questioningly.

Okane said, "They have been following you around lately, but for what purpose I do not know. We know that they have a secret hideout under a small shrine in your neighborhood. We have seen them enter the shrine, only to follow them and find the shrine empty. However, we have been unable to apprehend them or learn how to enter their hideout. Apparently, someone very clever is taking an interest in you, Brabham-san."

Bill's mouth fell open and he looked at Kurokawa, who also looked stunned and a little excited. Bill turned back to Okane and said, "Thank you for the information, I think it may be very useful to both Kurokawa-san and I. If I may ask, how did you learn that these monks were following me?"

Okane gave Bill a look like he was some sort of idiot and said,

"Well, obviously, because we have also been following you."

Bill said, quite nicely he thought, "Why?"

Okane answered plainly, "We are a very large and successful group for many reasons, Brabham-san, and one of those reasons is that we look after our assets."

"Oh," said Bill, partly flattered and partly worried. "That's very kind of you."

Okane said, "Yes, well, it was not solely for your benefit. You are dating my granddaughter, after all, and as I said, we look after our assets."

Bill nodded. "OK, so do you have any other random surprises in the briefcase for me? Perhaps proof that my long-lost father is alive and well and living in New Jersey?"

Okane, oblivious to the sarcasm, answered, "No, but I will be happy to have some men look into the matter if you would like."

Bill waved his hands in front of him and said, "No, no, please, that will not be necessary."

Hurriedly changing the subject, he then said, "Let's just have a look-see at what else is in the case."

He lifted up a cardboard divider to reveal several bundles of high-denomination yen, in other words, a boat-load of cash. He dropped the divider back on top of the money and looked at Okane, stunned.

Okane said, "That is a personal gift from me to you. He glanced over at Natsuko and added, "Perhaps you may use it to, I don't know, establish a nice home and a family here in Japan."

Bill looked at Natsuko and they smiled at each other. He looked back to Okane and said, "You are fantastic, Okane-sama. Truly fantastic. I am not sure that I deserve all of this. I feel like I now owe you a favor in return."

Okane waved a hand dismissively and said, "Do not worry about it, Bill-kun, I am sure that an occasion will arise when we will need your help again — you know how imposing family can be."

CHAPTER 48

"Well, that was...interesting," said Bill to his crew in the back of the Bentley as it took them home from the meeting.

Natsuko asked, "Did anyone else notice that the two lucky guys both received a briefcase full of cash while Sakura-chan and I basically just received more work to do?"

Bill answered sarcastically, "People are always the hardest on the ones they love the most. I'm sure he is just trying to build your character or something."

Natsuko smirked at him and asked, "Did I ever tell you how much I love you Bill? A really, really lot."

"Oh no," said Sakura, "now you've done it, Beer-san — Natsuko-san is going to hurt the one she loves."

Bill rolled his eyes and looked over at Kurokawa, who was staring blankly ahead and grinning. Bill pointed to him and said, "Look at this guy over here. I don't think I've ever seen him so happy before. I can almost see him carving little plastic shrimp in his head right now."

The girls agreed.

Kurokawa, who was not carving little plastic shrimp in his head but was nevertheless daydreaming about his new business, came reluctantly back to reality and asked, "What?"

Bill said again, "We were just saying that you look very happy."

"Oh, I am, Bill-san. Very happy. This is most excellent. And to think that the Yasei-kai also paid me money to start up a business. I don't know what I'm going to do with it all."

The car went quiet for a moment. The other three just stared at him, waiting for an explanation."

Kurokawa noticed this and suddenly became self-conscious. "What?" he asked, indignantly. "I didn't ask for it — it was merely a bonus for all of my hard work. After all, I single-handedly doubled their production speed while simultaneously increasing their quality. Because of me, they were able to meet their aggressive deadline."

Bill asked sarcastically, "You mean the deadline for placing all of the bombs throughout Tokyo, several of which were in businesses that are friendly with Natsuko's family? Yes, well done K-san. Good job."

Kurokawa's yard-long frown returned. "I had not looked at it that way. I suppose I took my undercover job too seriously. I am sorry."

"Bill!" said Natsuko as she tapped him on the arm, "That was mean. Let the poor man be happy for a change."

Bill said, "Sorry, K-san, I really was just teasing."

Natsuko then said to Kurokawa, "Don't listen to Bill. We all know that the timetable was irrelevant because, thanks to you, we learned about their plan and were able to stop them. You were very brave and you deserve your rewards."

Bill added, "Exactly. Don't listen to me. I'm just punch drunk on adrenaline right now. You are a good man, K-san, and I'm glad to see things go well for you. Enjoy that money and use it however you see fit. Speaking of which, what are we going to do with all this cash? Couldn't Okane-sama have written us a check? It's probably going to look a little suspicious walking up to the bank teller with a briefcase full of cash, don't you think? I mean, aren't they trained to ask questions about that sort of thing? What are we going to say? Oh, it's cool, I got this as a present from the Yakuza — it's perfectly legit. No, I don't know why some of the bills have bloody fingerprints on them, how odd."

Natsuko waved a hand dismissively. "It's all about style and presentation, Bill. A briefcase full of cash is far more exciting than a check stuffed into a Thank You card. Do not worry about it, we have banks that understand these things."

"Speaking of banks," interjected Sakura, "That guy from Tamiya Bank keeps calling me every day now on my suicide hotline number. I sort of feel bad for him. Do you think it would be OK if we let him off the hook now?"

The other three suddenly looked as if each of them had just

remembered that they had left the kettle on the burner. Bill said, "Oh crap, I was so busy with the Yasei-kai thing that I forgot about the bank completely. Crap. Yes, I think we have probably punished them more than enough now — especially that assistant manager. But, uh, how do we go about setting things right?"

Sakura looked at the two briefcases full of cash and said, "Simple, Beer-san, we are going to make a deposit. Here is the plan..."

CHAPTER 49

A black Bentley pulled up in front of Tamiya Bank and five people strode up to the front door, parting the small group of protesters as they did.

The protesters starting whispering amongst themselves. A careful listener could catch little snippets such as "Hey, I think that is the Prince of England." and "What is a prince doing here at a bankrupt bank?" One of the braver protesters shouted out to the Prince, asking him what he was doing at the Bank.

Bill, now with his hair and eyes returned to their original colors, looked toward Natsuko for an interpretation. The two of them had a back-and-forth in English, and then finally Natsuko answered the question, "Prince William has been studying several banks in the area in order to find the best one possible. Several weeks ago he identified Tamiya Bank as the best. Unfortunately, a vicious rumor was started about this bank, which led to the bank run that has since crippled it. We have reason to suspect that this rumor was started by a rival bank in order to gain the Prince's business. But the Prince is a loyal person, and he insists on doing business only with the best, so he is here to deposit a portion of his fortune in the bank, and to aid in its restoration. The bank should be open for regular business very soon. You will be able to withdraw your money then, however, the Prince asks that you reflect on this information and reconsider that choice. Good day to you all."

Natsuko, Bill, and Kurokawa turned back to the door. Natsuko and Kurokawa were flanking Bill just as last time.

Following the three of them was the limo driver, who was carrying Kurokawa's two briefcases, each one handcuffed to a wrist. Behind all of them was Sakura, who was acting as security again. The protesters were giving them all a wide berth, probably because of the menacing way in which she was holding the pepper spray and tear gas.

The bank manager met them at the door and let them inside, locking it again behind them. The lobby was empty, and all the cashiers had been sent home (after they had cleaned up all of their beauty supplies, of course).

The manager said to them, "I have to say, I was a little shocked to hear from you. After listening to the assistant manager talk about you all, and then for you not to have shown up, well, I was starting to think that he was somehow the victim of a scam. I'm sorry that I doubted you."

This was translated into English for the Prince. Bill had been warned that the manager spoke very good English, and so he should refrain from kidding around this time.

Bill replied in English, and in his best diction, "We are honored to return to your bank, and we are most dreadfully sorry for our extended absence. Many unexpected happenings have been preventing me from doing so. I do humbly apologize if this caused you or your bank any undue consequences."

The manager almost stuttered his reply in English, "Oh no, your grace, nothing of the sort. We are honored that you have returned to our bank. Please, come into the conference room. I am sure the assistant manager will be very glad to see you as well."

And he was. The assistant manager almost broke out into tears when he saw the Prince enter the room. He sprang up and practically skipped across the room to shake Bill's hand.

Bill said, "Good to see you again, my friend. I trust you have been well. I am sorry for the delay in getting back to you."

After translation, the man replied, "I knew you would return. I have been telling everyone here not to worry, but they kept doubting me." A conflicted look crept across his face for a moment and then he added, "I do admit to being a little worried when the number on Kobayashi-sama's business card turned out to be in error. And then not hearing from you..."

Natsuko asked, "Could I see the card?"

The assistant nodded and fetched it from his desk. He handed it to her.

Natsuko examined it and said, "Oh, I am terribly sorry. This is from the early batch of cards that I had received — they were printed with the wrong number on them. It is so hard to get good print work done these days." She then shook her head in mock exasperation, ripped the card up, and threw it into the trash bin.

The assistant manager looked serene. He turned to the manager and said, "There you go — everything is explained. Nothing to worry about, just as I have been telling you."

The manager gave him a 'we will have words about this later' look and said nothing.

The conversation was then turned over to Kurokawa who, thanks to Bill's coaching, proceeded to negotiate such things as interest rates, fund availability, expected percentage of reserves, and the ability for a representative of the Prince to audit the books periodically and without notice.

The manager complained a little about the last point, but changed his mind when the suggestion was made that the Prince may have to try another bank if the condition could not be met.

Kurokawa also made it clear that the Prince was very into helping the community and small business, and he would therefore consider it a personal favor if the bank would resume its Small Business Loan program. In return for which, the Prince would be willing to pose for ads and perform other functions to assist the bank in rebuilding its credibility with the public. Not surprisingly, the two managers agreed without hesitation.

After all the business had been settled, and the money in the briefcases had been counted and deposited under an account that listed Kurokawa as an authorized agent, it was time for drinking.

Sake was poured and enjoyed in quantity, although Bill's crew was careful not to drink too much. When the atmosphere seemed loose enough, the manager worked up the courage to ask the Prince about the story he had read about him in the newspaper.

Bill replied dismissively, "Oh, just baseless rumors. Well, I am sure that I do not have to tell you about rumors, sir. I have been spending much of my time in Japan in the company of Miss Kobayashi, who has been acting as my translator and cultural consultant. She is a very great lady, but there is nothing between us romantically. As everyone knows, I have a princess awaiting my return in England whom I love very much. I truly hope that she does not hear about these rumors — she comes from a long line of women who are prone to say the words 'Off with his head' rather more easily than I would like."

Bill made a slicing motion in front of his neck and smiled.

The manager looked worried for a moment and then realized that it was a joke and laughed.

Bill then leaned forward and said quietly, "Of course, just between us, the one about the vending machine was true — I never did get my bloody ramen. The blasted machine."

CHAPTER 50

Sakamoto was inside one of the warehouses that had served, until recently, as one of his adult film production studios. He was standing up and facing a wall with his hands held above his head by ropes attached to anchors in the wall. His legs were similarly immobilized. He was also naked, but not by his choice.

He flailed and tried to call out, but could form no words because of the rubber ball in his mouth. The ball had a rope through the center of it, which was tied behind his head to secure it in place.

In short order, a small girl walked up beside him. He looked at her pleadingly and said, "Hrrrrmmm! Hrrrrmmmm!"

The small girl said, "That is perfect! That's what we want to see — that's it exactly." She looked excited. Sakamoto wrenched his neck to watch her as she set up several cameras around the room.

The girl then said to him, "OK, give me that line one more time."

Sakamoto looked confused. He said, "Hrmm?"

The girl shook her head in disappointment. "No, no, no. Where is the pleading? I want to see the pleading again."

Sakamoto said, "Hrrrm."

"No," snapped the girl, "That's not it either. I think you need some coaching." She snapped her fingers. "Girls, give him a little motivation."

Sakamoto looked left and right a few times to try to see who was approaching. Unfortunately, since they were approaching from directly behind, he could not discern much about them.

He started to smell cigarette smoke as he heard them approach, and then suddenly each of them appeared on either side of him, smiling. It was One and Two.

Sakamoto said, "Hrrrrrm!" as he flipped his head from one to the other.

The little girl said again, sternly, "No, still not it. You've lost the intensity. Girls, give him some intensity."

One and Two then each removed the cigarettes from their mouths and started to slowly move them toward Sakamoto's face.

He tugged on the chains and kept turning his head from left to right and back again in order to avoid the hot ash. He yelled, "Hrrrrmmmm! Hrrrrmmm!"

The little girl clapped her hands. "Yes, nearly there. Let me see if I can help."

Sakamoto suddenly felt a hand firmly press against the side of his face, forcing his head against the wall as he was looking toward the left, at Two.

Two smiled again and slowly moved the cigarette toward his left eye. He struggled, but the little girl doubled the pressure. He yelled out, "Hrrrrrrm! Hrrrrrm!"

The little girl let go, and Two dropped the cigarette onto the floor and stamped it out.

Sakamoto nervously looked to his right. One was also stamping out her cigarette. He sighed and looked relieved.

"Excellent!" exclaimed the little girl. That was excellent. Very passionate. Well done. And you showed me relief too — or as it will appear in the film, false hope."

Sakamoto looked startled. He asked, "Hrrmm Hrrmm?"

The girl said, "Oh yes, false hope," and snapped her fingers again.

There was a sudden rattling of chains and the smell of leather and cheap cologne. Suddenly, Six Pints appeared beside Sakamoto and said, "Don't move. The more you squirm, the more it will hurt."

Six Pints was nearly naked except for a few chains and strips of leather. He made a show of starting to remove the bits down below.

Sakamoto screamed again and a yellow fountain of urine streamed against the wall. He shook violently for a few seconds, turned pale, and passed out.

Six Pints stopped undressing and said to the girl, "Can I get dressed now? This is embarrassing."

The girl nodded. Six Pints then scurried off to get changed in private.

The girl then went around the room and switched off the cameras. She walked up to the other two girls and said, "I will have copies of the tapes sent to your place — a little something to cheer you up when life has got you down."

The girls giggled. Two said, "Thank you so much for this, Sakura-san. We had dreamed of this for so long."

Sakura said, "No problem. Any time. Are you sure this is all you want to do to him? He's right there — and we have bats and knives and stuff?"

The girls glanced at each other for a second and then Two answered, "No, thank you for the offer, but we do not wish to be animals like him."

Sakura nodded.

Two then asked, "What will you do with him? You aren't going to kill him, are you?"

Sakura said, "No, I'm not going to kill him. I'll have to ask the boss what to do with him, but I suspect we will deliver him to the police along with the files that spell out all the nasty stuff that he has been doing. We'll let them deal with him."

Two smiled. "I am glad to hear that. It makes me feel better about working for you."

Sakura answered quickly, "You don't have to work for me, you know. You are free to go. We'll take you home — no problem."

Two said, "We have discussed it at length, and we would feel weird about going home to a normal life again. We love our parents, and we are glad that they know that we are alright, but living with them again would be...boring. We will visit them often, however."

"OK," said Sakura, "If that is how you feel, then I am happy to have you. And are you sure that you don't want to be called by your real names?"

"Oh no," said Two, "We like our new names — it makes us sound exotic and mysterious."

"I agree," replied Sakura. "Anyway, let's get out of here — this place stinks of cigarettes and urine." She then smacked Sakamoto hard on the butt.

One and Two giggled. They smiled at each other and then they each tried it once themselves before leaving.

CHAPTER 51

Miss Trezzor was replacing a book on the shelf when someone suddenly grabbed both of her arms and forced them behind her back. She yelped. "Let go! Help! I'll have you know I've sued for sexual harassment before — you won't get away with this!"

"We know, ma'am. I'm agent Gregory Peters with the FBI. You are under arrest for perjury, fraud, and a number of other crimes that will be made known to you in due course."

He then handcuffed her, read her her rights, and led her to the office door.

The office personnel sat stunned as their boss was paraded in front of them by two federal agents as they marched her to the elevator.

Meanwhile, Bill was standing outside of the building, just beside the exit with his back against the wall. He watched as Miss Trezzor was led to a black car and unceremoniously pushed into the back seat.

He took a long, thoughtful drag of a cigarette as the car pulled away, and then stubbed it out against the building and flicked it toward the retreating car.

Bill did not normally smoke, but he had spent too much time in the company of Sakura and had acquired her penchant for dramatic role-play. Somehow, the cigarette had felt...right.

He then popped a breath mint into his mouth and went inside the building.

As he walked out of the elevator, the whole office was staring at him. This had little to do with him personally, but they had just been discussing the federal agents and Miss Trezzor, so when the elevator had opened they were all half expecting to see more agents.

Bill looked around. "Hello everyone," he said nonchalantly. Whispering and hushed talking broke out instantly around the room. Bill ignored it and walked straight up to his ex-wife, Julie, who had been staring at him the whole time.

"Bill!?" she said with a mixture of excitement and confusion, "What are you doing here?"

Bill smiled. "Hey, Jules. It's... wow — it's nice to see you again." He felt the instinctive urge to hug her but stopped himself from actually following through.

Julie smiled. "It's...nice to see you too," she admitted, hesitantly.

They stared at each other for a few seconds, each feeling a little happy and a lot uncomfortable. Finally, Bill said, "Oh, yeah, why I'm here... I'm here to... Actually, do you want to go for lunch?"

Julie looked at the clock. "It's only eleven."

Bill glanced back at the elevator and then said, "I don't think your boss is coming back any time soon. Who is going to complain?"

Julie sniggered, "I suppose you have a point. OK, let's go."

They went to a little Italian bistro on the next block. They sat down at a table and after they had ordered, Bill began to explain the story of the COUGARS and Miss Trezzor's fraudulent claim of sexual harassment against him. Of course, he had to get a little creative with the source of the documents that he had handed her, claiming they were from a private investigator.

"Bill...I'm sorry. I don't know what else to say. I mean...what else was I to think?"

Bill shrugged.

Julie said hesitantly, "I've missed you."

Bill smiled. "I've missed you too, Jules."

"What have you been doing with yourself?" she asked.

"Well," explained Bill, "It's a tremendously long story, but basically I've been living in Japan."

"Japan?"

"Yep."

"How did you... Why Japan?"

Bill shrugged again. "Why not Japan? Actually, I've been working part-time at Fukushima."

"Bill," said Julie seriously, "that's dangerous. Do you really need the money that badly? Why don't you come back home? I'm not sure what is going on at the office now, but since I am the senior employee, I think that makes me the boss now. I'm sure I can hire you back."

She hesitated for a moment and then added, "Maybe we could... I mean..."

"No," said Bill quietly while shaking his head. "I'm sorry."

Julie looked hurt. "But...why?"

Bill took a breath while he gathered his thoughts. He then said, "Jules, I did love you — you know that."

"And I loved you," interrupted Julie.

"Yes, but you didn't trust me. And that's the problem. You didn't trust me."

"There's another woman, isn't there?" asked Julie, astutely.

"Yes," admitted Bill, "There is. And do you know what she said to me when I told her that I was going back to America to see my ex-wife?"

Julie shook her head.

"She said, 'OK, Bill — I'm going to miss you. When will you be back?'"

Julie had nothing to say to this and merely raise an eyebrow at him, hoping it would substitute as a witty comeback of some sort.

She suddenly felt extraordinarily awkward and did not see how she was going to be able to suffer through lunch like this. She stood up hurriedly, nearly crashing into the waiter who was about to serve their food. She said, "I'm sorry Bill, I just can't," and then ran out of the bistro.

The waiter looked at Bill, questioningly.

Bill said, "That's OK — I'm hungry. I'll eat hers too." He then thought for a moment and asked, "Do you have chopsticks by any chance?"

CHAPTER 52

Bill and his friend Kevin were at Bill's apartment, packing boxes. They took a break to eat some lunch and to shoot the breeze over a beer.

Bill said, "Oh wait... I have something for you." He then went to his bedroom and brought back a briefcase. He set it on the table and slid it over to Kevin saying, "A little token of my appreciation."

Kevin eyed him suspiciously and then opened the case. It was filled with cash. Kevin looked stunned for a moment and then he laughed — all the bills were singles.

"You're an ass. But you're funny — I'll give you that. I'm gonna miss you, bro."

Bill smiled. "Yeah, man, I'm gonna miss you too."

Then they clanked their beer bottles together and downed them in unison.

CHAPTER 53

"Omiyage! Omiyage!" exclaimed Sakura as she danced around Bill. He had just returned to Japan, and Sakura and Natsuko had been waiting for him in his apartment when he walked through the door.

He set down his bags and gave Sakura a hug. "OK, just a moment." He then went over to Natsuko and gave her a hug and a kiss.

Bill had learned quickly that Japan is a country brimming with social customs. One of these customs is that of *omiyage*, which are gifts that you are socially compelled to bring back with you whenever you take a trip. There is a form of this in America, of course, but in Japan it has been raised to an art form.

Bill handed one of his bags to Sakura. "Here," he said, "these are for you."

Sakura looked thrilled. She set the suitcase on the table and greedily flung it open. Inside were all of Bill's collectables.

Sakura looked up at Bill questioningly and said, "I don't want to sound ungrateful, Beer-san — these are very nice — but, you just visited America and you brought me back Japanese anime figures?"

Bill shrugged. "Yes, sorry about that — they used to be mine. I couldn't think of anything distinctly American to bring back for you — it was either these or McDonald's cheeseburgers, and you can get those here."

Sakura, unfazed, said, "OK, Beer-san. Thank you very much,"

and gave him another hug.

Natsuko smiled and said, "So, what do you have for me, Bill, a rice cooker?"

Bill looked at Sakura while pointing to Natsuko and said, "Have you been teaching her sarcasm?"

Sakura looked down at her feet. "Sorry, Beer-san."

"It's OK," said Bill jokingly, "just don't break her. I like her the way she is."

He turned back to Natsuko and made a show of patting his pockets while saying, "I've got yours here somewhere..."

"So, not a rice cooker, then, I'm guessing," ventured Natsuko.

He continued to search his person while saying, "I looked around all over and racked my brain looking for something to get you — someone who means the world to me, someone who has changed my life for the better, someone I hope I will never have to live without."

"Bill, I swear, if this really is a rice cooker then I'm going to leave you," explained Natsuko, only half joking.

"Oh, here it is," said Bill. He pulled it out of his coat pocket and held it up.

As Bill dropped to one knee, Natsuko started to shake with nervous excitement.

CHAPTER 54

Bill and Natsuko were both sitting on reclining beach chairs in the middle of, not surprisingly, a beach. They were sipping some sort of blue drink that tasted of foreign fruit and featured miniature beach umbrellas, which Bill could only assume were there to shade the drink from the sun. In reality, there only purpose had been to nearly blind him with every sip. Natsuko had sensibly taken hers out.

Their matching diamond rings sparkled in the noon-day sun as they each raised their glasses to their lips. Bill smiled every time he saw the rings. He felt, not for the first time, that he was truly a fortunate man.

He sat up, stretched, and then looked over to the couple next to them and asked, "How are you guys doing over there? Need anything? Another drink?"

Two voices rang back in concert, "We're good, thanks."

Bill had won four all-expenses-paid tickets to Hawaii from filling out a survey that came with his new rice cooker, which was fortunate because it was exactly where they had planned to spend their honeymoon. But what would they do with the extra tickets?

They had very briefly entertained the thought of bringing Sakura and Kurokawa, but then thought the better of it. Only half serious, Bill suggested giving the other two tickets to his old supervisor and Tina, since they were also engaged to be married.

And so here they all were on a sort of double-honeymoon, which turned out to be a lot more fun than he had originally thought it would be. Tina was always fun, and his old boss was not bad once he had a few drinks in him.

It was actually very nice to share the usual daytime activities with another couple — things like snorkeling over coral reefs, taking helicopter tours of the volcanic terrain of the islands, parasailing along the coast, and drinking to excess on the beach. However, they had all agreed that there would be no sharing of the usual nighttime activities.

"So," asked the ex-supervisor, "how is the power plant holding up now that I'm gone?"

"Everything is fantastic — no problems!" answered Bill, automatically."

"Yes, Yes," replied the ex-supervisor irritably, "Of course. But I'm talking off the record. How are things going?"

Bill said cheerily, "Actually, things really are going quite well. We've got the water filtration systems back on line and have rebuilt all the leaky storage tanks. We still have a ground water problem, mind you, but we are constructing a giant, underground ice-wall to stop the flow from reaching the ocean."

The ex-supervisor nearly choked on his drink. "You mean you are really going ahead with that? But the cost — how are you paying for it?"

"No problem," said Bill airily, "Sakura-chan got us funding from the government."

The ex-supervisor sank back in his chair. He looked deflated. Bill noticed this and said, "I have to commend you, sir."

The ex-supervisor perked up a bit. Bill continued, "I don't know how you managed to hold that place together for so long."

The supervisor was about to say something when Bill continued, "I mean, who would have thought that the place was crawling with saboteurs?"

"Saboteurs?" questioned the ex-supervisor.

"Oh yes, didn't anyone tell you? You remember that gang a while back that was trying to blow up Tokyo? What were they called...the Yasei-kai, I think?"

The ex-supervisor nodded. "Yes, I remember them. They somehow managed to mess it up and they blew up most of their own properties instead. Personally, I doubt that. I'm sure the government was involved — there's a lot that goes on that they don't tell us about, you know."

Bill agreed, "Very true. Well, anyway, it turns out that they were working on behalf of a certain coal company, who had been doing much more business since the disaster and hoped to keep that business by undermining the public's confidence in nuclear power. They were doing this by continually keeping the plant in the spotlight by means of sabotage. Honestly, sir, they were everywhere. After the Yasei-kai got shut down — or shut themselves down, whichever version of the story you believe — the plant lost some fifteen percent of its staff. So like I said, I have to commend you, sir, for doing so well under those impossible circumstances."

The ex-supervisor was practically radiating pride now. It was all a bunch of baloney, of course, but Bill thought that the man deserved to enjoy his honeymoon. And, in a way, it was the truth. After all, something really had infiltrated the plant — his curse. But telling the man that the plant was cursed would have sounded like a hollow excuse. It's like Sakura always said: sometimes a lie is best.

Tina, who knew a line of bullshit when she heard it, caught Bill's eye and mouthed to him, "Thank you."

Bill nodded and took another sip of his drink, nearly losing an eye from the umbrella but managing to pass it off as a wink.

CHAPTER 55

Bill slid a briefcase that was half-filled with cash across the desk. A distinguished-looking Japanese man wearing a very conservative gray suit, a black necktie, and a pair of yellow panties on his head said, "Oh my, this calls for better dress." He quickly removed the yellow panties from his head and then, after some rummaging around in his desk drawer, replaced them with a lacy, black pair.

Bill was starting to understand Okane Noboru's penchant for transferring wealth in this manner — it really made people's faces light up when they received it. The owner of his apartment complex certainly seemed to have enjoyed it.

The two men signed a few complicated looking documents and then nodded to each other. The previous owner said, "OK, the apartment complex is all yours. May I ask what you are going to do with it?"

Bill answered, "Ever since I was a boy, I had always dreamed of owning an entire neighborhood and letting all of my friends move in for free. I figured that it would be an awesome place to live. You might say that this is a small-scale way of making that dream come true."

"Very interesting, Bill-san," admitted the man. "Tell me, is there any place for an eccentric old man in your dream?"

Bill had been expecting this question. He was slightly against the idea of letting the man continue to live there, but the other three had convinced him otherwise. They seemed to think of him as more a sort of mascot than a perverted old man — it was curious. Bill looked at him and smiled. "You are welcome to stay for as long as you would like."

The man looked at the briefcase and considered this. Finally, he said, "You know what — I think I will move after all. Thank you for the offer, I really appreciate it. But I think maybe it is time to see the world a little. And besides, between you and me, this neighborhood is getting rather strange these days. Do you know I even saw two monks hiding in the hedges the other day? Peeping Tom monks? What is the world coming to?"

Bill tried real hard not to look at the underwear on the man's head and said, "Fair enough. Well then, I must be off." The two men stood up, and Bill collected his paperwork. They bowed to each other, and Bill walked out of the man's door and then right back into his own a few steps away. As he made his way to the top of the stairs, Natsuko asked, "How did everything go?"

Bill waved the documents in demonstration and said, "No problems. This place is ours now."

"Is he going to stay?" she asked.

"No," answered Bill, "He says he wants to see the world now or something."

"Good for him," said Natsuko.

Bill nodded.

"I think maybe we should leave his place vacant for a while just in case he changes his mind," suggested Natsuko.

Bill nodded again.

Natsuko continued, "So that just leaves the tenants in 1B and 2C. I already talked to each of them and told them about the new ownership. The lady in 1B's lease expires next month, and she already has plans to move in with her children because she is getting too old to live by herself. I think I would like to take her apartment if you do not mind. This way, I can have a place for my stuff, and you can have a place for yours."

Bill wrinkled his brow for a moment and said, "That actually sounds rather sensible. It could very well be the key to a happy marriage."

"Perhaps," agreed Natsuko. "Anyway, the young man in 2C was a little resistant, but after the mention of compensation he agreed to move out next month as well. I think it would be best if we used his apartment as a clubhouse. This would be a place for any and all of us to hang out together if we are feeling sociable. It would also become our new official meeting place."

"Oh," said Bill, a new HQ? Well, it isn't a cave carved into the side of a mountain yet, but it is an improvement over my living room. Sounds good to me."

Natsuko agreed and gave him a hug. As she did this, she noticed a new painting on Bill's wall. She had actually noticed it earlier, but never had a chance to ask about it until now, and so she did.

Bill looked at it and said, "It's a drawing that I got from a hotel concierge. He sketched this whole thing up in a matter of minutes — truly remarkable. I have no idea what a man of his talent is doing wasting it in a hotel.

"I think I do," stated Natsuko as she reexamined the signature at the bottom of the drawing.

"Have you not heard of Sadamoto Hayao-san?"

Bill said, "Yes, of course, I am a fan of anime and manga after all."

Natsuko pointed to the drawing and said, "This is his signature."

Bill examined it and said, "No way! Oh my god — I couldn't read it. Are you sure?"

"I am fairly certain, yes. He used to be a sort of family friend up until a few years ago, and then he just disappeared from the limelight."

"What happened?" asked Bill, enthralled.

"His latest work flopped. He was very proud of it, and he was crushed at the harsh criticisms that it received."

"What was it about?" asked Bill.

Natsuko scrunched up her nose and said, "I think it was a story about a boy and his magical potato."

Bill laughed.

Natsuko continued, "He could not handle the criticism. Many say that he went a little crazy. His wife, for one, tried to have him institutionalized but failed. Sadamoto-san then spitefully hid his fortune from her and disappeared. Rumor has it that he travels between low-level jobs while trying to find enlightenment or inspiration or some such thing. I guess the rumors are true."

Bill asked, "So what became of his fortune?"

Natsuko tilted her head slightly and answered, "No one really knows, of course. His fans like to believe that he has given it away to a random fan since he is known to be impulsive at times. I do not think we will ever know."

Bill looked at the drawing again and smiled. "Oh, I don't

know, maybe someone will find out. Do you know he was very, very pleased with me when I complimented his work and asked for his signature. I remember that after he signed it, he stared at me for a second and then scribbled something else on the drawing."

"What did he draw?" asked Natsuko, full of curiosity.

Bill shrugged. I don't know. It was just a few strokes. I sort of chalked it up to him adding a finishing detail — until now that is."

"About where did he add it?" asked Natsuko.

Bill pointed to a part of the map and said, "Around here someplace, I think."

They both studied the drawing for some time. Just when Bill was about to proclaim the whole notion as silly, Natsuko exclaimed, "Here!"

Bill looked. Just over one of the train stations there was the *kanji* character *kin*, which meant gold, money, or treasure. Below it were some numbers.

"A locker?" she suggested.

"A locker," agreed Bill.

"It can't be," explained Bill. "That was well before I gained my power; it was before I had my good luck."

"And you do not think that you could have been lucky on your own?" asked Natsuko.

Bill considered this. "Maybe," he conceded. "Still, it's not as if he left me a...key." His voice trailed off as he remembered about his keyring. He fished it out of his pocket and flipped madly between the keys. Finally, he found the odd one and held it up. "Or maybe he did."

"Bill, that's astonishing."

Bill nodded. "And that was without my power. Who would have thought? I wonder if the power even affects the past? Perhaps it has to affect the past in order to engineer good fortune in the present."

"I do not know the answer to that, Bill, but what I definitely do know for sure is that you should never say things like that in front of Kurokawa-san — he would have a heart attack from the worry and would probably ask you not to use your power until he has studied the topic at length."

Bill nodded. "Very true. Best not to freak him out like that."

Natsuko nodded too and then said, "Oh, and speaking of your power, when are you going to track down the monks?"

Bill put his keys back in his pocket and suddenly looked more solemn. "Funny you should mention them — Panty Man told me that he saw them lurking in the bushes not long ago. Truthfully, I was thinking that I should not look a gift horse in the mouth, but I must say that curiosity is getting the best of me. I think I'll pay them a visit soon."

"Have you given any thought as to how you are going to do it?" asked Natsuko.

Bill nodded. "Yes, in fact, I should see Sakura about a few things. Excuse me for a minute."

Bill then trotted down his stairs and out of his door. He turned right and walked two doors down and knocked on Sakura's door.

There was a pause, and then he heard footsteps pattering down some stairs. The door opened and Sakura was standing there in a robe with her hair wrapped in a towel and a toothbrush sticking out of her mouth at a jaunty angle. "Whaa?" she asked.

Bill said, "I need to borrow one of your girls — someone who can act..."

Sakura gave him a warning look.

Bill saw this and continued, "Not THAT kind of acting — just general acting ability. I also need someone good with a bow and arrow."

"Wheh?" asked Sakura.

"Mmm, maybe next Saturday if that is possible."

Sakura pulled the toothbrush out of her mouth and pointed it at Bill and said, "You got it, Beer-san. No problem." She then closed the door and trotted back up the stairs.

Bill reflected that Sakura was quickly becoming Natsuko's replacement as "the woman who gets things done." He considered himself very lucky that they were both on his side.

CHAPTER 56

A young girl was taking a walk around the small park near Bill's apartment when she noticed a building buried inside a cluster of trees. She walked over to investigate and found a small shrine.

She purified her hands and mouth as was the custom, and then dropped a few coins into the offering box. She glanced up at the large bells above her for a second and then shook the large rope vigorously.

At that moment, an archer imbued with good luck and natural talent shot a well-aimed razor arrow, which sliced through the string that bound the bells to the rope and continued harmlessly into the woods.

The bells fell and crashed down on the girl's head, who collapsed into a heap on the ground, seemingly unconscious.

In an underground room somewhere below her, one monk asked another monk, "Did you set the trap again, boy?"

The junior monk shook his head. "No, Master."

The senior monk shook his head in disapproval. "Shoddy workmanship, boy. What do you have to say for yourself?"

"I am most sorry, Master. Shall I fetch the Cane of Discipline?"

"Perhaps later," said the senior monk, "But right now we must check on that young girl. Bring the medical kit."

"Yes, Master."

And then shortly after that, a large, white marble statue of a fox spirit inside the shrine slid sideways on its base to reveal a hidden stairway beneath. A little bald head poked up from the opening and looked around.

"All clear, Master."

The two monks then cautiously walked outside to aid the young girl. They bent down and took her pulse, and then checked her pupils by prying her eyelids apart and shining a light into her eyes.

"She's fine," said a voice that was suddenly behind them."

The girl opened her eyes and gave them a smile. The monks twisted around to see Bill behind them, grinning.

Bill said, "Well done, Nenette-san. That was excellent."

Nenette smiled in reply.

The senior monk said, "I thought this day might come — for what chance do we stand against such a lucky man?"

Bill walked casually over to the monks and sat in front of them, cross-legged. He then said, "May I ask why you are following me, and what this shrine has to do with my good fortune?"

The senior monk looked at him unblinkingly and said, "And if we refuse?"

Bill sighed and stood back up. He motioned to Nenette and said, "Come along, Nenette-san."

He bowed to the monks and said, "Thank you for your time. I am very sorry for my deceit. Whatever your reasons for doing this to me, I most sincerely thank you for it."

He and Nenette turned and started to walk off. They got as far as the edge of the woods when the senior monk called out, "That was the correct answer. Please come and sit."

Bill flicked a smile to himself before turning back around and rejoining the monks.

"We represent a small sect of monks who have been tasked to merge and reconcile the worlds of science and religion," explained the senior monk.

"Tough job," empathized Bill.

The senior monk smiled. "It has certainly been...difficult. We have long since abandoned the idea of trying to prove the existence of this god or that god — frankly, the whole idea seemed pointless to us. So then we began to contemplate if it were possible to somehow awaken the spirituality of skeptics and atheists using science."

"How?" asked Bill, almost hesitantly.

"Chemically," said the senior monk.

"Chemically?" inquired Bill, visibly horrified.

"Oh yes," said the senior monk. "We have been working on a serum that will do just that. We found that by juggling a few things in the brain we could... Tell me, do you know anything about quantum theory?"

Bill shook his head, now mesmerized. "I've heard about it, but I can't say that I know much about it."

"You see," explained the monk, "it all comes down to something called quantum entanglement. We learned that much of the world is connected in ways we cannot imagine. Some particles here could be linked to some particles in another town, another country, another world, or even another galaxy."

Bill, not understanding where this was going at all, simply nodded.

"One day when contemplating quantum theory and the nature of gods, I had quite a revelation."

Bill leaned forward slightly and asked, "What?"

The monk answered, "That if gods do exist, then they must surely be hiding inside the randomness of the universe, remaining forever disguised as rounding errors in Planck's Constant."

The junior monk yawned. The senior monk swatted him and said, "Pay attention, boy."

"Sorry, Master," said the junior monk, sleepily.

Bill said, "I do not understand a bit of what you just said, but I appreciate the effort all the same."

The monk frowned and stroked his beard. "We created pairs of entangled particles and then we transmitted half of the pairs at the sun. The other half of the pairs were added to a serum that had been designed to deliver the entangled particles into the brain."

Bill looked at him blankly.

The monk frowned and stroked his beard again. Finally, he said, "It's magic. Does that work for you?"

Bill smiled. "Yes, yes. Fine — I get it — it's all very complicated and scientific. So, you make up this magic potion that somehow links a man's mind with a raging inferno of nuclear fusion and you inject me and my friend with it and then... what? What were you hoping to accomplish?"

"We were not sure — that is what science is about — hypothesis, experimentation, and observation. We thought maybe that your mind would become more connected with the universe and its wonders." He hesitated and then added weakly,

"Well, that or burst into flames."

He flashed Bill a smile and continued, "But after experimentation and observation, it appears that the serum has somehow imbued you with power over chance occurrences. It is a fantastic and frightening power."

"I agree," said Bill. "It is a frightening power. I think you two were lucky, if you pardon the expression, to have chosen Kurokawa-san and I. If someone like Sakamoto-san had this power..." He shuddered. "I think you should destroy the serum. I think it is too dangerous to exist."

The senior monk stared unblinkingly at Bill for a few seconds and then said. "Yes. We too came to that conclusion after watching you. It has already been done. We have destroyed the formula. Mind you, we still have one dose of serum left just in case."

Bill nodded. "I can see that you two are very wise." He then noticed the junior monk with his head to one side, his eyes closed, and his mouth drooling. He corrected himself, "Well, at least you are wise, sir. Tell me, is there an antidote? Could you make me normal again?"

The monk asked, "Do you wish it so?"

Bill shook his head. "No, I do not wish for it. And I am sure that I will never wish for it. But I am also sure that absolute power corrupts absolutely. So I can foresee a time in the future when the rest of the world may wish for it."

The monk gave Bill a small bow and said, "Yes, we have such an antidote."

"Good," said Bill, relieved. "Then please promise me this: if ever I get out of hand, then you must give me the antidote. You must stop me."

The monk bowed again and said, "You have my word. But, surely it is more wise to administer the antidote now."

Bill smirked. "But you are not going to, are you?"

"No," admitted the monk.

"Scientific curiosity," said Bill, knowingly.

"As you say," admitted the monk.

Bill then said, "I have one other request."

"Yes?" inquired the monk.

"If ever you find that I have become some sort of super villain luck-monster, could you do one other thing for me?"

"Yes?"

"Learn how to hide. Wearing white robes while hiding in the

bushes is a bit daft, don't you think?"

"Yes," admitted the monk.

"Well," said Bill while standing up and dusting himself off, "I guess that about sorts everything out. It was nice meeting you. I am sure I will be seeing you around. Later, then."

He bowed to the monks, one of which was now snoring, and collected Nenette, who was not snoring but nevertheless looked dazed and confused. She had no idea what any of the conversation had meant.

As they left the group of trees and entered the clearing of the park, Bill noticed the extremely old lady walking surprisingly easily along the walkway, and more to the point, she noticed him.

She stared at him, as if not certain of who he was. Bill hazarded a small wave. The woman yelled, "You! Come! I must talk!" She waved him over.

Bill shrugged and walked with Nenette to meet with the old woman. "Hello, dear lady, how are you today?" asked Bill, smoothly.

"Hello again, deary! I'm sorry for before. I should not have yelled at you. I...I do not know what you are, but what you said did come true. You said my luck would change for the better, and it did. Oh boy did it. First, my old hip popped back into place one morning, as did my back. I feel great! And then my grandson finally divorced that awful woman he was married to..."

Hearing this, Nanette stared from the old woman, to Bill, and then back again. She then excused herself and left the two to chat in private, not wanting to sit through another incomprehensible conversation.

Bill said to her, "OK, see you around. Thanks again for the help."

Nenette waved and left.

The old woman resumed, "...and then there was the sale on ribbons — you never can have enough ribbons. And then my dear cat Whisker-chan, who had been lost for a month, came scratching at my door last week. And then, and this is miraculous, I was digging in my garden and found a jar!" she looked at Bill, proudly.

"Wow, a jar," said Bill with as much enthusiasm as he could muster. "You can never have enough jars."

The woman nodded, sagely. "Damn right. But there was something inside the jar: a key and directions to a locker at a train station in Tokyo."

"My, my," said Bill, "How odd. Did you follow the directions?"

"Damn right I did. And you want to know what I found?"

Bill nodded, even though he technically already knew what was in the locker and had taken half of the spoils for himself a week ago.

The woman looked around and lowered her voice. "Gold!" she said in an excited whisper. "Gold! — lots of it, dozens of gold coins."

"Astonishing!" said Bill, hamming it up.

The old woman gave him a hug. "Bless you, deary. Bless you." As she did this, Bill could just make out a couple of monks on the edge of the woods, giving him the thumbs up.

CHAPTER 57

Kurokawa was doing very well. He stood in a corner of his factory and surveyed its operation with considerable pride. Everything was going well, and his new employees were picking things up quickly.

He had been able to convince several of the old employees of Yummy Plastics — the ones that were not directly involved in the Yasei-kai — to return to work for him. However, when he had made the same offer to Meat Cleaver and his associates, they had thanked him for the offer and the education, but had said that it really was not their thing. In the end, only Sally had taken the offer.

Kurokawa walked over to her workstation to check on her. Her station was by itself, several feet away from all the other stations. He watched her work as he approached.

Sally held a #10 hole maker (a sort of sharpened tube about the thickness of a thumb) high above her head in both hands and then tensed.

With a loud "Ki-yaaaa!" she thrust it down into a yellow block of plastic. She pulled it out and repeated this again and again.

"Ki-yaaaa! Ki-yaaaa! Ki-yaaaa! Ki-yaaaa! Ki-yaaaa!"

She turned the block and then erupted into another bout of stabbing and screaming.

When this was done, she set down the #10 hole maker and picked up a large, sharp sword.

"Ki-yaaaa! Ki-yaaaa! Ki-yaaaa! Ki-yaaaa! Ki-yaaaa!" she

exclaimed while slicing the block repeatedly.

After the entire block had been reduced to slices, Sally set the sword down and caught her breath.

Kurokawa picked up a random slice and held it up to the light. He shook it gently and watched critically as it flexed and wiggled. He set it down and chose two more pieces at random, subjecting them to the same scrutiny.

Sally watched him intently, waiting for his verdict.

Kurokawa smiled and said, "Very well done, Sally. Perfect Swiss cheese. Great randomizing of the hole pattern, and the slice consistency is as good as any machine. Very well done. You see there, Sally, everyone has a talent just waiting for the right outlet."

Sally beamed.

CHAPTER 58

Prince William — the real Prince William — sat on an ornate yellow and gold couch in the White Drawing Room of Buckingham Palace. He nervously gripped the head of some mythical creature that had been carved into the armrest as his grandmother, Queen Elizabeth II, peered at him disapprovingly over the brim of her tea cup.

She placed it down gently on the end table and asked, "So, how are you doing, William? In good health, I trust."

"Very well, Granny. Everything is splendid. And yourself?"

"Oh, I'm doing well. Every day it gets a little harder to get out of bed, but once I am up, it is not so bad. So, tell me, have you been anywhere interesting lately?" inquired the Queen.

"Not particularly, I'm afraid."

"Are you sure?" pressed the Queen. "Perhaps somewhere in Asia?"

"No," replied Prince William, shaking his head and relaxing back into the couch.

He was reaching for his tea when the Queen suddenly barked, "Do not think you can fool me, William!"

The Prince almost dropped his cup and snapped to attention. "But Granny, I swear I have not."

"I have seen the photos. I have seen the newspaper reports. Do you take me for a fool? I know my own grandson when I see him. If that was not you gallivanting around Japan, hanging on strange women and assaulting machinery, then who was it?"

"But Granny, I swear..."

CHAPTER 59

The four sat back in their chairs and breathed the fresh, night air. They were on the Ledge of Recollections, also known as the balcony to the upstairs apartment that was now serving as their headquarters and clubhouse.

It was one of those perfect, clear nights when the temperature was so perfect that no one noticed it, and the stars were so plentiful that it looked like a new galaxy had just arrived out of nowhere and double-parked over the current one.

There was some sort of festival going on in a neighboring town, and fireworks were going off in celebration. The four chatted randomly about nothing much at all as they watched.

Natsuko said, "I think Panty Man would have enjoyed this. I wonder what he is doing now?"

The others gave a few grunts and shrugs. Bill then said, "I'm sure he is doing fine. Actually, I think he might have started up his own business."

Kurokawa asked, "What makes you say that?"

Bill answered, "Well, has anyone else noticed the new vending machines around town? The ones that sell coffee, tea, and...used panties?"

"I have," volunteered Sakura. "I use them all the time."

The other three looked at her.

"To buy tea," she added while rolling her eyes.

They became silent again as they watched the next burst of fireworks, occasionally sipping their tea.

After a while, Natsuko said, "Oh, Bill, I have been meaning to tell you — you remember that manga artist that drew the map for you?"

"Of course," replied Bill.

"Well, it looks like you inspired him to resume his work."

"That's fantastic."

"Yes," agreed Natsuko, "He is working on a manga about an American named Bill who gains a strange superpower and starts fighting crime in Tokyo."

Bill nearly spit out his tea. "You're kidding."

"No," said Natsuko. "I promise you that he is."

Bill shook his head. "Poor guy — it sounds like such an outlandish story. It will never sell and he will be mocked again."

Natsuko smiled.

Another burst of fireworks broke out in the sky. When silence returned again, Natsuko asked, "Did you ever go and speak to those monks, Bill?"

Bill took another sip of tea and replied. "Oh, yes. They were surprisingly nice. It turns out that they were just trying to make some sort of spiritual enlightenment potion, but they botched the job and turned Kurokawa and I into luck-monsters instead. We chatted for a while and reached a sort of understanding, I think."

"It's just that..." Natsuko began saying while staring down at the neighbor's bushes, "...I can't help but notice that there are a couple of men dressed in camouflaged robes peering at us from the bushes over there."

The others looked around, muttering, "Where? Where?"

Natsuko pointed at them, and then they suddenly ducked deeper into the undergrowth.

Bill said, "All part of the understanding, I assure you. Think nothing of it."

Natsuko knew her husband well enough not to bother pressing him for information when he was feeling coy, so she moved on to another subject and asked, "How about the gas station owner, did you ever track him down?"

"Oh, yes," said Bill happily, "I didn't tell you? It turns out that, despite what Sakura hinted at, he wasn't killed after all."

"That's good news. Did you...do anything for him?" asked Natsuko.

"Well, funny you should ask," said Bill. "It seems that his insurance company paid him three times the amount of what the gas station was really worth. I hear he is building something completely new to replace it — a combination laundromat, game center, and tavern. How brilliant is that?"

Kurokawa then said, "Actually, that is very clever. You have a bored, captive audience waiting for their clothes to be washed, why not give them something to spend their time and money on?"

Another burst of fireworks bloomed overhead as the others nodded in agreement.

Bill then asked, "How about you? How has the friendly face of the Yakuza been doing in her charitable endeavors?"

Natsuko kicked his shin lovingly and said, "Fantastic. We are currently remediating the soil of several farms so they can safely be used again. And we are helping the families to move back in."

"Excellent," said Bill. "That is exactly the sort of stuff that I had in mind when I first convinced Kurokawa-san that we could use our power for something worthwhile."

Sakura then said cheekily, "And to think, Beer-san, that when I first met you, you said you probably would not bother to help people if you had a super power."

Bill shrugged. "I suppose I met some good people that changed my mind."

There was another burst of fireworks, and then Sakura said, "You know, this is really nice. I'm so glad I met all of you."

Natsuko said, "Aw, how nice. We love you, Sakura-chan," and then she leaned over and gave her a kiss on the cheek. Bill reached over and patted Sakura's head, while Kurokawa gave her a rubbery smile.

Bill said, "I have to agree with Sakura. I think I am happier now than I have ever been. And to think that it all started because of some really bad luck that I had in America."

"Like Saiou's Horse," suggested Kurokawa.

"Exactly, K-san. It just goes to show you that it's a crazy old world, and your luck can change on a dime."

"Especially if you run into us," giggled Sakura.

Bill chuckled too. "Yes, especially if you run into us."

"Speaking of which, where do we go from here?" asked Kurokawa.

Bill sat up, somewhat excited, and said, "Actually, I had this idea: we could go after..."

"Bill," interrupted Natsuko.

"Yes, Natsuko?"

"Perhaps not tonight. No business. Let's just enjoy the

fireworks."

Bill nodded. "You're right, of course. Sorry, K-san, another time."

Kurokawa nodded and the group fell into silence as they sipped their tea and watched the brilliant flashes of light in the sky. And somewhere in a nearby bush, a monk was smacked on the head by another monk. "Pay attention, boy, the fate of the world depends on us."

The junior monk rubbed his head thoughtfully and said, "I think the world can look after itself for an hour or two, Master. Can we not just watch the fireworks?"

The senior monk stroked his long, white beard and said, "Very well, boy. But just for an hour."